HOPE
ABLAZE

HOPE
ABLAZE

Sarah Mughal Rana

WEDNESDAY BOOKS
NEW YORK

Published in the United States by Wednesday Books, an imprint of St. Martin's Publishing Group

HOPE ABLAZE. Copyright © 2024 by Sarah Mughal Rana. All rights reserved. Printed in the United States of America. For information, address St. Martin's Publishing Group, 120 Broadway, New York, NY 10271.

www.wednesdaybooks.com

Book design by Michelle McMillian

Library of Congress Cataloging-in-Publication Data

Names: Rana, Sarah Mughal, author.
Title: Hope ablaze / Sarah Mughal Rana.
Description: First edition. | New York : Wednesday Books, 2024. | Audience: Ages 13–18.
Identifiers: LCCN 2023036255 | ISBN 9781250899316 (hardcover) | ISBN 9781250899323 (ebook)
Subjects: CYAC: Poetry—Fiction. | Family life—Fiction. | Identity—Fiction. | Muslims—Fiction. | LCGFT: Novels.
Classification: LCC PZ7.1.R34434 Ho 2024 | DDC [Fic]—dc23
LC record available at https://lccn.loc.gov/2023036255.

Our books may be purchased in bulk for promotional, educational, or business use. Please contact your local bookseller or the Macmillan Corporate and Premium Sales Department at 1-800-221-7945, extension 5442, or by email at MacmillanSpecialMarkets@macmillan.com.

First Edition: 2024

10 9 8 7 6 5 4 3 2 1

This book is dedicated to all my hijabi sisters.
You are so strong.

HOPE
ABLAZE

One

There have been many times in my life when I was con-
fronted with moments that made me think: *this is it, this is
where I revoke my brown card.*

And my Amma trotting a black goat into our home was one
of them.

"*Is this even legal?*" My eyes widened as I glanced up sharply
from the kitchen counter, cluttered in baking supplies. My hand
darted forward, tucking my poetry notebook behind a bowl of
batter.

"Shut up, beta," Amma said, as if this were a normal practice,
bringing furred four-legged things meant to be mutton kebobs
into our house.

"I'm frying jalebis! This isn't hygienic!"

Amma was not having it. "Oho chashm-e-baddoor"—she
whacked the back of my head—"who will save us from the evil
eye? Did you hear the news?"

Not this again. When Amma fell down a pit of paranoia
because of the neighborhood's rumor mill, she would order a
goat from Uncle Mahmoud, the local Syrian butcher, before
slaughtering it under the name of charity. As if all the negative

energy would suddenly disappear because the world had one less goat.

Amma continued, "Aunty Farooqi told me there's a new aunty in town. Sister Ayesha who moved down the street. Farooqi said, 'This Ayesha is opening a catering business'! I think she's jealous of ours! She's giving us the evil eye! She's even going to call it Aunty's Punjabi Kitchen."

I gasped in mock horror. "The nerve."

Amma didn't register the sarcasm. "Her name is so generic too. Are we calling our business Aunty's Sindhi Kitchen?" Amma all but sneered. "No, because we're all Pakistani."

Before I could reply, the haze of burnt fried dough and sugar syrup hit my senses. As I yanked down on the door of the gas stove, the black goat bellowed and struggled against the frayed rope tied around its neck, its slitted blue eyes peering up like *save me!* For a wavering second, I empathized with the goat.

Earlier, in the morning, my older sister had warned me that Amma would be up to her usual antics, and it'd be better for me to escape and hang with the poets to *make use of the summer before senior year.*

My teeth gritted. But nope. Amma spammed me with WhatsApp messages, threatening me into frying jalebis for an emergency client's order. All morning, the undeniable scent of sticky mithai had the uncles across the street from the Al-Rasheed mosque popping their heads into the doorway with that *I know I'm on a diet, don't tell my wife, but remember to save me a bite* look. I'd promised to share leftovers.

Across the counter, Amma began packing a plastic container of unburned jalebis to distribute to the neighbors. Her eyes darted to the bowl of batter. My poetry notebook stuck out like a sore thumb.

"What's this?" The disapproval hardened her glare.

"Schoolwork?"

"Nice try," Amma said but left it. My heart fluttered in relief. "I'll be back by the afternoon and then you can go visit Mamou at the prison."

I opened and then shut my mouth. *Afternoon?* I was supposed to meet the poets at the shawarma restaurant for a critique circle. We always met up around a plate of pilaf and döner kebobs. This would be the third time I'd be blowing it off—in a row.

"Can you come earlier?" I asked.

"I'm finalizing a client's menu for a small wedding and then I have a delivery up north," she explained. "Why?"

"Well . . ." I fumbled for an excuse, desperate to see the poets. "What do I do with the goat while you're gone?"

She whacked me again. "Oho, the goat isn't bothering you, ignore it. We'll fatten it up and have the butcher slaughter it in a few days."

"But—"

She raised a brow, silently urging me to talk back just so she could whack me again. Ridiculous, I know. I decided to change the subject.

"Amma, when you go, can you leave the door unlocked? My friend is coming to drop off my physics textbook," I said.

Amma nodded and popped a piece of fried dough in her mouth, pecked my forehead, and left. I glanced at my notebook, my heart sinking.

I recalled a time when this wasn't the case. When Amma didn't mind if I escaped with the poets. That was before Mamou went to prison. Now she despised our poetry.

Maybe this was a sign. All morning I'd had a bad feeling strangling my chest. It happened on the days I was supposed to visit my uncle. Today after morning prayer, when I sat down to revise my verse, my mind was a blank wall, the well of inspiration all but dried out.

After flicking a match and lighting the stove again to fry another round of desserts, my sister sniffed her way into the kitchen. "You're still here?"

I wiped my floured hands on my apron. "I burned the dough because of the freaking goat."

"What about the other poets?"

My stomach lurched as I filled the piping bag. "If I go, who's going to finish the client's order?"

Zaynab had the audacity to shrug. "You should've left when you had the chance."

"Did Amma even ask you for help?"

"I told her I couldn't." Zaynab began stuffing her face with the orange goodness. "I have a law school event that I'm prepping for tonight. Next time, just tell Amma about your plans."

"Easy for you to say." I fought the urge to roll my eyes. At every turn, Zaynab's studies were a proffered excuse. Amma ate it up. Zaynab was out there fulfilling brown pedigrees by applying to law schools. But Zaynab was good at that, saying no. As the oldest she'd had more practice with being firm with what she wanted. I was always caught between both extremes.

Suddenly Zaynab paused mid-bite. "Oho, Nida."

"What?"

"Is that your notebook?"

I whirled around and—

The goat nudged my notebook off the kitchen counter, nibbling on the edge. I snatched it away before more damage was done, wiping the wet, ruined pages against my sweatshirt.

My poetry letters were damp, the same ones I was *supposed* to work on for my performance next week at the Poet's Block.

"I guess that's a sign from God," Zaynab said.

"Of what?"

My sister nodded her chin at the half-chewed notebook. "You blew off the poets. I guess the evil eye was the goat all along."

Her words were meant as a joke, but it stung. I swallowed uneasily.

"Which evil eye?"

I turned and saw my friend Alexis poke her head into the kitchen.

"Your mom let me in," she explained. "I'm dropping off the textbook you let me borrow—*is that a goat?*" Her eyes became blue saucers.

"Yes . . . that is a goat," I said nonchalantly.

"It's chewing on paper!"

"Yes . . . it's chewing on paper from my journal."

"Why are you acting like this is normal?"

"We sacrifice goats for charity. But according to Zaynab, the goat is cursing me with the evil eye."

I met Alexis last year, in the eleventh grade. She was the first white friend approved and vetted by my Amma's paranoid standards. *A gori of our block*, Amma decided, which was as welcoming as she gets.

Alexis skirted a wide berth around the furry creature. "Why would you have the evil eye on you?"

Zaynab interjected, "Nida was supposed to write a piece her spoken word performance, but she flaked because she was too scared to ask Amma. Now she's stuck frying desserts. So, I think God's trying to show that she shouldn't blow off her commitments."

"*I can speak for myself*," I cut back in, an edge to my voice.

My friend glanced between us. "And I think your sister has a point. Summer vacation is almost over. You can go after you're done here."

"I can't." I gestured miserably at the kitchen. "After finishing this order, I have to visit my Mamou."

"But if you don't practice, you can't perform. You even said no to that poetry contest that I showed you last week!" Alexis put out her arm to stop me from grabbing the piping bag.

"Because I didn't have time to submit a piece. And I hate contests." I pointed between Zaynab and Alexis. "I don't like when you gang up on me. It's weird."

"You're weird for self-sabotaging your own opportunities." Zaynab snatched another plate of fried desserts before, thankfully, retreating down the hall to our shared bedroom.

Alexis began rolling up her sleeves. "I need your apron."

"What are you doing?"

"I'll fry the desserts while you practice your spoken word letter."

"Don't you have to go home?"

She shrugged, grabbing the spatula. "My parents were fighting again. I'd rather be here, frying . . ."

"Jalebis."

"Frying jalebis." She smiled.

Just like the first day I had met her, Alexis defied my expectations. "Do you know how?"

"How hard can it be? It's like funnel cakes, right?"

"Sure," I said before trying to snatch back the spatula.

Alexis was taller so she held it up over her head. "Let people help you, Nida." For a moment I was silent. Then she added, "But I have a condition."

"Condition?"

"Just promise me that you'll consider entering that contest I showed you."

My smile dropped. "My poetry letters are private. I don't like contests." I looked away and picked up the piping bag.

Ever since my old English teacher had sent an email about the National Students Poet League (NSPL), encouraging me to enter, Alexis and the other poets rammed the idea down my throat, telling me it'd be a good way to gain some national recognition. Like in their eyes, being good at something without recognition didn't make it a legitimate hobby.

Alexis gently removed the piping bag from my hands. "But you perform at the Poet's Block. What's so different about a competition? You could even win money."

My stomach squirmed. NSPL's prize for first place was a $5,000 check, publication in a renowned national magazine, and a spoken word performance on the news. The competition was the paragon of talent, and I had no intention of playing in the big leagues. But a wave of guilt coursed through me.

Technically—just technically—Alexis was right. She knew about Amma's debt and our small catering business. She knew that if I placed in a competition, with this recognition, I'd be booked for all kinds of public performances. But I wanted to say, *I didn't tell you all this for it to be thrown right back at me.*

"The Poet's Block is different because it's designed for only Muslims from our city. Besides, everyone knows me as Abdul-Hafeedh's niece, that's why my poetry is meaningful to the neighborhood. It reminds the families of my uncle's work. A national competition is different, it's risky."

Alexis began piping swirling designs of batter onto the hot oil and *wow*—it really was like funnel cake. She glanced up from the frying pan. "But you've performed at other competitions. Didn't you win last year at that tournament, MIST nationals?"

"MIST is an all-Muslim tournament. The judges are less likely to misjudge my words."

What I didn't say was that years ago, when my Mamou went viral performing online and across the country, his words were twisted against him. The public saw my Mamou as radical—which is exactly what my Amma feared would happen to me.

Alexis seemed to read my mind. "What would your Mamou say?"

I flinched. "You don't know my Mamou like I do. My Mamou's poetry—"

Landed him in a federal prison. I bit my tongue. It was the kind of nasty thought that reminded me of bruised fruit, something my Amma would let slip, not me.

"I can't force you, but I want you to think about it." Alexis pointed at my notebook. "I'll finish frying jalebis, it's so easy—see, I haven't even burned it!—and you can finish your letter before you visit your uncle."

I sighed and untied my apron.

"Deal."

Two

The visitor's entrance to the federal prison resembled my high school, twin shiny white doors, the building an array of red-brown bricks rising above a concrete staircase.

I let out a steadying breath. Checked my face in the compact mirror I'd brought with me, just to make sure my usual piercings weren't there. Everything looked orderly: my hijab was changed into a low turban form; my Allah necklace engraved in calligraphy—a gift from my incarcerated uncle—was left on my desk at home. I had even unclipped my nose ring that Amma brought from Karachi.

But the anxiety wouldn't ebb, not until I was past the security check-in.

During my visits, my uncle always claimed to be doing as well as anyone could be in prison. But I wondered, as I looked around—how was Mamou Abdul-Hafeedh *actually*? To the rest of the world, he was the notorious poet, a fox of Karachi, never backing down from a fight. He was good at concealing his pain behind a full-mouthed laugh.

But now there was talk from the courts about extraditing Mamou to Pakistan. They called us lucky because he wasn't trapped like the others in Guantanamo Bay. If he was extradited, I wouldn't stand for it. We needed him here, to appeal the verdict. We'd only just been granted visitation rights.

My fingers shook at the thought.

In the visitation room, I spotted my Mamou on the other side of the glass partition, prison telephones strung along the ends to talk to inmates. The yellow walls were plastered in posters. Mamou sat at the farthest seat, studying one about prison education, stoic guards posted at the exit behind him.

Mamou Abdul-Hafeedh was ten years my Amma's junior. Prison had beaten his youth into a gaunt skeleton frame, all bones tucked under a shield of thin skin. Still, with gaping dark eyes and rich brown skin, one stolen glance from him was all it took to bridge his world and yours; he dipped his hands into the cage of one's mind, ran his nails through the swell of one's thoughts, and took long pauses before he spoke.

And when he finally did, my uncle said exactly the right things, as if he were free therapy. Because he knew firsthand the lengths one would go to hide their troubles behind a carefully gathered smile.

If I wrote Mamou as a poem, he would be concise one-liners delivered like a gut punch, the kind that would make you either outraged or emotional enough to cry.

But his first greeting to me here was a different kind of one-liner. "Beta, you're losing weight!"

"Mamou," I groaned into the pay phone. "I swear, you say this every time I see you."

"Why is Zuha not feeding you?"

"Amma is feeding me just fine. Wallahi, my blood is fifty percent curry, thirty percent basmati, and twenty percent roti."

His jaw dropped. "Did you willingly do math?"

It was kind of sad that I was proud of that joke too. "Excuse me, I have an eighty-five in algebra. And I've been eating Amma's food without complaint, including all her sabzi."

"Look at yourself! Tell her enough with the sabzi, she needs to feed you more meat!"

I glanced down at my baggy jeans and Jordans. "My Js are still fresh."

Suddenly, his next words morphed into a wet, wringing cough. I shot up, but with the partition between us, I couldn't even pat his back.

Mamou swatted the air flippantly. "It's only the dust," he said, and my jaw clenched at his non-answer. "Tell me, how's Zaynab, how's little Mohamed?"

"They're fine. But I have some good news."

Unexpectedly, the light in his eyes dimmed. "Good news," he stated, less than thrilled.

Maybe he was used to good news always plummeting into more bad news.

"Yeah," I continued. "Last week, I received an appointment— *finally*—from Justice Behind Bars. And they're open to taking on your legal case!"

There was a reason I had researched for months, scouring every legal aid association that I could find. Justice Behind Bars, if they agreed to my appeals, would not only cover our legal fees, but also find us an expert terrorism attorney to replace the court-appointed one.

Several legal aid organizations were hesitant about Mamou's circumstances, because not only was he a Pakistani immigrant likely to be extradited, but his small, somehow relevant criminal background cast a long shadow of doubt on his innocence. Too many believed that Mamou and the rest of the Al-Rasheed Five's charges of conspiracy to commit terrorist-related crimes were true.

We had donations from the Al-Rasheed neighborhood, bless

their God-fearing souls, but Amma was suspicious of the media catching wind of it. After so many years, the guilt had nestled right into her blood like a parasite. Even she believed her brother's terrorism case was drawn-out and shut; hopeless.

But *finally* I felt a glimmer of hope. The Justice Behind Bars board of directors was willing to rally behind Mamou. His incarceration was wrong, and they seemed to realize it too.

Mamou frowned. "The board confirmed this?"

"There's still a lot to iron out, and they want to talk to you, but after all these years of silence, I think this is a good sign."

Grudgingly, some of that hope flickered back into his eyes. "I see."

I grinned. "And you always say I'm wasting my time."

He shrugged. "Nida, you *are* wasting your time. Most of these organizations can't work miracles. A girl your age should be worrying about her studies, meeting friends. Not lawyers."

I shrugged back. "I'm not just any girl. You always said, I'm your legacy."

"Now I'm saying, I wish you'd be just any girl."

"Then I guess I should give up poetry." I spoke with exaggerated sweetness, knowing I had him there.

He sighed and pinched his nose with his free hand. "Enough. Tell me, when's your next performance? When I saw Zaynab, she mentioned you're entering some contest?"

I struggled not to scowl. "I decided against it, it's too public. It's risky."

"Everything is risky, beta. I've been saying that you need to expand your horizons, share your work with other people."

I stared at him, unsure if I should protest his words—after Alexis had pointed out how I avoid slam contests.

"At least share a letter with me. Or is that *too public?*" he mimicked in English.

Mamou was the one who had proposed the idea of writing poetry letters. After my parents' divorce, we'd moved to a small neighborhood, where we were one of the only Muslim families, and in our first week of living there, someone had complained to the community watchmen about our Quran and nasheed recitations during Eid Milad-un-Nabi, a time to celebrate the mercy of our Prophet, Peace Be Upon Him.

I couldn't understand how a holiday had turned into a nightmare. But Mamou had crouched, tapped my journal, and said: *The sharpest sword is the tongue, beta.*

That day, I wrote a poetry letter. My letters weren't words but small moments where I imagined I had the strength to confront my aggressors.

I dragged myself away from those memories. "I wrote a couple bars at home," I finally muttered.

"A couple bars?" he imitated again in English. "Is that what the youth call it? You are a shayar, a poet, and your tongue is Urdu. I will always call your letter a sher," he said.

Sher, a word for an Urdu or Persian couplet. But I was no shaeirah. My poetry was purely English.

"It's just slang," I said, reluctantly. "Besides, I left my journal in my bag."

Mamou raised a brow. "Who needs a journal when Allah has given you a tongue," he answered, simply.

There in the visitation room, I closed my eyes and spoke short verses into the phone, my typical rhythm muffled and staticky. It felt cold and wrong. Still, Mamou cocked his head, listening attentively to my English. I could speak Urdu but not enough to master the art of constructing ghazals or free-flowing nazms the way he could. At least Mamou looked pleased.

"It's been so long," he said, "since I've heard your poetry. You did good."

I shrugged away the compliment. "You haven't shared your poetry in years. It's not fair."

"Inmates are given the barest crumb of recreation time. I can hardly write. I'm a hypocrite, may Allah spare me." He winked, but beneath his words, he sounded bitter.

"After you're released from here, you'll have to make up for lost time."

His humor faded. "Stop saying that. You're wasting your childhood, Nida. You say no to opportunities—to competitions. You could do so much with your words, but you choose to waste it here, in this room."

My cheeks heated in embarrassment.

He continued to ramble about sacrifice, about the immigrant experience and the price of education, about the beauty of my art and how I'm wasting the family legacy. But as I glanced at the line of inmates on the other side of the partition, gazing at their own loved ones behind a glass screen, a pang resonated in my chest.

I interrupted his rant with a glare. "I understand the value well, of all the sacrifices our family has made—Amma never finished her degree after immigrating. I would never let her waste the tears she sheds day and night drowning in her worries. But I also understand the value of my own uncle. That's something neither Amma nor you had to teach me."

Three

On my commute home from visiting Mamou, a massive crowd surged around Wirth Park for the evening political rally downtown. Police patrolled the perimeters as signs were pushed into the grass by the Democratic Party volunteers. I kept myself busy by swiping through my phone.

Amma messaged me, ranting how her client asked for a steep discount like every other customer. But we couldn't comply when our landlord was pressing us for our late rent.

As I asked how the rest of the delivery went, my phone buzzed, the adhaan for Asr reminding me of the evening prayer. I hurried down the field toward the park. Cars swerved to a stop as a group of joggers cut across the street. My knees bounced to an R&B playlist humming through my earphones, my nose wrinkling at the scent of gasoline permeating the air.

On my right, hoopers were trading insults in a game of one-on-one. Their curses echoed through the quad alongside a stereo blaring Kendrick. As I passed, they rattled the fence before hooting and cheering, each friend gassing the other up.

In my distraction, my foot snagged on a yard sign, scuffing a poster of Mitchell Wilson.

There were dozens across the park. From what I recalled, Wilson was a Democratic candidate in the upcoming Senate election, a war veteran of the Afghan invasion, and a liberal man who envisioned a better state that would reflect *our changing values*—or so claimed the evening news, according to Aunty Nadia.

The primaries of the US Senate election would determine which candidates would make the final ballot. Tonight was Mr. Wilson's political rally.

Wilson seems like a decent enough man, Amma had once said. When I demanded why, she retorted, *Jaanu, he took the time to visit our mosque more than once, he cares about the Muslim vote.*

It would be my first time voting because my eighteenth birthday was in a matter of days.

My phone buzzed again with a second reminder to pray.

I gazed around. Police milled on the sidewalks, directing traffic on the blocked roads. At the far end of the park, the border of trees was bereft of people. After locating a spot, I laid out my silk pocket prayer mat from my bag. Every Muslim knew the ideal criteria to pray in public: in a park and under a tree. I pulled out my black abaya from my bag, buttoning it over my jeans before tightening my dark hijab. Then I raised my hands to begin the worship.

Suddenly, something gripped my shoulder, jerking me from prayer.

"Hands up. *Hands up.*"

"What?" I turned but the hand shook my body. *Roughly.*

Two men loomed above my mat, their shadows swallowing me. My tongue went dry when I took in their jet-black uniforms and the walkie-talkies looped around their hips blaring ear-shattering static. Their eyes scoured the length of me, lingering on my hijab.

They were cops.

"Hands up."

My hands lifted. Slow and visible, like I was taught.

Nida, this shouldn't be new to you. The morbid thought didn't ease my panic.

"Do you see that?" snapped the cop on the left, his dark hair swept under his cap. "She has one of those. Check it." He jabbed a finger at my scarf.

I flinched.

"Hands up higher," he barked. "I won't repeat it again."

"Yes, sir," I said automatically. That's another rule that my uncle had taught me. There were many rules. *Make sure your mouth is shut,* my Mamou's warning thudded in my chest. *Make sure you obey.*

His words weren't just fusses and fears, they were cynical prophecy.

Don't move, Nida. Do. Not. Move.

The cop on the right suddenly tugged on my hijab. "We need to search you."

"Search me?"

"Yes, for security."

My hands began shaking hard. The full reality of what was about to happen hit me at once. "Sir, but why?"

"Stay still!"

My lips opened, different words somersaulting over and over in my head. *If I don't say anything, they'll remove my hijab.*

"She could be hiding anything in there. Remember, we can't take risks with Wilson's rally," his colleague said before pulling a walkie from his belt. "There could be others." His gaze locked with mine. "Who else is with you?"

"No one!"

But he was already gazing around as if hunting for another hijabi. "No acquaintance? Collaborator? We had a security alert of a threat. And then we found you here."

Collaborator?

At my hesitation, he nodded at his colleague before nudging my backpack. "Search it all."

If I was hiding anything dangerous under a flimsy piece of cotton on my head, then what was I hiding under my shirt? Inside my pants? My socks? What about the rest of the visitors of the park playing behind me? What were *they* hiding?

Why was I singled out?

It didn't matter that I was on public property outside the vicinity of the political rally that was scheduled to be held in *several* hours. I'd learned since Mamou's arrest that the little details never mattered when it came to people like us.

One of their hands grasped my hijab and my desperation kicked in and I tried to keep my tone calm. "Sir, please, I could show my ID, and proof of my residence. I only came here to pray. I have to go back home."

But the cops barely registered my words.

He yanked my hijab, unraveling the material—unraveling my dignity. Now I only wore a white headcap. I felt bare naked. Violated.

It was the equivalent to the cops forcing me to undress. I'd spent years covering my hair, only for the authorities to treat the decision like it was nothing.

"*Please.*" My voice caught. "I came to pray, on God I swear."

His eyes were cold and a fathomless black. His feet were rooted to the ground. Nothing I said could've moved him.

Amma might've told me to comply, to forget Mamou, and oaths, and *Ameens*, but I had rights. "Please," I tried one last time. "Not in front of everyone."

He cocked his head. "Why wear it? You're in America now."

In any other circumstance, I'd have scoffed, *As if I wasn't born in this country*, but at the moment, all I could think of was my exposed hair. My hands reached to cover tendrils of it. It was an instinct; I moved before my brain caught on to the action.

The officer's hands shot out, wrenching my arms down, painfully.

"Elijah, what's the delay?" a new voice interrupted from behind the cop.

It belonged to a man flanked by two security personnel. My jaw dropped. It was the same man I'd seen in those blue posters.

Mitchell Wilson, the Democratic candidate. He was tall like my uncle, with a protruding gut, dressed in a checkered suit as charmingly gray as his hair, and a snug blue tie. If I were younger and asked to draw what an American politician looked like, it would be him.

My heart still raced, palms clammy, but I was less afraid. Seeing him brought me an awkward sort of relief. *Didn't Amma say he'd visited our mosque?*

"Who's this young girl?" Mr. Wilson's sharp gaze assessed the situation, the cops poised above me. He appeared almost disinterested.

"A suspect who isn't complying with security standards. We had an alert. Then we found her," the cop in front of me reassured him.

If I wasn't paralyzed by fear, I would've laughed. Security standards? I was a high school student. But my bravado dissipated as quickly as the wind.

Mr. Wilson's brows pinched together as he studied my black abaya and hijab. His frown deepened. "That burka, it's like she's a bank robber," he murmured to himself.

It took a moment for me to register his comment. I gaped at him. To make sure I wasn't imagining this.

"Exactly, sir. She was making her way to the rally with her flag, sir."

"Flag?" I shrieked. "What flag? This is my prayer mat!" But it was like I wasn't there. One of the cops kicked the mat forward, his heel dragging it on the dirt, before tossing my scarf down as if they were weapons.

"There's been a misunderstanding. That's my hijab and mat!"

Mr. Wilson waved his hand dismissively. "Oh, you poor thing. I find it unacceptable that someone is wearing this burka in a country of human rights. This is a place of values, not a place to promote barbarism. There's no need for your father to force you to wear it, you can come out of it now." His words were calm, like he knew better, making it feel worse. He nodded at the cop. "I'll meet you back at the rally, Elijah. Thank you for your work."

His security personnel nudged him forward toward the rally's setup. Mr. Wilson was nonchalant, with that grin of his, that confident tone, as if he hadn't just shattered a girl's worldview.

"I can't stand Muslims," his security guard remarked, and Mr. Wilson casually smiled.

My body was numb. *What just happened?*

One of the remaining cops peeled off my headcap. I didn't stop them as one of them stuck two of his long fingers through my hair, ignoring the way I clenched my teeth. I didn't stop them when they rummaged through my pack, tossing out my extra headcap, charger, poetry journal, and phone.

"See, what's this?" One of them kicked around the black prayer mat embossed with the holy Kaaba in the center and Arabic calligraphy on the tag. "What country is this even from? This looks like the ISIS flag."

But—

I'm a US citizen.

I'm a US citizen.

I'm a US citizen—

It didn't matter what the truth was when the only female citizens that were seen as free to them were the ones with exposed hair. But I wanted to shout it anyway.

I'm a US citizen.

After what felt like an hour, the cops nodded. "All clear," one of them spoke into his walkie.

By the time the guards left, I was shivering in the open sunlight. Only one thought coiled tight in my chest. A terrifying thought. *I wish I wasn't Pakistani.* I clenched my teeth tight, to keep them from chattering. *I wish I could be someone else.* I hated the thought, but I couldn't banish it.

I bent in the grass and scooped up my things. My hands trembled as I brushed away the dirt staining my journal. Hugging it, I knew tonight I would be pressing my anger into its pages until it was a mess of blue ink.

I imagined uncapping my pen and writing: *Dear Mitchell Wilson.*

I would write a letter, like I did with all my emotions, and I would pretend that I had the guts to tell Mr. Wilson how wrong he truly was. I could envision the words of my letter holding my frustration the way an Amma consoles a child.

Mr. Wilson may have visited our mosque, but he doesn't know anything about us.

But he didn't just say those words. He agreed with everything the guards accused me of.

How could a man who swore up and down to protect this state not be able to protect one young girl?

Dear Cops,

You wear nafrat packaged into black button-ups;
gilt gold badges, stiff straight caps.
You wear khofnak,
disguised as poesy and promise,
their gestured odes in the form of a hand to their badge
like a hand to a bible.
But the scariest is when these people
are no longer scared of being racist.
Their worship of Ms. Liberty
becomes worship of the paint over their monuments
as they cry, These are our human rights,
but the right is just a pretty way of saying, We prefer the
    shade of white.

Dear America,

My Mamou was sponsored to the United States by Amma
years after she immigrated to America.
He was cargo,
packaged, preened, and shipped across the seas
to a home he imagined to be so welcoming.
Upon attending college,
trying out for the debate team,
he was met with jeers and rolled eyes
at his stunted English and hard rolled accent.
Indeed, my Mamou was the package that cracked.
He was dropped in a land of circling vultures
    bent on devouring him.

Dear Mamou,

Against all odds,
you were accepted into college with all the student loans that
    would bury you long after.
You worked
    part-time as a school cleaner,
    part-time as a speaker,
for nights of slams and rants.

That same accent that your peers snickered at,
that same accent they mocked—
    their shrills ringing in your ears hours after you'd walked
        home
—was put to the gift that Allah demanded it be
    made for.
An accent spinning words like gold embroidery,
lifting them high for audiences to behold.

Post 9/11,
the time of the Iraq invasion,
you shifted your spoken word to charged odes and dangerous
    verse,
shouting about the American invasions
that disguised wars as liberty.

Senators would visit Al-Rasheed mosque,
but Mamou made a point to walk out,
      taking issue with their mess of Iraq and Afghanistan,
      taking issue with their support of drones sent to Pakistan.
Your viral reputation riled the youth.
Immigrants called you inspirational,
Non-immigrants called you radical.

Every Islamic event you frequented,
every protest you attended only to be arrested,
you performed with the fire of a bright-eyed Muslim.
Many hated you for it.
Because this man,
      unable to vote,
      unraised in this country,
using that poet tongue through a long, proud beard,
you called it for what it was.

But of course,
we all should've known
      brown men who don't keep silent
      are bound to become this country's target.

Four

Zaynab drove down to pick me up because Amma was an hour north delivering a client's order. During the car ride I recounted the frisking to Zaynab. My voice was hollow. My fingers shook.

I kept my tears inside and it hurt. My burning eyes were so swollen by the time we pulled into our neighborhood, I struggled to open them wider.

"We're here," Zaynab said quietly.

Al-Rasheed was a cluttered line of immigrant-owned concrete storefronts. Most of the shop signs were written in various dialects of Arabic script. At the end of the block, the green mosque seemed to penetrate the sky with its long earthy minaret and shining dome—the only polished aspect of the dense street. Beside it was the Poet's Block, a tented cement rectangle with peeling white paint. The only clean color against the neighborhood's dim setting.

Heaps of people crowded around the tent's entrance. I spotted Uncle Mahmoud the butcher in the midst, walking from his Syrian meat shop. There was the local paan and chaat store owned by Aunty Farooqi, who made the best golguppa, filled with spiced chickpeas, to slurp during late nights. There was the Uyghur baker, Uncle Ehmet, who was known for his patterned, lamb-stuffed naan that sold out every morning. The bakery was co-owned with his Uzbek wife Aunty Sahnoza, an expert in various mithai and halva assortments. Behind them stood Uncle Daoud, a Christian Syrian who ran a spice shop.

More and more people streamed toward the Poet's Block: the elders who owned Asian fabric stores run illegally in their basement, clothes directly imported via suitcases from Karachi and Peshawar, Pakistan. I even saw Uncle Choudhry, the mechanic who fixed any broken electronic for a small fee and the promise to promote his business cards for his three other shops.

Al-Rasheed was a different side of America, a quilt of a brown enclave riddled with skeletons of run-down apartments and shabby barely-there townhomes. It was divided into mini quarters filled with immigrants. Community cleanups were attempted and abandoned, the filth never vanishing, as if no matter how many times we picked litter or trimmed the overgrowth of weeds, Al-Rasheed would always retain a stubborn but symbolic layer of dirt and dust.

"That's weird. It's not even prayer time but all the elders are out," I said before it hit me. "They found out, didn't they?" I turned to my sister in outrage. "You told the neighborhood about the frisking!"

"No! I told the poets and Amma! But you know how everyone is, they can't keep their mouths shut. . . ."

"Someone leaked it." I groaned.

Zaynab finished parking our old minivan in the small dusty field behind the Al-Rasheed mosque—which also served as a sad version of a parking lot. "I can wallah that I only texted

Jawad. He said he'd bring the poets. But the aunties and uncles are here now, and they're waiting for you. You can't ignore them, Nida. Or else they'll cause a commotion!"

"This is ridiculous."

I wanted to wallow with the poets while downing three cups of chai and a heap of cake rusks. Not deal with the neighborhood's overzealous, overprotective elders.

"They've seen our car," Zaynab continued in a low voice. "If we leave now, the aunties will assume the worst, stalk you home, and demand to pray all night long. Better to see them now, show them you're in one piece, and then they'll go."

I shoved my way out of the van toward the Poet's Block.

A huddle of students stood outside the entrance, like they were in detention. Typically, the Poet's Block was reserved for slam poetry on the weekends, but every Friday, it was the headquarters of our community meetings—especially in the event of an emergency.

"What's going on? Why aren't you inside?" I spotted Jawad first, the unofficial leader of the Block.

He was a good foot taller, which was why he was much better at ball than me. He was a pretty boy, built like a baller, with dark curly hair, wide eyes, and rich black skin, and when he spoke, it was velvet smooth. That voice did him a lot of good in spoken word. Like his father, the Somali Catholic convert-made-imam at the mosque, just by speaking, he made heads turn.

"The Block's been hijacked," Jawad said immediately. "The aunties came out of nowhere and they're demanding to see you."

"You leaked the frisking to the entire neighborhood," I hissed.

"Wallah, it was my mom. Now get rid of them," he hissed back.

Jawad and I were friends by virtue of us liking the same thing and going through the same thing. Our uncles were best friends and acclaimed poets. In fact, they'd kick-started the Poet's Block two decades ago before their arrests. Now Jawad was continuing his uncle's legacy, performing at the Poet's Block on weekends just like me.

Apparently, his legacy didn't come with having a backbone against the aunties.

With a deep breath, I forced my way inside the tent.

The first one to see me was Aunty Sahnoza. Tears filled her eyes as she folded me into her arms. She cursed in a mix of Russian and Uzbek. "Oh, those goons!" Over my shoulder, she gestured at someone. "Oi, Ehmet, bring the donation box."

Her Uyghur husband brought forward an old halal yogurt container filled with dollar bills.

"Take it, Nida."

"What's going on?"

"We must discuss what to do about those goons who hurt you," Ehmet explained slowly. "Everyone has been waiting."

"Everyone?" I repeated. "How many aunties are here?"

Instead of answering, Sahnoza yanked me deeper into the tent. "Come, come." I glanced helplessly at Zaynab, and she shrugged.

Inside the Poet's Block, thirty uncles and aunties were squeezed together on plastic fold-up chairs or cross-legged around the room-length floor table. A fan blasted in the corner, a small mercy in the humid air buzzing with flies. A haze of steam from freshly brewed chai with the sweet scent of cardamom lingered across the tent.

Elders from every South Asian motherland huddled together on the Persian carpet, and at the center, I spotted Aunty Farooqi wailing into the dupatta of her shalwar kameez. Aunties patted each other's shoulders in some austere version of comfort.

"May those officers be cursed! We must help our poor child," Aunty Farooqi ordered the room. She was my Amma's best friend, an Azad-Kashmiri who'd emigrated from the port city of Karachi together with my Amma.

"We should call the police center and complain about their officers," Aunty Nadia said. She owned the Punjabi Pak grocery shop across from the mosque. In the garage, she ran an illegal urban farm full of organic desi chickens.

"No, stupid, that won't do anything. They will protect their own," Aunty Farooqi argued.

"But they hurt our Zaynab, we must do something!"

Aunty Farooqi glared with all the heat of a Dundicut pepper. "*It happened to Nida,*" she snapped. "Not Zaynab."

"Tobah, toba-aaaah," Aunty Nadia wailed again.

Aunty Sahnoza dragged me forward toward them.

"Oho, those goons deserve punishment. Let's message Cousin Ahmed. His brothers charge fifty bucks per hit. One phone call, they'll take care of the problem," Aunty Farooqi offered to the council.

Because she's my favorite aunty, out of respect, I withheld my horror. But that was Aunty Farooqi's solution in every conflict— either engage in a Facebook smear campaign or hire her Punjabi in-laws to jump the offender.

At the front of the room, atop a small podium, stood Elder Arif. He was one of the older Pakistani uncles, a former tribal Pashtun leader who'd emigrated from Waziristan between the territories of Afghanistan and Pakistan. He was a pudgy, muscular old man, with russet-brown hair that brushed his ears the color of ginger qahwah and a long henna-stained beard.

On the podium, he slammed his cane, calling the room to attention. He was also in charge of council meetings only on the condition that someone sponsor the gatherings with chai, the traditional way.

"Oho, Nida is here," Elder Arif announced. "Come, Nida, come to the front. Oh good, she has the donation box."

The aunties' eyes scoured every inch of me as if they expected my body to be sporting bruises. I tried for a smile, but it came out weakly. "Assalaamualaykum," I greeted the room.

Aunty Farooqi stood with her hands on her hips. "Nida, we must begin with some prayers and Quran readings—" but she was cut off as others chimed in from every direction.

"*May Allah make Wilson burn in hell!*"

"*I emailed the mosque to lead a du'a for you!*"

"*Send me a video. I will spread it through the WhatsApp prayer groups!*"

The aunties continued to surge forward like this was some Hajj pilgrimage in Saudi Arabia rather than our run-down Block.

Then Elder Arif whistled with his two fingers, commanding them to silence. He tossed a wad of twenty-dollar bills at my chest. "Add that to the donation box."

"Uncle, I cannot accept the donations. You all need it more," I protested.

"Shut up, beta," he said. "We do not need this money. Those goons hurt our daughter. We must donate money in your name!"

I blinked hard, my eyes stinging. Most of these elders worked long hours in their respective shops—convenience stores and restaurants—while others worked at the factories around the ring roads or drove Ubers all day long.

Elder Arif addressed the aunties. "My sisters, we must be patient. We will call and lodge a complaint! We will sue Mitchell Wilson!"

Aunty Farooqi wasn't having it. "Oho, naïve old brother, do not waste your time complaining. These are dirty politicians! I warned you all, the evil eye is out to get us because of that jealous

Sister Ayesha." Her eyes cut to me. "Take the donations quickly! I have Cousin Ahmed on speed dial."

"Okay, no." I shoved the money back into their hands. "No one is jumping a very protected politician."

Aunty Farooqi grunted. "Beta, don't refuse the money, that evil eye won't just disappear. Chashm-e-badoor." She slit her hand against her throat with a fond grin. "I can always order another goat to slaughter."

"We are not slaughtering another goat. The one you gave my Amma is still at home!"

Zaynab came up from behind me, grabbing my shoulder before speaking up. "Uncles, aunties, as you can see, Nida is fine and in one piece." To soften the blow, she touched Elder Arif's arm. "Please, go home and rest. You've done more than enough. Because of you, Nida isn't in tears anymore."

I scoffed at that.

"My Amma will continue to update you on . . . the situation," my sister wisely called it.

And because she's the elder sister, they all nodded at her.

"The meeting is adjourned." Elder Arif slammed his cane again before shouting in Urdu, "Mahmoud bhai, bring my cup of chai!"

Welcome to Al-Rasheed, the most chaotic Muslim neighborhood in the state. A brown mecca, some claimed.

With the half-assed meeting adjourned, the aunties and uncles dispersed, some kissing my temple, others pulling out their small prayer beads and bottles of water to bless, rolling up their sleeves like they were prepared to battle a holy war on my behalf, their personal jihad. For the first time that day, I felt myself truly smile.

The imprint of the morning frisking was still on me—not on my skin, but down to the marrow of my bones, and I didn't think it would leave anytime soon. But that was okay. I had this: aunties, uncles, the poets, Amma, Zaynab . . .

I had Al-Rasheed.

By the time the last of the uncles had retreated, the poets had swelled into the tent.

"Thank Allah," Jawad announced by way of greeting. "You should've seen them, Nida; the elders took us by surprise. Now I know why we're called terrorists."

I settled a glare on him, and he pretended not to notice.

"Elder Arif threatened to whack me with his cane if we didn't leave for what he called 'an emerrr-gency council meeting.' Some council they have." He paused, taking notice of the container in my hand. "Why are you holding a yogurt tub?"

"It's my pity donation box. Are you going to donate too?"

He smirked. "No."

With that, Jawad directed the rest of the poets to form a circle. He pointed at a random boy. "Ahmed, you're going up for a rap battle against . . . Hania."

With his other hand, he unflicked the metal tea dispenser and began filling two Styrofoam cups with steaming chai.

"So, about the frisking, you doing okay? Did the aunties exorcise the nazar out of you?"

"I wish it were an evil eye," I answered honestly. "Also, I hope that chai is for me."

"Last week the mosque was vandalized," Jawad reminded me. "The imams are worried about security, and another shooting. None of the news outlets cared about the vandalism. With the election, tensions are high, and it'll only get worse when the candidates schedule their election debates. When you're out of the house, take it easy."

"I did take it easy. The cops found me because I was trying to pray in the park."

Jawad finished filling one cup. "Next time, wait to get home to pray. They could've seriously hurt you, Nida."

My gut clenched. *I wanted to pray on time. I did nothing wrong.* But of course, Jawad knew that.

My eyes shut, briefly, fingers gripping the pages of my journal.

"Hey," Jawad murmured. I felt his hand gently prying the notebook from me. "If this is all too much for you, we can get out of here."

"No, it's fine." My voice felt shaky. He searched my face.

"We can always go to my house. My mom made barris and goat."

Jawad's mother was my Quran teacher, and growing up, I'd spent every Sunday at her house, eating hilib ari—a type of braised goat with a plate of pilaf. It reminded me of Pakistani mutton karahi and pilou. But those times were different—we were younger and closer. He was busier now. He had a group of friends from the neighborhood and school where they played pickup basketball. He was the executive of a dozen different clubs. He was a people person.

Ever since high school, everything between us stretched far and distant like an impassable canyon. I guess a part of growing up meant slowly losing the friends closest to you.

"I can't," I finally muttered.

"Are you here to practice then?" He gestured toward the podium.

"No. I think I'll write instead."

He smiled slightly. "You're in the right place." Balancing our chai in the crook of his arm, he stepped back, his Nikes scuffing my Js.

"Easy! These are my babies." I crouched to have a good look. The retro Jordans were my prized pair, bought years ago after I won my first basketball game. Still in pristine condition, a testament to my care.

Instead of apologizing, Jawad dangled the chai underneath my nose. "Do you want the chai or no?"

I pretended to sniff it. He shoved the cup closer to my mouth until I snatched it away.

"You're forgiven," I decided after a sip of the toe-curling goodness. For a second, everything felt normal again.

I followed Jawad to the back of the tent. At the front, the poets readied for the first round of a rap battle on the mini podium— which was a stack of bricks. We sat cross-legged around the low table.

Instead of paying attention to the poetry, I riffled through my notebook filled with old letters. A fly landed on the pages. I swatted it away.

Jawad's hand reached out to graze my journal. "I know writing a letter helps you. But sometimes I think it's unfair that the rest of the world has no idea what we go through."

"You tried," I reminded him.

The Al-Rasheed Five resulted in five arrests. After Jawad's uncle returned from a trip to Somalia, bringing money to relatives overseas, he was arrested under terrorism-funding-related charges. He was held in Guantanamo Bay, the most notorious prison base in the world housing suspected terrorists, known for torture and brutality. Even through prison, his uncle's poetry was famous; it was showcased once in an art display at the Louis College of Criminal Justice before the Defense Department confiscated it.

At that time, Jawad posted videos of his spoken word. It backfired on his entire family. Jawad's father was under scrutiny as a Somali imam.

As if recalling it all, Jawad's eyes darkened.

"If I talked about today's incident," I continued, "how much good would it do for any of us?"

"I don't know. But our words have to count for something. I heard you said no to the NSPL competition, even with your teacher's recommendation."

"I did," I admitted slowly.

"Then what about my anthology?"

Everything inside me was twisting and screaming *yes*. The Block's best performers were publishing an anonymous poetry anthology under pen names through a small Muslim press. Using our connections with slams across the city and a national Islamic institute, they would distribute the anthology to different educational organizations.

Even under a pen name, Amma would say no. She'd tell me to focus on school. It was senior year, and I had deadlines, assignments—college applications. With my low-B average, I was barely at the benchmark for a reputable physics program.

But there was also *this* legacy.

My gaze drifted around the Poet's Block. Amma thought the slams were a hobby, something to forget after graduation when we embarked on jobs and corporate careers. Just the reality of it made my palms moisten. Would that be me after I graduated? Ruminating fondly on the Poet's Block as some memory?

My jaw clenched. Poetry wasn't a phase to me. In some ways it felt like my forever. I wasn't just *Nida, Abdul-Hafeedh's niece, Siddiqui,* or whichever title the others thought up. I wanted to carve out my *own* legacy the way Mamou did.

But imagining it was easier than actually doing it.

"I have to ask Amma." I broke the heavy silence. "The anthology goes against her rules."

"Why do you have to ask her? It's under a pen name, she'll never know."

I froze. A brief disappointment flashed in Jawad's gaze. The sad part? He looked unsurprised at my silence.

"I don't like telling you to go against your mom," he said. "But I also know it's not just her. You're scared. And you're using her as an excuse to never put your work out there."

He stood up, joining the others in the rap battle.

Suddenly, everything felt too real. Too loud.

I gripped my pen, the sensation a rippling calm, before writing my first words.

Dear Mitchell Wilson.

My finger touched the splash of ink. And then I wrote more.

Here, in private, my eyes burned feverishly. From withholding tears that I was too stubborn to shed. *Not in front of them. I don't want any looks of pity*, I told myself. Pity was simply the inability to do anything about someone else's pain. It reminded me that we were helpless against it.

I tried to write more but my skin crawled from the ghost of foreign touch. A tear marked a path down my cheek.

The tongue is your sword, Mamou would insist.

His mistake had always been hope. He hoped our words would be heard. He hoped our words would matter. He hoped our words would create change in a nefarious world. Writing was, to be truthful, a terrible way to cope. But it was the way I lived.

By the time I finished three different letters on Mitchell Wilson, a full hour had passed. Jawad finally returned to me because of a commotion at the entrance of the tent.

"Nida," he said, calling me over. "Deal with this."

I got up. "Deal with what—oh." My eyes widened. "Alexis?"

My friend stood awkwardly at the entrance of the tent, a small bag in her hands. Her expression was scrunched up apologetically as soon as our gazes met.

"I'm sorry," she immediately began. "I know it's weird for me to be here. But I heard about the frisking from Zaynab. I can't believe you didn't call me!"

I crossed the room toward her. "I haven't had time to text anyone. I haven't even seen my Amma. But Alexis, you're not supposed to be here. The other poets don't invite non-Muslims. It's a safety thing after the arrests. I've told you this."

Alexis held her hands up. "I know, I know. I'm leaving. I just wanted to make sure you were okay."

"You should've called—"

"I know," she interrupted again, shoving the bag into my arms. "I only wanted to drop off comfort food. That's what you did too, remember? You brought me snacks after my parents' divorce."

"Oh," I said, a mix of guilt and confusion welling inside me. I felt bad. She'd driven all the way down to Al-Rasheed.

The hairs on the back of my neck prickled. The other poets watched us. I turned to Jawad pleadingly. "Can she stay? Just for an hour?"

His eyes narrowed. "Only if we get some of those snacks." He faced Alexis. "This is a onetime exception, just for Nida. Believe it or not, we've had spies here on behalf of intelligence agencies. It's a safety rule, Lexie." He explained this monotonously, as if he'd repeated the same line to others a hundred times.

"Alexis," she corrected. "Thanks. Your name is Jamil, right?"

"Jawad," he corrected back.

"Right, sorry."

Around us, the other students resumed the rap battles, filling the seats at the front of the tent. "So, this is the inside of the Block?" she asked, almost unimpressed. I didn't blame her. It was a simple run-down tent. But that's where the magic began.

I yanked her forward toward the circle of performers, excitement blistering inside me. I was wary too, but I'd never had the chance to show Alexis the Poet's Block. "Yeah." I grinned. "I'll introduce you to everyone."

For the rest of the hour, Alexis hung around for a few rounds of battle, snapping and hooting alongside us. Thanks to Jawad's glare, she left after an hour. When the last of the poets finished their performances, my phone buzzed with a text from my Amma.

AMMA
Oho come home nows! Where u r?

NIDA
Ok. Coming.

I collected my things, readying to leave until I realized I'd misplaced my notebook. I retraced my steps to the chai station, but I couldn't find it. My pulse stuttered.

I texted Zaynab.

NIDA
Did you go home with my notebook?
Just double checking.

After waiting a few moments, Zaynab didn't answer. I searched again but Amma spammed me with more messages.

By then, the Poet's Block had all but emptied out, only a few students lingering. Jawad was outside, disposing of the trash bags.

Zaynab must have it, I reassured myself. That strange sensation returned from this morning, like something undeniably terrible had transpired.

My notebook is gone.

Five

I sprinted the short five-minute walk back to our townhome, attempting to quell my panic.

After unlocking the front door, I was immediately bombarded with the noise of our small television in the corner of the living room. Pakistan's *Geo News* blasted on-screen with the anchors cursing in Urdu through vaguely threatening insults in what they called political debates. The room was dim because we kept the lights off until sunset to reduce the cost of electricity.

At the kitchen counter, Amma was surrounded by six bottles of water, the holy Quran opened in her right hand as she riffled through its pages chaotically, her white dupatta tossed over her head to cover her hair. She was dressed in a dark russet shalwar and soft blue lawn-style kameez. "Bismillah," Amma huffed on the water bottles.

Aunty Aleema, one of our neighbors, stood beside her, reading a prayer book aloud. My twelve-year-old little brother, Mohamed, sat at the kitchen table with his Sunday summer school books open under their supervision.

"Amma salaam, I'm back!" I called out.

Amma's head jerked up, eyes slitted. "Oho, Nida, finally.

Come here right now. Drink all this water. I spent the past hour blessing it with the three Qul. I knew there was severe nazar over you from that Baji Ayesha next door."

Aunty Aleema put down her prayer book. "Oh, my Nida, I heard all about how the cops stole your things and beat you."

My jaw dropped. "Who told you this?"

"Baji Zuha."

"Amma," I hissed under my breath, but she pretended not to hear.

"Aleema, they left Nida in tears—" Amma practically cried.

"That is not what happened," I interrupted. "They only took my hijab—"

Aunty Aleema gasped. "They took all your clothes off too!" Her hands covered her mouth. "Tobah, tobah! Your honor!"

"No!" I shrieked before she went off on *that* tangent.

Mohamed squinted his eyes at my body. "I don't see anything. Amma told everyone the cops beat you up. She said you had broken bones."

"That didn't happen—"

But Amma nodded dejectedly, eyes downcast. "I know. They're animals."

I gave up.

Aunty Aleema went back to praying as Amma gathered up the water bottles.

"Nida, come now. Drink the water."

"I promise I will, but where's Zaynab?"

"Oi! I said drink the water now!"

"Amma, it's an emergency," I pleaded. "My notebook is gone."

"How can you be so careless?" Amma paled as some horrible realization struck her. "What if those cops took it?"

"But I had it with me an hour ago!"

My sister appeared at the entrance of our shared bedroom. "Hey, I was just about to order takeout."

"Did you bring my notebook home? I can't find it."

She took in my disheveled expression. "No, I didn't. Wasn't it at the Poet's Block?"

On cue, my phone buzzed with another text.

JAWAD
You left your notebook near the podium.
I'm coming over to drop it off.

"Oh, that's weird. Jawad found it," I announced, half-embarrassed.

For some reason, my dread was still present, weighing down my chest. I could wallahi that I hadn't left my notebook at the podium. I hadn't even stepped foot *near* the podium. How did it get there?

Zaynab must have read my expression. "You've had a rough day, that's why you misplaced it. How about we order from a delivery app, my treat? I'm sick of leftover korma."

"You can afford takeout?"

She smirked. "No. My college has a reimbursement program as part of their 'Cultural Orient Express' or whatever to make people try other cuisines. I made fake emails and Photoshopped the food receipts, so I was reimbursed for meals."

I pressed my hand to my chest. "That's genius."

As she ordered takeout, I went outside and sat on the porch, nursing a bottle of Amma's blessed water. A shaft of light from the weak setting sun splashed on my cheeks like its energy had been swallowed away too.

I stared across Al-Rasheed, wondering what about this place made the Mr. Wilsons of the world so terrified.

There wasn't a wall spared from blasts of graffiti—the type of art that came from angry refugees. Arabic script danced across the brick apartments with all sorts of national flags ranging from Jordan to Afghanistan, dressing the walls of tight alleyways before the road abruptly ended. Others showed odes of poetry. The art was back from Mamou's days.

At the entrance of the neighborhood, convenience stores and a gentrified mall brought most of the traffic. Trailing from the commercial stores, townhomes and gangly apartments were stacked together in a version of a residential area, housing the people of Al-Rasheed, with an occasional green (more like yellow) space between buildings.

I knew my rented house like the surety of the sun rising and setting. Home was chipped red paint, the yellow dock weeds stabbing up from the wooden porch. It was the occasional yells of Aunty Farooqi and her husband arguing next door. The scent of haldi spicing the air.

But after today, entering the racket of my neighborhood brought me an anxiety I could not explain, as if I half expected Mr. Wilson and his security to be right at my heels. My skin itched from the sensation.

It was fully dark by the time Jawad approached my town house. I waved at him.

"I can't believe you left this at the tent," Jawad said from below the porch, tossing the notebook upward.

I managed to catch it. "Would you like this Quranic-blessed water in exchange?"

He studied the bottle suspiciously. "No, thanks."

His gaze went up to meet mine.

"But you can reconsider the anthology. It would be weird for me to do it without you."

I cradled the notebook. "It's not that easy," I whispered. "Not after today."

"Our uncles always said how the Block is a good way for Muslims to rediscover their artistic history and traditions, but in some ways, it's like a bubble. Someday, the Poet's Block will disappear. We'll move away. Grow up. The next generation will forget. I won't always be living here."

I lurched up at his statement. For some reason, that hurt. Or maybe, change hurt.

He gestured to the neighborhood. "You have to ask yourself, is the poetry in the Poet's Block, or is the poetry inside you?"

Dear Journal,

Mamou said the art of letter writing is the inferior gift
    derived from oral traditions.
Ancestral stories passed from grandmother to granddaughter,
thick in dialects before erased through the sanitization of
    translations.

Mamou said our tribe recited poetry,
from Mughal court poets to bazaar storytellers,
from oratory to written stories.

Mamou said when a child of Islam was upset
they had choices like any human being.
But only theirs could be guided by the hands of religiosity.
Islam was peace but in a country of people who declared you
    their enemy. . . .
Mamou said, It was important to show them what peace
    means to a Muslim,
to write out anger into something beautiful,
something that could be wholly mine,
something disguising rage into pretty rhymes.

Dear Alexis,

On the first day of school
my gym teacher asked why . . .
why my headscarf was getting in the way
of my dribbles and handles in the class basketball game.
I wanted to ask why . . .
why I had to abide by
this notion that my clothes
were a form of control.

I was banned from competing for being "out of uniform,"
for refusing to strip to shorts and an immodest T-shirt,
for sticking to my religious beliefs,
humiliated by a teacher for my barbaric "modest" motifs.

Until the popular girl stood up and said:
"Mr. Daniels, it's racist to think
a girl can't have the right to her own beliefs
in a country that applauds itself on diversity,
and multicultural plurality.
Last time I checked, this is a free country,
so let the Muslim girl wear her hijab and sweatpants in peace."

Alexis, that wasn't the first time
nor the last time you defended
and encouraged me.
You're the shield who can say things
that I can't say alone.
Our friendship is new,
a feeling of safety in a room full of finger pointing.
Mamou told me friends are precious jewels,
you are what your people are.
My people are you.

Dear Alexis,

I never made friends easily.
After Mamou's arrest
I never understood Amma's paranoia,
but no worry,
America would soon explain that to me.

Amma was stalked by FBI spies.
Intelligence branches conducted surveillances across Muslim
    enclaves,
even visiting the Muslim Student Association at Zaynab's
    campus.

In the months following the media frenzy
targeting Mamou and the rest of the Al-Rasheed Five,
    our electricity was shut,
    Amma's tires were slashed,
    her accounts doxed, and our Toyota van tailed by
        unidentifiable cars.

Zaynab made her first friend at a campus
    café;
that friend turned out to be a spy
for the same police department

attempting to map where local Muslim families prayed, ate,
    worked, and studied.
It was something out of a dystopian movie.

Alexis, you became my first friend outside the Poet's Block.
You were the popular girl,
we went three years in high school
hardly acknowledging each other.

Junior year physics class, Mr. Mathews made us partners.
You came over. You tasted Pakistani food. You were amazed.
    You asked questions and I never minded.
Between your parents' decision to divorce,
you saw yourself in my separated family,
our home giving you warmth.

Maybe that's why I was eager to trust you but hesitant,
like the way I approached a firefly.
Its light would be so tempting to cup in my hands,
but it could wink out at a moment's notice.

Friendships are scary.
You invest your hopes in a person
but very rarely do you see a return.

Six

The next seven weeks passed blissfully. I tried hard to forget about Mr. Wilson's frisking. And by late October, during the long weekend, two months into my senior year, I was returning home from playing ball with the block's kids, the memory shoved to the back of my mind. I waved at Aunty Sahnoza from the Turkic quarters of Al-Rasheed—a nickname for the group of Uyghur immigrants that had recently settled in our neighborhood.

"Nida," she greeted. "Farooqi was looking for you. She said she found a package with your name. Something about a competition."

"A package?" I began fanning myself with the neck of my Raptors jersey. Despite the fall season, we'd been handed the late heat.

"You know how she is. I saw her trying to open it. Go before she shows the entire neighborhood." She pinched my cheek and went back to her gardening.

I rushed over to my home, spotting Aunty Farooqi sitting on our shared porch, her woolen shawl flapping from the wind. Her husband was in the garage below, preparing for their barbeque party that afternoon.

"Oho, Nida baby." She smiled all crookedly with her tobacco-lined teeth. "How's my beti doing?"

"Salaam, Aunty. I'm good, Alhamdullilah."

Her nose wrinkled. "Nida, baby, take a shower. You reek."

"Thanks, Aunty. Aunty Sahnoza said you had a package."

"Oho, patience. Your aunty wants to talk to you." She patted her chest, coughing deeply with those smoker's lungs before speaking through another mouthful of tobacco. "The package came for you an hour ago. I told them I'd take care of it." She finished her chewing, winked, then spit the tobacco into her plastic water bottle.

Aunty Farooqi always had an unending pile of Nestlé bottles stashed against the border of her porch, filled halfway with the black tar of spit tobacco. Normal people had a trophy shelf—Aunty Farooqi's were her precious tobacco bottles.

"Aunty, you know there's a trash can for a reason, right?"

"Oho, I know there's a trash can, baby. Almost put my husband in one."

I smothered my laugh into a cough. Their morning arguments could be heard down the block. Not that it was my business that Uncle Jihad had forgotten their wedding anniversary, anyway—

"You know we're supposed to be caring about the climate and all. You should recycle the bottles."

"Well, tell the climate to care about me! It's so damn hot!"

I searched around. "About that package . . ."

She patted the cardboard box stashed beneath her rocking chair. "Right here, baby. It says N-S-P-L!"

I did my best to school my expression. Aunty Farooqi spread

gossip like wildfire, our version of a security guard. When something strange happened, she was the first to shriek it down the street, a little bit of exaggeration mixed with the truth.

Aunty Farooqi handed me the cardboard box. On the right corner, there was an emblem of a microphone with the initials NSPL looping in a circle.

"National Students Poet League," I read, stunned.

"What else does it say? I can't read this fancy English!" Aunty bobbed her head.

"Maybe that's a good thing." I laughed nervously.

"You know, when I was young, I couldn't step foot outside my village without having my sisters and my Ami with me. You kids have too much freedom." With a deep *harrumph*, she went back to her rocking chair and Facebook scrolling.

I bent down to the box for a closer look, a mix of dread and hope blossoming in my chest. I tore through the tape. Inside, there was an envelope, a purple magazine, and a card with a formal invitation to the *Fifteen Minutes* segment show, scheduled for next week.

Shock reverberated through me. *How is this possible?*

In a daze, I stared at the congratulations letter for placing first in NSPL's contest.

First? I never entered the competition.

The letter stated the monetary prize would be presented during the *Fifteen Minutes* segment. I flipped through the copy of this week's *American People*, a well-read political magazine. There was a three-page feature on NSPL. Each page included a poet and their winning piece along with a submitted photo and biography.

There I was in the first spread, with my high school picture eating up the entire space. A picture and poetry piece I didn't remember submitting.

Based on the invitation, I was expected to perform alongside two other winners at *Fifteen Minutes* before a live studio audience. But shock scattered any remnants of satisfaction. I never entered this contest. I didn't want to. So who did?

My fingers fiddled with the magazine pages as I sank to my knees.

Dear Mitchell Wilson, the first line read.

It was my poetry letter addressed to Mr. Wilson.

"I knew it!" Aunty Farooqi snapped from over my shoulder. "You won something!"

I crumpled the letter in my hand. "No, I didn't."

She tutted her tongue. "You cannot lie to me. My baby won, I saw the words *mag-a-zine* and *con-grat-u-lations,*" she enunciated slowly but proudly in English.

"Aunty, it's a misunderstanding, I didn't enter!"

"Did you hear that? My baby won!" Aunty squawked it aloud and the other neighbors took notice. "My baby is famous! She's in a magazine! Call *Geo News!*"

"Aunty!"

"What's that? Nida is famous?" Uncle Jihad lowered the Punjabi music blaring from his stereo on their side of the garage. He jogged up our shared porch, a freshly grilled piece of tandoori chicken clutched in his right hand that he passed to his wife. He was a big, towering uncle, more facial hair than actual person, sporting an impressive gray beard that tickled his chest.

"No one is famous, Uncle," I gritted out. "I said it's a misunderstanding."

"What's a misunderstanding?" my Amma chimed in from our doorway and I stilled.

Oh no.

"Nida, what's going on?" Amma demanded at my silence.

Aunty Farooqi stared between us, and I think she read my

panic, because her foot nudged the package behind the rocking chair before she shot up.

To my surprise, Aunty Farooqi changed the subject. "Did you hear, Fahad's engagement didn't go through! The girl expected four gold sets from the start! I knew my Fahad picked a gold digger for his rishta!"

To my relief, Amma fell for it. "Oho, post his résumé in the group chat I sent you; the mothers will see his accomplishments and offer hands-in-marriage right away."

"I already did." Aunty pouted.

"Then we pray," my Amma decided as I made a face. All the aunties were in wedding mode, sharing their children's résumés as if that was the way to parse out a potential spouse. But Pakistani parents were nothing if not efficient. These days, the mothers gathered over chai and cake rusks, in a poor attempt to matchmake for their children.

"You go tell your Zaynab that my Fahad is now a free man, okay?" Aunty Farooqi continued. "Maybe she'll be interested."

"Yes, we'll tell her," Amma reassured.

But Aunty Farooqi wasn't having it. To make extra sure, she pointed at me with her husband's half-gnawed bone of tandoori chicken. "You tell her too, Nida baby. Fahad must be married by the end of the year!"

"All in ease, behen-ji." Uncle Jihad went back to the garage, where the smoke of his traditional charcoal grill clogged the air. "I'm hosting my barbeque tonight. Many young men will be here, we can find a suitor for Zaynab that way." He turned to me. "Will you watch the cricket match, puttar? It's India versus Pakistan. We have the morning's halwa puri that Farooqi made taza taza." Uncle Jihad gestured at his jade pajamas and a conservative green T-shirt with the Pak flag stretched so tight, it showed a little too much of his round gut.

"I can't, Uncle-ji."

Because I just won a contest that I never entered.

He shook his head. "Amreeka has corrupted you, puttar," he said, before walking deeper into the garage. "A true Pakistani must love cricket! Zuha, get your bloody puttar's head checked!" He pointed to his skull in emphasis.

Amma shrugged. "Already did."

Aunty Farooqi and I held our breaths as Amma slowly returned inside.

"That was a close one," Aunty had the nerve to say. We glanced at the NSPL package, and she leaned in. "You have to tell your Amma, Nida baby. You won a contest. She'll find out sooner or later."

"Thanks, Aunty," I murmured.

Back in my bedroom, I set down the NSPL package on my desk.

Someone had entered the competition for me. Without my permission. But how? Who had access to my poetry letters?

I'd brought my journal to MSA meetings, to MIST practices, to the Poet's Block. Even at home, Zaynab and Mohamed had seen it.

Despite my confusion, a knot of joy swelled up my throat, brief but selfish. For that momentary second, it felt good to win a contest.

Maybe it was okay to dream and hope. This was validation, right? My poetry could be accepted outside the bubble of the Poet's Block. Maybe I could make it something more—make Mamou really proud. Step out of his shadow and make a name for myself.

That's the thing about recognition: after a small taste, you always wanted more.

But reality crashed against the fleeting hope. *Your poetry style is out there, in front of a national audience, to be exposed and judged.*

A sharp ache built up behind my rib cage. It grew heavier, until I had to lie on my mattress, reminding myself to take slow, deep breaths.

It's just a poetry contest. No one cares about it outside our own circles. None of it matters. It shouldn't matter.

But it did matter. Like on the day of the frisking, I felt violated. My eyes stung from tears.

Someone had read my poetry letters. Someone who knew my personal address, phone numbers, emergency contact . . .

Would Zaynab apply for me?

But I didn't dwell on the possibility. She was my sister; she wouldn't. Better than most people, she understood what it felt like to have your privacy invaded.

I wiped my cheeks and shoved the letter into my pocket.

"Nida! It is *emer-gency*!" Amma hollered from the kitchen.

A fog of smoke hung in the house, smelling of freshly ground coriander seeds and cumin. Amma stood at the sink, washing her mortar and pestle. For her catering business, she used it to hand-crush her spices along with garlic and ginger paste, refusing the store-bought jars full of soybean oil. She said it affected the taste of her curries.

"Good you're here," Amma said. "My rotis burned! Clear the smoke!"

The half-broken smoke detector, which hung by a thin, dwindling wire from the ceiling, began beeping.

I grabbed the kitchen towel from the counter and swatted it against the ceiling until the detector smashed against the ceiling and miraculously shut off.

I debated ways to break the news about the poetry contest. Maybe the promise of the cash prize would soften the blow.

Oh God. A national *magazine. This is real. This isn't a fever dream. She's going to kill me.*

"Amma, I have to tell you something," I began.

Amma riffled absentmindedly through her catering notebook. "Tell me after. I have an important request," she said.

I frowned and put the towel down. "Amma-ji, this is really important."

"Oho, when you need something, you're always at my ass. Who feeds you roti?"

"I'm gluten-free."

"Who feeds you roti?" she demanded.

I put my hands up. "Okay, okay, you."

"I thought so."

A little sheepishly, Amma passed me her phone and switched to English. It was another rule of hers. This year, she'd decided her children should speak to her in English for half their time at home. Amma was frustrated that despite living in America for two decades, she could only form broken sentences.

Amma pointed at the screen. "Look."

A green light emanated from the device. The dread worked its way through my body, but it was too late. I couldn't run away from WhatsApp and the group chat called *Moms of Al-Rasheed.*

Every day, my Amma begged me to update her social media statuses. For example, during the end of a school term, Amma would snap pictures of our report cards, upload them onto her status, and type:

Mashallah, Subhanallah, Alhamdullilah, Ya Allah
blessed me with smart kids. #DuasComeTrue
#MuslimMoms #MuslimMomPakistani #PakistaniKids
#Immigrantlife

Or the worst was during Eid, after we'd trek to the mosque. She'd take photos of our Eid outfits and post:

Grow up fast, almost marriage ready! Off for the Eid Khutbah #Spiritual #Islam #MarryMyDaughterPls

Amma always wondered why we're prone to the evil eye. When you're broadcasting your children's grades to the Pakistani virtual world, eventually you get the evil eye.

"Not this again." I groaned. "I have to tell you something important. It's life-altering news!"

Amma, cleverly, ignored me. "I need you send nice massage—"

"*Message*," I corrected her English. "Not massage."

"Nice message to Aunty Faiza, the one on—"

"Yes, it's always the one on Wind Drive next to Uncle Khalid, I know."

Amma pinched my ear. "Oho. Send nice massage thanking her for the box of dates from pilgrimage. Say her, *Reza family always in our prayers*. Use other nice words in English. And add those things."

I raised a brow. "An emoji?"

"*Moji toji*—whatever, use one."

"Amma, I just found out that I won—"

"I have such useless kids," she complained before drifting over to the living room.

Then my phone pinged. And I almost dropped it.

ZAYNAB
The national news is featuring your spoken word!

NIDA
What?!!!

ZAYNAB

Your videos from last year's MIST competition!

                                                    NIDA

                                   Why am I on the news!

ZAYNAB

I'm almost home. Wait for me.

My phone buzzed again with a mailbox notification, this time from my school email.

The subject line read: *NOTICE: Defamation of Mr. Wilson*

Dear Nida Siddiqui,

I have been retained to act on behalf of Mr. Mitchell Wilson regarding your published poem. If you have legal counsel retained, please have them contact me with regard to this letter.

My client advises that you have uttered untrue statements about him in a public forum that have severely damaged his reputation in a quantifiable way. Therefore, my client has instructed me to serve you immediately with a cease-and-desist letter. If you do not cease these defamatory statements and withdraw and apologize publicly for said statements, my client will proceed with a civil suit against you. Please note that these can be very costly and time-consuming. However, if you agree to retract your statements and make a public apology, my client will not pursue litigation.

To indicate if you accept our offer, please contact our offices as soon as possible to resolve this matter.

Sincerely,
McCarthy and Co.

I quickly exited from my inbox. This couldn't be real. The email felt like a hand reaching out to smother me.

"Amma," I said shakily. But there was no time to process before I heard her gasp.

"Nida, why did the aunties send me a picture of you in the news?"

She grabbed the Jadoo remote and flicked from *Geo News* to the state-news channel. The familiar sight of Marissa, the Friday anchor, popped on-screen. And to my wild surprise, my high school photo was floating beside an image of Mitchell Wilson.

In bold words, the headline stated: *Muslim Student's Letter Linked to Terrorism Directed at US Democratic Senate Candidate.*

Marissa's voice filtered into the stunned quiet.

"Eighteen-year-old Nida Siddiqui won first place in the acclaimed National Students Poet League contest, featured in *American People* magazine. But after an alarming set of accusations about US Democratic Senate candidate Mitchell Wilson, this young girl's history was brought to the surface, one linked to Islamic jihad and a family member convicted of terrorism."

Mamou Abdul-Hafeedh's mug shot sprung on-screen in black and white, his beard scraggly and untamed, his puffy eyes outlined with dark circles.

"Nida Siddiqui is the niece of convicted terrorist Abdul-Hafeedh and shares the jihadist ideologies of her uncle. In a public letter issued to candidate Mitchell Wilson, who is now threatening to sue the local student for defamation and slander two weeks before the tight Senate election race, Nida Siddiqui had this to say."

The news zoomed in on a cropped image of the *American People* feature. Marissa took that as a cue to begin reading my letter aloud, the one that won me the NSPL contest.

"Turn it off," I whispered, but Amma ignored me.

The reporter's voice was high, monotone, and completely empty. "In her letter titled *Dear Mitchell Wilson*, Nida Siddiqui penned . . ."

My eyes squeezed shut.

Marissa read the letter.

It was so isolated. No rhythm. No varying tone. Just cold words. Even the way she pronounced the Arabic jargon was over-enunciated. The poetry was not mine anymore. It was theirs.

The newscaster continued to butcher the rest of the letter and the accusations I railed against Mr. Wilson, pausing only when she was prompted by an on-air "political analyst" to discuss my identity.

"Nida Siddiqui's family emigrated from Pakistan twenty years ago, a country declared by experts as the haven of jihadist terrorism," the analyst explained coolly.

I flinched. *That's not my Pakistan.*

"Pakistan became a hot spot in America's war on terror. In Washington's efforts to curb groups like Al-Qaeda, Pakistan has had a rough history of collaboration, with militant groups sending men undercover to the United States in the name of jihad. Abdul-Hafeedh, under links of funding these groups, and a history of violence after his immigration to America, was arrested."

No! I wanted to shout.

There wasn't a summer that went by when I hadn't lived with my Baba in Karachi. But the way the newscaster described my homeland was not the Pakistan I knew. Not the land of 108 peaks and green valleys, not the land of desert and blue sea. Not the land of all geographies.

My nails dug into my palms.

"Nida is an avid spoken word artist who's performed before fundamentalist gatherings. The most infamous is the Poet's Block, a group her uncle, the convicted terrorist, founded in a local

Muslim enclave, which led to his arrest. Now his niece is following in his footsteps. In the next clip, we see the type of dangerous rhetoric that indoctrinates young Muslims."

The news played videos of my slam from the Poet's Block and MIST. The clips were mismatched and disjointed, edited into out-of-context lines.

My jihad is the strife of my own identity/But I swear by Allah, needlepoint, my words are swords that cut down my enemies.

In the staticky video, the small audience snapped and some Muslims shouted *Ameen.*

It was so *eerie.* I didn't appear as a girl spitting verse to inspire. I looked like the monster they made me out to be. The media ate it up, dissecting the videos, misconstruing verses, and accusing me of things I'd never done.

I was aware that during slams, the audience would film me. But they were local Muslims who filmed videos for the sake of our memories. I'd never foreseen the day America would weaponize my own poetry against me.

Beside me, Amma flinched.

Then a new person was speaking. The headline named him as Attorney Benjamin McCarthy, Mr. Wilson's lawyer.

"These are unpatriotic people slandering Mitchell Wilson before a tight election in a poor attempt to deter the Muslim vote," Mr. McCarthy commented. "These verses are nothing but lines from their holy Kor-*aan*, used to inflame our political climate."

Why did I use the word sword? Why did I say Allahuakbar? Why did my tone sound so angry?

"What is this, Nida?" Amma whispered before shaking her head. Then she repeated it louder, harsher. *"What is this, Nida?"*

Tears streamed down my cheeks. I didn't remember starting to cry. "Amma, I don't know how this happened!"

"You don't know? You don't know how a politician wants to sue our family?"

Her eyes snapped to me, and she was a ghost from the past. She reminded me of the night of Mamou's arrest.

"Are you delusional? Are you sound of mind? Like your uncle!" She paced before the television. "Why would you risk using Arabic in your poetry? Why those—those words of blood, sword, *death*. We understand it. But they"—she jabbed her finger at the outside world—"they would never understand our religion. We could hand them our book, we could explain our prayers, but they will always hate us for being different. Or have you forgotten what they did to your Mamou?"

"Of course I haven't, Amma!"

The gravity of our situation hit me. Mr. Wilson was richer and more powerful than I ever could be and had his entire political career at stake. The lengths a man would go to win were beyond me. That much I understood.

"Amma, what's happening?"

We both whirled to see my brother out of his room, staring wide-eyed. Seeing Mohamed and his bleary brown eyes, identical to my Baba, softened Amma.

"Mohamed, go to your sister's room. Grab Nida's journal."

Mohamed glanced nervously at me. "But why?"

"Listen to your Amma," Amma said.

Many things happened after that.

Mohamed scooped up the rose-pink journal. My sister arrived home, joining our disjointed family. She pulled me tight to her chest, her hijab rough against my cheek. At Amma's glare, she quickly let go. Her expression matched the solemnity of the room.

They're like twins, I observed hollowly. *Equally empathetic but unflinchingly rational.*

"There are two vans that just parked on the curb of the block." Zaynab spoke quietly. "I don't know if it's only the news."

The police might search our house. In fact, it was likely. They could accuse us of *conspiracy to commit jihad-related activities*, and who knew what else they would conjure.

I'd seen it done before. In my old neighborhood, our neighbors called the cops on us more times than I was invited for playdates. The justification was always the same. They claimed we were engaging in hostile behavior during our annual Ramadan prayers and the Quran readings Sister Almeera hosted. Our old apartment had been bugged after Mamou's arrest, before we moved back to Al-Rasheed.

Another time, my Amma was pulled over when we were driving to Detroit for a wedding. We were held at a detention center for eighteen hours because they were suspicious of our proximity to the Canadian-American border, while we were dressed in traditional shalwar kameez and dupattas. That was the day Amma decided she was better off forgetting her oaths, and rituals, and *Ameens*. She was better off not wearing the hijab to survive in this country.

I felt the past repeating itself in the present.

Amma handed my journal to Zaynab. "Take this. It's better to be safe."

It's better to be silent, she meant.

"I need you to get rid of the journal."

My world stopped.

"*What?*" I yelled.

"Think about our izzat," Amma continued. "Where is our honor?"

But it's just a poetry journal, I thought meekly. It *was* a poetry journal.

"Zaynab, stop looking at her!" Amma snapped to my sister. "I said get rid of it."

My hand snatched the journal from her grasp before they could stop me.

"Nida!"

"Amma, this is going too far, even for you! You're using this as an excuse to get rid of years of my work! We could hide it!" I turned to Zaynab, practically pleading. "I promise, I won't show it to anyone. I'll—I'll hide it. I won't ever use it."

"Are you stupid? Crazy?" Amma argued back. "If you keep it and that politician tries to investigate us, to sue us, your journal is evidence! They'll see all your private writings; they'll make up all kinds of things about you like they did with your uncle!"

"Amma, I said I'll hide it! Wallah!"

"*Nid-a*," Amma warned.

She snatched it back, but my fingers wouldn't loosen.

"Nida!" She tugged harder and I let go.

"Amma, you can't do this! You can't!"

Zaynab glanced at Amma with an unsure gaze. "Nida is right," she said gently. "This might be an overreaction. It's only a journal. Everything will blow over. We don't have to go this far."

"Exactly," I agreed, but Amma shook her head firmly.

"No. Put it through the shredder and then stuff the scraps in the garbage. I'm not taking any chances. Nida's not using her head. This could ruin her entire future. I always knew her Mamou's antics would hurt her too. Look where he's brought her."

"Amma, you're using that as an excuse! You never liked my notebook! You're angry so you're using this as a chance to get rid of it so I'll never write again!"

"And so what?" Amma shook her head. "Look what it's done. I always told you to stop following your Mamou."

Zaynab swallowed hard before locking gazes with me. "I-I'm sorry Nida." Her eyes reddened from her tears. "*I'm sorry.*"

I ignored her, unable to see past my anger. It enveloped me, clouding my thoughts. Was she saying sorry because of *this* or . . .

"It was you, wasn't it?" I whispered. "You entered the contest. You took my letters! You've been going on and on about how this is a good opportunity for me. Now you agree with Amma! You always have!"

Zaynab's eyes widened. "Why would I take your letters without your permission?"

But I turned away. Who else could've entered the contest?

All the defiance drained out of my sister. A part of me wished she would try to do something more. Amma would listen to Zaynab. She was the elder sister of the household. Her opinion held more sway.

But . . . she didn't do anything.

In their eyes, if the journal's contents vanished, it would be a kind of cathartic release for them all. With the pages gone, so was the evidence of my mistakes—my words would never hurt anyone ever again. Our family would heal, and the news would forget, and eventually, my name would disappear like every other news cycle.

But they didn't understand what it was like to watch years of work turned into scraps.

They claimed it was the price of safety.

Nothing felt safe about it.

Dear Anger,

My anger was persistent,
speech coated in saliva each time I spoke.
You could mop the floor with all the words.

But Amma taught me, anger can be leashed.
It's a mad dog,
some pats and dangling treats, it's defeat.
I listened to Amma. She is smart. Street smart.
But the only problem is when anger has no face,
you have no target.
So my dangling treat would be school and grades,
would be smiles and thanks.
They said, Keep your head down, Nida, be smart, Nida.
Be quiet, Nida.

Dear Amma,

Where is your mother's intuition?
I wanted to scream.
That mother doesn't have a mother's intuition.
I wished she defended me but I knew in a legacy of silence
what worth are words,
> *when you've been told all your life*
> *your words have no worth.*

Dear Zaynab,

I watched you tear my poetry
    in two pieces,
        then three,
            then four,
                then more.
My thoughts snarled like a frothing animal,
twisting and turning,
tumbling like the boys racing down Wirth Park's hill.

Out of pure instinct I lunged, trying to save even just
a lick of paper,
before I realized
I wanted you to burn it.
My fingers snagged on a loose piece like a cry for help,
the rest becoming a million shreds sobbing to the floor.

To write is to show the world your heart
before letting them stomp all over it.
That kind of permission was dangerous,
because consent didn't matter for our art
when we never had ownership to begin with.

Dear Journal,

After Zaynab shredded my poetry,
I walked to the bathroom with the lighter we used
to get the gas stove going,
clutching the last torn sheet of my journal in my fist.
The ink on the page was the final stroke of my pen.

My hand hovered above the running sink water.
Grip so hard, that page cut like a knife until my palm was
    smiling red from bleeding.

With shut eyes I made a vow, murmuring:
"I will never write to you again."
And then I burned it.

There went my Muslim words,
with my Muslim hands,
and my Muslim paper,
consumed by red flames
that ate and ate at the paper,
consuming all in its path, until there was nothing Muslim
    left.

Dear News Anchor,

Your headline was the kind crafted for a tweet,
its limited character count perfect to go viral.
Headlines are powerful, twelve words, black bold font,
with short simple tweaks
you could get the people to love or hate you.

I was your headline, just another headline, a type of headline
to be the fear that America magnifies,
for a family hunched over their breakfast table to mull over,
with the television blaring from the living room.
On a relaxed morning, they half-mindedly listen to their
    newscaster,
sipping their coffee and nodding their heads,
confirming the picture that'd been designed by past presi-
    dents who'd used those same headlines to declare wars.

Isn't that how they'd invaded us? We were numbers in their
    eyes and a list of recycled adjectives:
    Muslim, terrorist, violent, brown, jihad, oppressors of
        female rights, and uncivilized.
It was a strange thing to witness how fear was created then
    displayed.
I was helpless to it, witnessing a car crash
    over and over again.

Dear Wolf of Al-Rasheed,

The fairy tale goes the angry wolf huffed and puffed.
Amma was huffin' and puffin' in this tale,
almost blowing the house down.

She paced in a straight line,
tasbih in her left hand before switching to her right,
reciting her Astaghfars
    and her Alhamdullilahs
        and her Subhanallahs,
           —who'd tell her that no tasbih will save her beti from
                that beast anger.

Amma's lips pursed tight, like chewing on sour fruit,
    biting in, in, in . . .
    hoping to find a solution worrying at the pink skin.
"Zaynab, tell your sister, she must fix this,"
    like I wasn't right there and listening.

But Amma's fear was the wolf preying on her love,
face crumpling like my journal papers scrunched in her fist.

"Tell Mr. Wilson you are sorry."
Amma loved her pain, choosing it over truth.
Maybe that's why her talons gripping my shoulders hurt.

"Tell Mr. Wilson you are a liar."
She rattled those shoulders,
making sure I was heeding,
reliving her brother's arrest,
praying then fearing
at repeated history.
"Nida, kasam se. Fix this."

Dear Amma,

Zaynab is better at it. Being a daughter of yours.
You and I don't have a normal mother-daughter
    relationship.
I could never relate to stories of a mother being her
    daughter's best friend.
You have two, what was the use for me?
The first daughter was there to embrace your hopes and
    dreams,
the second is an afterthought.

Every morning is a game. I'd stand at the kitchen counter,
you would cook, work, or clean.
I'd wonder what to answer when you asked me how my day
    went. How much did you care? And how much of my
    honesty would hurt?
My mouth would flap open and closed,
a gaping fish, but no sound would spill out.
"Salaam, Amma," I'd finally greet.
I'd wait to see if you'd ask more.
You wouldn't.
I would try to say, I did this, I did that . . .
but a client's call would ring in a blaring ding
and you'd brush past me without realizing
that I was talking.

Language is a border
that cleaves across generations:
  a mother on this side,
  a daughter on the other side,
separated by two throats
croaking syllables in odd sounds.
I spoke America.
You spoke Pakistan.
That made it harder.
You wouldn't understand what I'd be explaining and
I would be confusing your words into a jumble.
You with Sindhi and Urdu.
Me with English.
A dialogue where a mother couldn't understand her daughter.
I'd learned to stick to simpler sentences.

My day was good
and school was fine.
Always fine. Never bad,
but inside I was crying. I wish—
It was a mantra at that point.
I wish, I wish, I wish I could speak willingly,
wanton and free. I wish I could tell you about the colleges I
  am applying to, I wish I could show you the performance
  at the Poet's Block without a wall of your resentment.
I wish I could sit and speak to you
—talk to you.
I wish the things I liked had value to you.

Dear Odd One Out,

Amma calls my poetic yapping and snapping
a Himalayan cuckoo.

Warbling its screeching chitters,
bobbing its head
at first morning dew.

But caught between Amma's icy lectures
and Older Sister's scorching reprimands . . .
    I am the bird raised outside the nest,
    eager to flap its wings fast,
    never to take rest.

Seven

The next day was a blur of news vans. Journalists of all kinds—local and national—piled on our porch only to be promptly turned away by Aunty Farooqi and her explicit Punjabi threats.

Zaynab even suggested that a televised interview could provide our perspective and clear up the accusations, but Amma shut that down. In the evening, she snapped at me to keep the blinds shut.

If my stomach weren't empty, I would've hurled.

If they know where we live, I realized, *how long will this last?*

"There will be more of them." Amma rubbed at her forehead before squaring her shoulders. "I'll message the imam, and the community council, to be wary of any lurkers around our house. But do not go outside alone at night. If you go out, take Zaynab or ask Aunty Aamiina and her son Jawad."

I hated that Amma couldn't even meet my eyes. The shame made it impossible to be in the same space as her.

In my bedroom, my phone buzzed with messages from the

community. I skipped to Jawad's contact, ignoring his questions. I knew what had to be done.

NIDA

See, Jawad? You asked me for my decision about the anthology. You got your answer. I won't do it.

There. Text sent. Like ripping off a bandage.

My poetry letters were a signature style passed down from my Mamou, and his father, and so forth. If I ever published anything under a pen name, it would be recognizable to artists in the poet scene that I was the same writer from NSPL. Every poet had a specific cadence, rhythm—lilt and tone.

It was better to be cautious, as Amma would say. My eyes stung.

Next, I disabled my social medias. Already my notifications were popping off from random news sites tagging me in their posts. Some were angry commenters under my old poetry posts. I imagined them as invisible faces smashing at their keyboards without any guilt. I had messages from random Muslims, encouraging in their comments, but others accused me of unconscionable crimes.

My email kept pinging, filled with interview requests. But my eyes caught on two. The first was from NSPL and the second from JBB. With an empty heart, I opened the first.

Dear Nida Siddiqui,

I am writing on behalf of the executive team of the National Students Poet League. Our most recent publication has stirred national controversy in light of your considerable accusations. An executive decision has been made to pull this year's magazine and revoke your first-place award. When choosing our winners, our internal judges

mark on several criteria outlined in the judging manual. But despite
our careful work, human errors are made. We apologize for the inconvenience. We adhere to a strict policy of inclusivity and open dialogue,
but we do not condone hate speech, dangerous views, and incitements
of violence. Initially, we were moved by the honesty in your piece. But
recent context clarified the troubling history of your family.

We hope you can understand.

Thank you and best,
Elizabeth Edwards
Chair of the NSPL

I couldn't even react. I hardly blinked. I wanted to laugh.
Numb, I opened the second email from Justice Behind Bars. I
skimmed its contents, the last of my hopes plummeting.

Hi Nida,

*It's Katherine. We spoke on the phone last week. I'm afraid JBB
must delay any more development regarding the representation of
Abdul-Hafeedh. The board's requested another round of evaluation.
To be frank, the credibility for your case is being called into question.
There's a fine line between justice and criminalization, but in your family's unique circumstances, we cannot work with associates involved in
condoning terror-related rhetoric and violence.*

*However, nothing is definite until the board reaches a decision. I
understand this was not the news you were hoping for, so I apologize for
the inconvenience. You'll hear from me soon about the board's decision.*

I sank down against the door in sheer disbelief. Every other
legal aid organization had had the same response, the same fears,
and now JBB was another on the long list of rejections. We had
no one left to turn to.

How would I face Mamou? The dim spark in his eyes when I mentioned JBB's decision—would that light be extinguished too?

Outside my bedroom, my ears trained on Zaynab's footsteps entering the kitchen. She began exchanging murmurs with Amma. My eyes squeezed shut as their words filtered through the door crack.

"What was she thinking, writing those letters?" Amma said.

It was just poetry.

"Amma, she didn't know."

No, I knew better.

"She's ruined this family. First her Mamou, and now her. It's their blood. It's poisoned. It's cursed! Someone has done black magic on us!"

My fists clenched. *Zaynab, defend me,* I silently urged.

"Amma, she can hear you!"

"She ruined us, our izzat, our reputation! This whole house is ruined!"

Amma was right. I ruined us. I ruined Mamou's chances.

"Amma, please."

Their voices rose louder.

"This morning, three clients canceled their catering orders. Thousands of dollars gone. And we're behind on rent. Now what? Tell me. You think pretending will solve this? You think when Mohamed goes to school, he'll be safe? You think your sister will be safe? Her future is ruined. All the sacrifices, all the work I've done, our honor, izzat! I've prayed that Nida doesn't turn out like my brother. I've prayed she stops with her writing—"

A protest escaped my mouth before I clamped it shut.

Zaynab, say something to her, tell her I'm sorry, I silently pled. *Tell her the words I'm too much of a coward to say. Tell her I didn't know better.*

"*Amma, you're angry. I understand. But you never tried to understand her writing. You were like her once. And now you're taking out your regrets on her.*"

I sat up. Regrets? Which kind of regrets was Zaynab talking about?

"*Enough. Stay within your limits,*" Amma hissed, extinguishing my sister's argument.

I was tempted to scream *stop* at Amma, because I could hear her, and her words were worse than any label thrown at us. Because *she's* my Amma. And *they* were strangers.

Ya Allah, guide me.

At my desk, I ripped out a fresh sheet from a new journal. To fix this, I would tell the world I was a liar. I would take back that Mr. Wilson was complicit in an illegal frisking, that he had made comments about my religion, about my family.

I would release my statement and send it to the journalists clogging my email. It wouldn't solve what was out there already, tainting our name. It was pure mitigation but that was the best I could hope for.

Flexing my fingers, I tried to visualize the lies I'd write, and how I could clean up this mess.

The blue pen pressed against the page.

My fingers gripped it until my nails turned white. My head was stuffed with the newscaster's voice overenunciating my poetry, cold, callous, and unapologetic.

I crumpled the paper before tossing it at the bin. I grabbed a new sheet and tried again. And again. And again.

Fifteen more times before I changed it to: *Dear Nida.*

I can fix this, I will.

I was pathetic.

Eight

I wrote a letter. I called myself the liar. I'd never imagined writing a letter addressed to me.

Dear Nida . . .

I stared at my half-tried verses, jaw clenching until it cramped.

I grabbed a fresh page. But at the next stroke of my pen, no ink trickled out.

My hand paused. *That's weird.* Uncapping a new pen, I pressed it against the journal. Ink dripped onto the white, but the pen wouldn't write.

I did it again. Grabbed a fresh page. Uncapped a new pen.

Yet every word I wrote was gibberish.

I tried writing my name, but the pen wouldn't obey the command of my own hand. I jerked it across the page, wrestling with it as if it were animated. Both my hands yanking it up and down.

Frustrated, I tore the paper. Same routine. Grabbed a fresh page. Uncapped a new pen. And began to write. When the pen pressed lightly against the white, a hole tore into it.

Sweat ran down my forehead. I didn't understand why my body felt so exhausted.

I tried again but the pen wasn't the issue. The paper wasn't the issue.

For another hour, anything and everything I tried with the pen *wouldn't work.*

Finally, an idea struck me. After rummaging through my math notebook, with the same pen, I wrote out an equation.

Then I tried another one. That worked too.

So I pressed it again to write my statement to the journalists, but the pen slipped from my fingers.

I wrestled it back to write a verse of poetry, but the words became illegible and the paper ripped in half.

It wasn't just the pen. The papers took on a life of their own. Something invisible tore them apart.

Staring at my hands and the flutter of paper around me, I backed away from my desk. Something was stopping me from writing.

I gulped uneasily. What about my spoken word? If my pen didn't work, I had my tongue.

I stood like an idiot in the middle of the bedroom, opening my mouth wide to recite a memorized verse. But my tongue wouldn't obey. It was arrested in my mouth, a useless muscle.

If my pen wouldn't work, if my tongue wouldn't work, then I had my phone. I opened my email to type a statement to one of the journalists, to lie and neutralize the entire scandal. But as I began typing, my fingers stopped working.

I was in denial. Maybe I was hallucinating. Maybe this was a dream.

In the bathroom, I splashed cold water on my face. In the mirror, my gaze was haunted, eyes puffy from unshed tears.

I would try again to write something—anything. If not to fix my reputation, at least to undo the damage brought against Mamou. I'd promised Mamou, I—

A sharp pain tore through my arms and chest, making me stumble.

I tugged at my shirt just as a blue string erupted from both my wrists, disappearing into the yellow carpeted floor. Before I could cry out, a third string enclosed itself around my throat, gnarled and twisted, choking my sounds.

The string was thick, the width of two fingers, almost like rope. When I tried to touch it, it wasn't corporeal, the blue string passing through my fingers.

Is this the evil eye?

I pinched both my arms. I slapped my face. It wouldn't disappear.

I tried to reason with myself—as reasonable as anyone could be in my predicament. *Maybe this is a dream.*

I stood up but the blue string followed me. Even though I couldn't touch it, it felt heavy, like I was being weighed down by blue chains. I screamed.

Zaynab barged into our room. "Nida!" She looked me up and down, frantically. "What happened? Why did you scream?"

"My wrists, look!"

"Did you hurt yourself? Where?"

"Look! Don't you see it?"

"I'm looking," she said carefully, like I was delusional.

"It-It's a blue—" My mouth stopped speaking. I could not *talk*, the blue strings binding my lips shut. Whatever this was—it wouldn't allow me to tell her.

My sister's eyes narrowed. "I think you need to rest."

When I stayed silent, she threw up her hands and left.

The blue strings tightened like a warning before easing.

What was happening? I huddled on my mattress, staring at the string. Did Allah do this to me?

More horrifyingly . . . *How can I ever write again?*

My mind couldn't help but piece it together. The blue string had only appeared when the poetry ceased to work. And the poetry had only ceased to work when I tried writing lies about my accusations against Mitchell Wilson.

I was cursed.

My mind, dazed from this revelation, conjured the memory of the first day I wrote poetry. When I was little and Mamou introduced me to Urdu poets, I began performing my spoken word alone to the four corners of my shared bedroom. When I finally mustered the courage to share some verses at my first poetry slam, Mamou told me that in the long lineage of our family tribe, performance came with a sacred responsibility.

A silent oath was forged, one with rules that demanded I respect the laws of my poetry and never use it for ill purpose.

As a child, it was difficult to remember a time when I spoke and someone *heard*. When my words weren't a light wind brushing against skin but easy to ignore. Poetry altered that very reality; people at the Poet's Block finally took me seriously.

Until the day that I abused it—when I let my family tear my poetry journal apart. The same day I burned the poetry and vowed to never write again. And the day I tried to lie with verse.

Trust is a greedy thing, like gifts. You expect it but you never give it. I stopped trusting my pen and tongue. But the pen also stopped trusting me.

Dear America,

In the aftermath of the Paris terrorist attacks,
national emergencies were declared across Europe,
their ramifications exploding in America.

Muslims were tracked for the sake of security.
Hate crimes increased,
just another forgotten statistic in a long spiral of sadistic
    attacks
written off by bureaucrats into simple numbers.
Election cycles ran,
Muslim bans were enacted,
politicians failed to mention how their own military con-
    tracts
bought millions of Muslims' data through prayer apps.

We were dogs—
spied, identified, and traced.
Our cries went unheard,
authorities sweeping through brown enclaves like we were
    cattle herds.
Politicians called it securing America's safety.
But what about our safety?

Dear America,

Ever come home to pointed guns?
What honor is left of a man
returning from a visit to his family in Pakistan,
only to be greeted with an arrest and guns?

The weekend of my Mamou's return
from the Pakistani provinces Sindh and Khyber-Pakhtunkhwa,
he attended a night of slam
with four of his friends he called his Islamic brothers in tow.
They bowed down in sujood of the Tahajjud prayer
in the peaceful walls of the Al-Rasheed mosque,
only to walk home to arrests,
for allegedly participating in an overseas terrorist training
  camp
"attempting to indoctrinate local Americans in jihad."

They called them the Al-Rasheed Five.
Labeling the destruction of lives
with the perfect documentary name like our pain was a
  spectacle,
the type of trauma porn to grace online streams,
helping filmmakers create another hard-hitting piece.

In the court hearings that proceeded,
the prosecution played unrelated footage on a screen,
brought prejudicial evidence,
things like images and videos of militants at the Pakistan
    borders
singing Allahuakbar in gritty ways, saying
        "Here's proof he traveled overseas
           for terrorism recruitment before propagandizing
           America into unpatriotic thought";
      saying, "his poetry slams recited in both Urdu and Arabic
      were radical recitations of the Holy Quran,"
linking these together like random puzzle pieces,
pointing fingers at Mamou and the four other defendants,
even parading around anonymous witnesses
claiming coincidences like it was evidence.

They said, explosives were planted at Al-Rasheed Block
—later discovered to be cheap fireworks—
but the authorities glossed over the nuances, slapping
    Mamou and his acquaintances with terrorism-related
    charges.
Just more mass arrests
where dark-skinned and bearded men were rounded up
    through the streets,
deported, arrested, or locked into Guantanamo Bay.

We were patterns,
cycles waiting to be repeated,
reincarnations of each other,
just different souls
  replacing skin and bones.

Dear Mark Oster,

My Mamou was never silent.
In viral videos of his spoken word
Mamou name-dropped politicians running for re-election
*   like Mr. Oster.*
Mr. Oster, who served in the Central Intelligence Agency,
before running for election,
who supported drone strikes in Pakistan, Afghanistan, and
*   Syria*
and hated that for once he became an unwanted target.
Just a casualty of Mamou's silver tongue
instead of the millions of civilian casualties overseas.

In court, Oster testified
about a "threatening" run-in he had with my Mamou.
But behind the straight white teeth
was a man of the thickest anger.

He despised the sight of Muslims in headcaps.
He despised brown folks who stuttered in broken English.
He despised being humiliated by a combination of both:
*   an immigrant man who spoke more truth than he ever*
*   could.*
Because of Mr. Oster, Mamou was sentenced to life in prison
for a crime he never committed.

Nine

After prayer, my phone buzzed. I was tempted to shut it off, but my eyes caught on the name.

ALEXIS
Nida! Congrats on first place, I knew you'd win!

I'd forgotten to message Alexis. But her message had a whole different meaning. The world paused along with my heart.

NIDA
What do you mean, you knew I'd win?
How'd you know I was in the contest?

ALEXIS
Who else entered for you? And now you're
$5,000 richer!

My fingers shook until the phone dropped from my hand, landing on the prayer mat.

Young girls are fed one hundred different versions of heartbreak, but no one prepares you for the heartbreak of a friend's betrayal. What was worse was how I'd accused Zaynab—*my own sister*—without even considering Alexis.

NIDA

How could you enter without my permission!?

ALEXIS

What do you mean? You won a national contest!

NIDA

Didn't you see the news? Besides, they revoked my award. But even if they hadn't, you invaded my privacy! You went through my journal!

ALEXIS

Nida, your letter went viral, I saw the videos online and your follower count! So many people love your work! Look at the bigger picture, you can use this to your advantage!

I flinched at the phone screen and Alexis's enthusiasm. I had trusted her. I had let her meet the poets. She was the Poet Block's only exception and she'd abused it. But how did she enter the contest? How did she have access to my personal information?

My eyes prickled with tears. I thought Alexis understood, from our heart-to-hearts, about the risks of the contest and the ramifications for not only Mamou but my entire family.

I glanced again at the message and her words saying *bigger picture*. How could I look at the bigger picture when my world was falling apart?

Dear Curse,

That night,
I dreamed of my curse.
I sat in a room with no walls or doors
but light emanating in a blush of gold
from the world's in-between planes.
The blue strings clamped on my limbs.
I was caught in a web.

It spoke to me, and the light disappeared
like the orange of sundown
before plummeting into night
where the shadows grew long.
It was a suspended moment
that was sudden but drastic in its difference.
The blue string said:

Dear Nida,

Do not keep writing and staring at me.
I am one pen amongst thousands. To an artist, I am a
   sacred responsibility.
I refuse to be here. Do not keep clutching my body,
I refuse to be written.
I refuse to be sketched on that page of cold white horizons.
I refuse to be held by a girl who abandoned me to that
   barren landscape.
I refuse to be your edict, when the pen was God's first
   creation.
I refuse to be awakened and commanded to false instruc-
   tions.
I refuse to be the girl's mandate, for the Lord can foresee
   the lies I will write for a human,
      when the first pen was ordered by the Lord to scribe
         mankind's decree.
Do not keep writing and staring at me.
I refuse to be here. I refuse to be here.

Sincerely,
Your Personal Pen

Dear Pen,

I wrote and wrote
but you took control,
large hands clutching me between your fingers,
digging your nails into my skin,
cracking me open to bare.
I wrote and wrote
but you did not want to be commanded,
You said, Wallah, not by you, not anymore.
I mourned you.

Ten

In the morning, the blue string was still there. I tried to yank it, to cut it, to run around my room praying it would disappear. At any attempt to write, it snagged around my limbs, preventing me.

Eventually, Amma ordered me to the kitchen. "Nida!"

When I went to her, she was sorting the chai cups. At my appearance, she placed her hands on her hips. "Nida, you haven't eaten. Go eat with the aunties in the living room."

"The aunties are here?" I ignored her concern about my lack of food.

"They are here to grieve," Amma told me.

"Grieve? For what?"

Amma smacked a jar of elachi on the chai tray. "To grieve for you, of course!"

I peeked into the living room. All ten aunties turned to me at once.

"My jaan!"

"Poor thing!"

"Oh, mera bacha!"

Each aunty crushed me into their arms, their bangles scraping against my cheeks, their rose and attar perfumes invading my sense of smell.

"Nida, you're famous!" Aunty Nadia claimed.

"What?" I muffled into her hijab.

"When I saw the video, I was so proud. I forwarded to my sister Habiba. My jaanu's performance was so good! Like your Mamou!"

Well, this was unexpected. "Aunty, you misunderstand. The news thinks I'm crazy."

"—and I sent the video to Rubiya, Habiba's sister-in-law's cousin's daughter, the news journalist." She continued waving her arms without a care for my protests.

"Nadia baji, you're about to knock the chai over!" Amma pointed out.

"Save the chai!" Aunty Sobia shoved us away from the counter.

"Oi, Nida baby." Aunty Farooqi snapped her fingers. "I told you, you girls have too much freedom around here. That's why you have the evil eye on you! There's all kinds of nazar for girls like you."

"*Oh*," all the aunties collectively murmured.

"That's not true," I protested but inside I wondered, was the blue string a manifestation of the evil eye?

"She's right." Aunty Nadia munched on a zeera biscuit. "Why didn't I think of this? Zuha, you have to call the butcher and order a goat to be slaughtered. We must do Nida's sadaqa, her charity!"

"The evil eye? From who?" Aunty Sobia was actually buying into all of this.

Aunty Farooqi beckoned everyone forward. "I warned you, that baji Ayesha that just moved down the street, she's no good! She opened a catering business, rivaling yours. She's jealous of your girls, they're prettier than hers!"

Even my Amma was nodding now. Pakistanis blamed nazar, the evil eye, if things went wrong. Their solution? Slaughter a goat. It didn't matter if you were vegan. And it definitely didn't matter if you didn't like mutton. Distributing goat meat to charity was the solution.

"I'll call Ahmed bhai," Amma muttered, searching for her phone. "I'll tell him to get a goat prepared."

"Nida baby." Aunty Farooqi placed her hand on my head, flashing those tobacco teeth at me. "You did what I told you, right?"

"Hmm?"

"You told your Zaynab that my little Fahad is free and ready to be engaged?"

"No, Aunty, I forgot because I've been all over the news. But I don't know if Zaynab wants to be engaged. She's focused on school."

Her grin wilted. "What? Repeat that, Nida baby. I didn't quite hear you." It sounded like a warning.

"I just meant—" I stammered. "You know, work, education . . ."

You need more buzzwords, Nida.

"Zaynab wants to be a doctor?" I sounded unsure. "No, wait! She wants to be a lawyer. She has to focus on her lawyer studies." There, that was the golden word.

"Useless." Aunty Farooqi shook her head. "You all are useless!"

"Oho yaar, forget talk of engagement. Nida hasn't eaten in days!" Amma raised her voice above the commotion. "She'll only eat on your insistence. She refuses to listen to me!"

My gaze flared at her. She couldn't do that. She couldn't act like she was not crying to Zaynab, saying I was tainted like our uncle.

I wondered if Amma would be happy to learn about my curse. In Islam, the prayer of a mother was amongst the most powerful. Amma's prayers had been granted—I'd never be able to write again.

"I'm not hungry," I told everyone.

"You're upset, Nida," Amma retorted. "And throwing a tantrum by not eating. I even made your favorite. Spicy pakora."

"Well, I don't need pakora."

Amma scoffed. "You could never resist pakora."

She was right. My eyes were already glued to the hot frying pan on the gas stove. A deep mocking, oily sizzle beckoned me forward as if to say, *Eat me now.*

Amma didn't just fry crispy golden-red spiced pakoras. No, Amma was a genius. She stuffed spinach and potato in there, so it wasn't *just* battered fried goodness, it was battered *potato* fried goodness that tricked you into thinking you were subtly inhaling a portion of veggies when really, it was more calories and grease than nutrients—

I should stop. I had some self-respect. But I craved those pakoras badly. *No pakoras today.*

"Oho, Nida, you'll get weak. Don't take on so much tension," Aunty Nadia reprimanded me with a squeeze to my cheek. After snatching their chai cups, the aunties filtered back to their so-called grieving circle.

Alone, I focused my glare on Amma, but she ignored it. I hated how she continued to pile food onto a plate, nonchalantly. Her gazed roamed from pot to pot, probably thinking, *Would Nida like mutton karahi or bhindi today?*

"Do you want roti or pulao?" Amma instead asked, as she ladled on squash raita next to the pakora.

"Nothing. I don't want *any* of it."

Amma put both pulao and roti on the plate, before squeezing in a spoonful of kachumber salad. In the background, the aunties blasted 102.9 Punjabi Radio with DJ Uncle Adil ranting about the next Pakistani elections. Were we sure they were here to grieve?

"Amma, stop serving me food!" I spoke over the radio.

Amma turned her face away like the thought of looking at me still hurt her. Anger was one thing but shame hurt worse. Amma valued her izzat—*honor*. It's why she felt angrier about the tarnishing of our reputation than the possibility of hurting me. That's why my words were intentional, I wanted them to pinch Amma until she was forced to acknowledge me. Until the pain of my words was impossible to ignore.

It worked. Amma clenched her jaw so hard, I swear I felt my molars ache. "If I say you'll eat, you'll eat. I am finished with your disobedience."

"If I eat, I'll puke. Besides, I should go. I have to finish schoolwork," I lied.

"I don't care. If I cooked, you're eating. It's almost Maghrib. I'm not blind to your tantrum. You're acting like little Mohamed!"

Amma's eyes glowed red in irritation and . . . was that remorse?

"I spent hours cooking food, *for you*," she added more quietly.

My fingers curled and the anger building up from the day bled into my words. "I didn't ask you to cook for me. I didn't ask for any of this. If I get weaker, that's on me. I'd rather get sick than eat."

"Just listen to the nonsense you're saying—"

"I'd rather be sick than eat your food."

That stunned her to silence.

You see, food was never just food in our house. It was the glue that forced us, even in our bickering, to join together and acknowledge each other's presence. Amma used food as her apology and her thanks. This was the first time I rejected both.

My memories played it like a broken record. My eyes saw

Amma blaming me, over and over. And my ears heard my Amma declaring how I'd ruined our family name. My release used to be poetry, but my words weren't so poetic anymore. And I couldn't fix this by scribing an apology.

"Nida!"

I shouldered past her.

"*Nid-a.*"

In my religion, a mother had heaven beneath her feet. In my anger, I was closing the doors to that heaven, praying my Amma's footsteps wouldn't sound behind me, blessed and all.

Amma was witnessing how it felt for family to turn against you in less than a day. What I'd forgotten was my Amma was well equipped in this feeling. After all, she didn't have her husband. And she'd lost her only brother for the same reason as the trouble I'd brought to our entire family. Everything pointed back to a cursed poetry journal.

Amma grabbed my arm before I could flee. "All the peace in the house is gone because of you. And still, you have no thanks for me, no appreciation!"

"This is what you choose to do? Blame me? What about what they're saying on the news? How is that my fault? That's screwed up, Amma. And you—you can't even have my back."

"Lower your voice! It's this stubbornness of yours just like Abdul-Hafeedh."

I flinched at Mamou's mention.

"If only—" She paused.

"If only what?" I said, because I liked digging deeper into open wounds.

"Nida, do you have any respect for your mother to keep giving me responses like this? All you do is cause fights in this house!"

"But I'm not—"

"Enough! Voice low!"

Why is she always against me? It's always Zaynab who does things right. Why can't I do anything good in her eyes, anything to make her proud? Why do I love the things she despises?

"Amma, what's happening?" My sister stepped between us. I hadn't heard her enter the kitchen.

Seeing Amma's glassy eyes, Zaynab's gaze snapped to me. "You're making Amma cry!"

She turned to my sister, pleadingly. "Tell her to stay and eat. I won't have any sukoon tonight if she stays hungry."

Sukoon—*peace.* It felt ironic.

Seeing them together, against me, for something I never did, for something that was out of my control, was like a needle digging into my skin. Small and hidden but so painful.

Suddenly, it was too much. I took a step back. "Amma will cry regardless of what I do. I need to go."

"Now you're running away from the argument. She only wants you to eat and you've made a fight from it."

My sister always had this way of involving herself in everything and then arguing why she was right.

"You both think I cause arguments, but then when I try to walk away, I'm the one at fault? I don't want to be here. I didn't want to fight. I didn't want to be told how I'm to blame for everything. If you or Amma had taken a second to think, you could have asked me how my name landed in that contest, even though, for years, I've always been against them. But you didn't. I didn't enter the contest. It was Alexis who entered, without my permission." I spoke in a rush of English to my sister.

From beside her, the anger in Amma deflated. She couldn't understand what I'd said to Zaynab and that made it so much worse. I couldn't even explain it to her. Not in English. And hardly in Urdu.

"What did she say?" Amma asked my sister.

I lifted my hands and squeezed them together, hoping they'd stop trembling.

"She'll talk to you tomorrow," Zaynab told Amma. "Let her go."

Zaynab let me walk away but on her own conditions. A very Zaynab thing to do. And she got the final word. I hadn't even asked Zaynab how her law school event went. I wanted to ask but we'd all argued instead.

"No, call her back!" Amma pleaded.

I fled the kitchen as her pleads changed, calling me *ungrateful* to my back. She said more words, deep, dark, and rough. I ignored those too.

Wallah, I felt selfish for making Amma my anger's punching bag. I knew it was unfair, but I was so exhausted. *Amma doesn't feel sorry for destroying my journal. Of course she doesn't.*

Before I slammed my door shut, I stole one last glance behind me.

Amma sat at the table, absent of her family but below the family portrait. The food sat untouched, probably cold. I knew her red fingers were blistered from hand-crushing chilies all evening to make my favorite raita. Amma couldn't right her wrongs. She always thought with food she could. It'd worked for years. Except now.

Her eyes drifted to our family portrait, probably reminding her of a home that no longer existed. I imagined her wondering about her mistakes that led her here. Regrets too.

Amma's eyes filled with suppressed tears. She stuffed her hiccups into her arm so the aunties bickering in the living room wouldn't overhear. A red kind of hate simmered in me. I hated myself so deeply, I turned away.

The image haunted me for the rest of the night.

Dear Amma (and by extension, your stupid goats),

Charity goats are your thing.
I understand,
I understand the call of devotion,
    of submission,
    of unadulterated affection
    to Allah and the daughter He blessed in your
        name.

When Baba left,
the intensity of unrequited adoration
found its passion in the habits of worship,
    the intensity of motherhood,
    the fondness of faithfulness,
    the devotedness of spirituality.

It means my pain is your pain.
It means my struggle is your struggle.
It means when I walk out that door, hijab down my neck,
    the scarf is around your throat, threatening to strangle
    you too.
Because we love our faith and the risks in wearing it
even when bigots condemn our community
and we're left to brace for the aftermath, invisibly.

I understand, I understand
    why you slaughter your charity goats in comfort,
    why you entertain the aunties' dramatic efforts,
    why you take these actions before our problems become
        worse.
Because in a world that disclaims the goodness of a religion,
renouncing piety and inflaming society,
all you have is your faith
to quell your anxiety.

Eleven

After Isha prayer, Zaynab returned to our bedroom, bobbing her head to the aunties' radio blaring Pakistan's *Coke Studio* from the living room.

She began rummaging through our side desk. "Have you seen my law school binder? It was here."

"There," I said stiffly, pointing at her mattress.

"Okay," she said.

My eyes landed on the wall behind her. I despised our odd silence. Should I try to speak first? But I always did. She was the one who got involved between Amma and me. Sometimes, being around Zaynab was equivalent to walking on eggshells. I never knew if my words annoyed her or if she'd flip out.

My mind drifted to the conversation I'd overheard between her and Amma. "Zaynab," I said before I bit my tongue. Dammit. I spoke first.

These days, even simple words didn't come easy.

"You can't do that." Zaynab put down her binder. "Spit it out."

"I overheard the conversation you had with Amma."

Her lips turned down. "Amma was angry. You can't take what she said to heart."

I ignored her. "You told Amma that she was blaming me for everything because of her own regrets. What did you mean?"

If it was possible to frown harder, Zaynab accomplished it. "I'm not sure Amma wants me to tell you. Especially not now."

It was my turn to say, "You can't do that. If you were in my place, and Amma took your personal things and ripped them apart, you'd want to know the real reason why!"

"Listen." She sat down on my mattress. "I don't know much. I just remember after Mamou's arrest, when we moved to a new house in Al-Rasheed, I found an old notebook in a box that I thought belonged to Mamou. It was full of Urdu poetry like nazm! And some of them *were* Mamou's . . . but some were Amma's when she was younger. They were dated to the time when she moved to America. But she took it from me and never answered any of my questions. She said I wasn't allowed to tell you or anyone else. I think she got rid of it."

"What? And you're sure they were Amma's?"

"I don't know. She didn't confirm anything, but it looked like Amma's handwriting, and she was terrified when I found it. That's why I couldn't tell you. And she'd kill me if she learns that I told you this."

I flinched. Was it Amma's poetry? How could I ever ask her? And what was the point in finding out more? Amma despised it now, enough to rip apart years of my work without a second thought. Enough to destroy Mamou's old things and never tell me.

"I won't tell her that you told me," I whispered. "But you could've explained this to me before. You could've trusted me to hide something this big."

Zaynab returned to her side of the room with an angry jerk to her movements. "Trust? Your friend entered that contest without your permission, *a gora*, and you blamed me. I don't know what trust you're talking about."

"How can you blame me? You and Amma took my journal! I wasn't thinking straight. I never actually believed you entered for me."

She gaped in disbelief. "Do you really think that low of me? We share a room, for Allah's sake. You shouldn't have blamed me in the first place!"

"I shouldn't have to watch you rip my poetry apart. You could've defended me!"

"I did defend you! I told Amma to let me hide it."

"No." My voice hitched. "You barely protested."

She sucked on her teeth. "I never agreed with what she did. But I knew Amma would do something drastic. You know how she gets when she's paranoid. It's exactly like the spiral she fell into after Mamou's arrest."

"No. I don't get it."

"Nida." Her voice wavered. "Believe me. I didn't want to take your journal, but I thought going along with it would stop something worse."

"But this was the worst. It just shows you never valued my poetry in the first place!"

"Nida, it all happened too fast. If I could go back to change what happened, I would! I'm sorry."

I wasn't ready to let it go, but I did believe her. "Then I'm sorry for thinking it was you who entered the contest."

A fragile silence settled between us until she held up a container of hair gel like it was a truce. "Have you looked at yourself?" She picked at a strand of my limp hair. "There's nothing that rejuvenating hair can't cure."

"What about the Quran?"

She nodded solemnly. "The Lord comes first, of course. But He gave us hair too."

"Fine, but I have to ask you a favor."

After propping me up on the mattress, Zaynab took a bottle filled with water and spritzed it onto my head.

"What favor?"

"It's about Mitchell Wilson. I think we should email his attorney, the one who sent the cease-and-desist letter. I want to ask for a meeting to neutralize my accusations and to release a joint statement."

She dropped the spray bottle. "No way."

"I have to," I protested. "If I don't, Mr. Wilson will sue us!"

"Nida, that's the oldest trick in the book. Famous people threaten to sue to scare people poorer than them into silence."

"Even if it's to scare me, Mitchell Wilson can *still* afford all the legal fees. He's going to use this scandal in his campaign by dragging not only our family name, but Mamou's name through the mud. That's why JBB is reevaluating Mamou's case, because the backlash puts more doubt on *all* of our innocence. We need to take back some control. If I email Mr. Wilson and ask to release some kind of statement with his team and call everything one big misunderstanding, we'll clean up this entire mess."

"That's not how scandals work," Zaynab warned me. "He's playing dirty. If we contact him, and he agrees to a statement, we'll have to lie about how he treated you. So, no, I can't help you." She returned the gel back to the hair basket and stood up. But I darted in front of the door, blocking her from leaving.

"Move," she demanded.

"No. You're the one studying law. You're good at this legal stuff. And you're good with people!"

It was true. I had a way with words if it involved a pen and paper. And that's how people knew me: I was my uncle's niece, the poet carrying his legacy.

But Zaynab . . . she was people smart. She steered herself around strangers expertly, the way she talked on their level, reciprocating their emotions, the way she never once broke gaze. She could meet someone new and find out their entire life story within an hour; she could saunter down Al-Rasheed and greet every aunty by their first name, asking about their children, friends, job, and worship.

Zaynab's eyes darkened. "Folks around here won't be happy. You haven't seen what they're saying down at the mosque and Poet's Block. They're angry on your behalf. Group chats are blowing up, letters are being emailed to our reps, and the poets want to stage a protest when the Democratic volunteers decide to canvass here this weekend, to solicit the Muslim vote. You understand that, right?"

I swallowed hard. My plan meant downplaying Mitchell Wilson's actions. By releasing this statement, I would be undermining Al-Rasheed and all their anger. But my mind was made up. "I can't sit by for the next two weeks until the election and do nothing."

She was silent for a moment. "Then when you meet him, I want to be with you. It's dangerous to roam around a group of Mr. Wilson's supporters who happen to be complete strangers. And reporters will be there too once they catch wind of you meeting with the same man that you accused of racism."

She had a point. Zaynab squeezed my shoulder and for the first time, I didn't feel like I was carrying this burden completely alone.

"Thanks," I mumbled.

Zaynab opened her laptop before cracking her knuckles.

I sent a silent prayer to Allah that it would work.

Dear Parasite,

The last thing I'd expected to see
was the parasite who'd wormed into my life,
seated three feet from me,
sipping from the same teacup I'd clutched in my hand,
since four years old.

Mr. Wilson lifted the mug like an ode of thanks,
grinning my way.
Red washed over me, the anger pushing up my throat,
instead of yelling . . . I swallowed the urge to weep.

Mr. Wilson's attorney sat to the right,
in an identical crisp black suit.
A costume of diplomacy.
After Zaynab's email, Mr. Wilson's attorney wanted to
     discuss our options,
suggesting a joint media statement with Mr. Wilson's elec-
     toral team
to clean up his Senate campaign.

That morning, Amma rushed into the living room
forcing a rare smile
she'd hardly shined my way.
Her hair was smoothed into a low bun,

and she was wearing her best blouse and black pants,
the outfit she reserved for Zaynab's graduation,
dressed up more for white men than she'd ever dressed
     for me.

Amma offered English tea and zeera click biscuits,
to impress the man she'd cursed behind private doors.
What was it with Pakistanis wanting to smile and please the
     pale men
who'd done nothing but spit
at the likes of us time and time again?
They'd lie down by choice to have the honor to be walked
     over.

I couldn't help but think,
by Amma's urging expression,
I was ready to be bulldozed.

But . . .
behind Amma's careful smile was a sea of fear.
The kind of fear that made the anxiety take control,
where nails bit into palms, and teeth sank into lips,
until blood rose to the surface and speckled skin.
But Amma's fake smile was so believable.
She'd had a lot of practice hiding her emotions,
with her mother and brother,
it was their favorite game. To blend in and keep silent in
     new surroundings.
A game she grew up with, more than tag.

For a politician, Mr. Wilson spoke very little.
It was his attorney blabbering on about solutions.

About a potential press conference for Monday morning,
about us signing a non-disclosure agreement.
Mr. Wilson and his media team promised to stand
    beside me
in a show of solidarity.
The problem would be fixed, the harassment would end,
the past would be shoved behind us, never to be seen again.

You can fix this, Nida, *the attorney said.*
Amma nodded hurriedly. You fix, Nida.
Mr. Wilson and the attorney exchanged looks,
her broken English their inside joke.
Amma didn't even notice.

The room was suffocating. I cleared my throat.
I told myself, Fix this, Nida.

Dear Democracy,

I thought votes were part of a democracy
where choices were given
to secure individual autonomy.
But two candidates didn't feel like much choice,
just driven by dollars under the fancy name of lobbying.
I thought Mr. Wilson was supposed to represent half the
*   state as a party nominee,*
but why didn't I see candidates
with the same skin color as me?

Twelve

On Sunday morning, at ten o'clock sharp, Zaynab and I went to meet with Mr. Wilson's media team on the outskirts of Al-Rasheed. That same day, his canvassing team made their way around the suburbs, a mix of college students urging the brown enclave to vote blue, and to discern voter incentives. The Muslim vote would be key in this election race.

According to the canvasser app, Al-Rasheed was an undecided neighborhood. But I knew Al-Rasheed wasn't undecided. They were only conflicted. On the one hand, they didn't want to vote for the man who'd condoned the frisking and physical harassment of a Muslim high schooler. The only problem was that Al-Rasheed also hated the next best option. A Republican candidate hostile to Muslims. That's the issue when you only have two political options.

The Democratic Party volunteers noticed me too. One of the college canvassers not-so-subtly pointed toward me. *Wasn't that girl on TV just yesterday?*

Wasn't she the one who accused Mr. Wilson of illegal frisking and Islamophobia?

There were others, just as loud. *People were talking about her on the canvassing chats, saying she's a Republican mouthpiece paid to slander Wilson before the date of the election,* they said, as if I weren't standing three feet away.

My mouth dried. *I don't even know who I could vote for.*

Eventually, the media team leader approached us with a large bag and a canvasser notebook tucked under her left arm. Her black turtleneck was rimmed in the kind of rough-looking fur that made my neck itch.

"You must be Zaynab and Nida Siddiqui, correct?" After putting her hand out for a shake, she said, "I'm Vivian, part of the publicity team. Senate candidate Mitchell Wilson informed me about the planned press conference for today."

We nodded as Vivian led us to the side of the street.

"Before we meet him, I'll need a photo," Vivian continued.

"I was told we'd be meeting with Mr. Wilson outside the community center," I said. "Where is he?"

"Oh, you know how it is with politics—meetings and more meetings. He'll arrive shortly. In the meantime, we can get started. I'll need photos to submit in our press releases as well. It's standard."

Zaynab's eyes narrowed but Vivian pretended not to notice.

"Also, Nida you'll be canvassing as well, correct? As a show of solidarity after the conference?" she continued.

I recoiled at the frank way she put it. "No. I'm not part of his volunteer team. I'm just here to neutralize my accusations." My alarm bells began ringing incessantly.

Vivian's brows furrowed. "There was a miscommunication. Let me call Mr. McCarthy to confirm. Would you mind holding onto my bag for a second?"

She handed me her bag and clipboard. The bag was surprisingly heavy. At first glance, hats and pins stuck out, scrawled with *Vote Wilson!* in cheeky blue.

Around us, residents of Al-Rasheed who were returning from work stopped and stared at the canvassers. Some pointed at the volunteers' T-shirts sporting Mr. Wilson's picture and slogans.

Even Uncle Jihad stood outside his shop in the parking lot, shooing the canvassers who tried to approach the building. "Dafa ho jao, racists!" he shouted. *Get lost racists.*

And from behind me, a familiar voice: "Nida baby, what are you doing holding those *things?*" Aunty Farooqi paused on the sidewalk, grocery bags looped around her wrists.

"Salaam, Aunty."

But she didn't return the greeting, studying the clipboard in my hand.

"Nida baby, are you volunteering for that . . . what's his name? Tilson? Ah yes, Kilson's campaign?"

"It's Wilson and no, Aunty, of course not."

"Then why are you with Kilson's team and those posters?"

"I . . ."

I stopped, taken aback that I was recognized in my own hypocrisy.

"Nida baby, do young Muslims bend their spine for Islamophobes so easily?" With that remark, she continued down the sidewalk without a second glance.

"Did Aunty just say I don't have a spine?" I gaped at her.

Zaynab shook her head. "I warned you. Aunty Farooqi was angriest on your behalf when the news went off about us. We should've told her about our plan that we'd be doing a press conference with Wilson's team. She probably feels betrayed. If we stand out here any longer, the other residents will recognize us and spread gossip. They'll misinterpret our intentions."

"But we can clarify them, right?"

Zaynab opened her mouth to reply but paused. "Where's Vivian?"

I glanced around, noticing that Vivian was no longer beside us. She was standing farther down the sidewalk, away from me.

Snap!

It was the unmistakable click of a camera. Zaynab's face dropped, and an understanding spread across her features before, in one swoop, she knocked the bag and clipboard from my arms. My sister shoved me behind her like she was my shield.

"*You liar.*" Zaynab turned on Vivian, practically seething.

"Zaynab, what just happened?"

"Vivian here isn't just a publicist!" she snapped.

Vivian grimaced before collecting her fallen bag. The spilled pages of the clipboard revealed empty data forms for canvassers.

Vivian looked calm, and unalarmed. "It was a pleasure to meet you both."

She walked away, following the other canvassers. A pair of photographers followed at her heels.

Zaynab grimaced. "This was . . ."

A setup.

"She made me hold Mr. Wilson's voting merch and the clipboard," I realized.

"While she distracted us, the PR team snapped photos of you conveniently in front of the other canvassers," Zaynab said. "They did it to make you look like one of *his* volunteers. I don't know who she was but that's not a regular publicist. They're playing dirty."

I was shaking. "They never cared about a joint statement. If those photos reach the media, they're going to make my letter look like a bunch of lies. They'll say I supported his campaign."

"We're such idiots." Zaynab groaned.

"I can't believe I fell for that," I said, more stunned than angry. "Does that mean Mr. Wilson isn't even showing up for a press conference?"

Zaynab whirled now. "Who cares about a media statement? I told you, trying to cover for them never works! They play dirty!"

"I can't just do nothing!"

"We can't *do* anything. It's better to let this all blow over."

But this wouldn't blow over until the election was over. To everyone, I seemed like the Democrats' enemy. To the Republicans, I seemed like an ally. I was caught in between.

I watched, helplessly, as the canvassers rang the doorbells of our neighbors, trying to convince my own people to vote for Mr. Wilson.

"What do I do now, Zaynab?" My voice was small, but it softened her anger.

"We need to go home and tell Amma, okay? We'll tell Amma, and we'll figure out a game plan."

I didn't move.

She stepped close, bending until we were eye to eye. "Hey, we got this, okay? Wallah. It's just pictures. It's not the end of the world, yet." She kept repeating this, her encouragement infecting the air until I was nodding along.

"Yeah. You're right."

It wasn't the end of the world, *yet*.

Together, we walked deeper into the neighborhood, toward the mosque. To my surprise, a group of uncles and aunties huddled in the center of the road, threatening to greet the volunteers with the underside of their shoes. Some lashed out colorful insults. It was a sea of languages: Punjabi, Pashto, Farsi, and Urdu.

Even the college kids from the Poet's Block blocked the canvassers from venturing farther into the neighborhood, forcing the team to retreat.

"Now they're really going to think Al-Rasheed is crazy." Zaynab snorted.

"More like brave. Everyone has more of a spine than me," I said quietly.

I wanted to be satisfied at how Al-Rasheed came together but I didn't deserve it. I wasn't the one out there risking my neck.

———

Back at our house, Jawad's mother stood on the porch.

"Aunty Aamiina?" I said.

Zaynab disappeared inside the house, leaving me to her. Aunty Aamiina was not only Jawad's mother but also the wife of the local imam. She was the kind of Somali aunty always feeding everyone in gatherings, staying behind in iftars to clean, hollering *Yalla* to get praying Muslims to stand shoulder-to-shoulder.

She wore a light blue jilbab that made her dark eyes seem larger, more perceptive. Her smile was warm as she patted my cheeks. "I've been so worried about you. You missed your Quran lessons too! I was hoping to see you."

"I know, I'm sorry. But I couldn't leave after this mess. I was stuck at home."

She nodded in sympathy. "I emailed the journalists who covered that awful story about you."

"Really?" I was touched that she went to all that effort.

"I made everyone do it." She gestured around us. "There's an email template being forwarded through the WhatsApp groups. I've had my students send emails to the news network demanding they take back their accusations, and to apologize for their poor professionalism."

"What? How many people sent them?"

"Hundreds. We shared them all over our networks."

A slow horror slithered through me. Aunty Aamiina had good intentions, but what they did was risky. I could already envision the headlines, some news anchor claiming Al-Rasheed is an enclave of radicalism for supporting me.

"Please don't take that chance for me," I said thickly. "I don't want the mosque to be in trouble. I don't want any of you to be investigated because of my mistakes."

She whacked my head, her tone wrapped in worry. "Oi! Enough!"

I rubbed my temple. "Ow."

"None of this is your fault. We won't stay quiet. The audacity of them to come after an innocent girl, for them to say those horrible things about your uncle—"

"My uncle and I aren't exactly innocent," I corrected her.

My uncle loved to stoke fires with his poetry. He was the flint to dry tinder, hoping for embers to ignite. Drawn to controversy so his verse was heard by more. Even before his arrest, he had a criminal record from trespassing and creating spoken word mobs, and a list of accusations for so-called incitements of violence.

"All the videos shown on the news, I wrote those verses," I continued. "I used Arabic words, and adjectives that confirmed so many biases against Islam. I made everything worse at home. Amma was so angry. I shouldn't have played around like that." I angled away, tears of frustration brimming my eyes.

Aunty Aamiina tilted my chin toward her. "Nida, it doesn't mean you regret your words. Stand your ground. I just heard from Aunty Farooqi that you were hanging around those volunteers. She said you were working with Mitchell Wilson's team?"

My jaw clenched. WhatsApp chats were faster than just about anything around here.

"No, Aunty. It was a misunderstanding."

She crossed her arms and waited for some brilliant explanation.

"Actually, it was a mistake," I admitted.

But there was something else I felt, something that made me stare her dead in the eyes. The pool of dread in my stomach only grew larger. This election wouldn't result in any wins for Al-Rasheed.

"Aunty, no matter what happens, Mr. Wilson won't be disappearing. Even if he doesn't win the election, it wouldn't change a thing. Not before this election, and not after. We're a swing state. Wilson is a Democrat. Most community members might have to vote for him because his Republican opponent is worse, someone who's had a history of terrible immigration, corruption, and healthcare policies."

She sighed. "It that what this is about? I don't know the answers either, Nida, but that doesn't excuse the way that man treated you. And the way the media is treating your family."

"But, Aunty, we also can't *not* vote. Bringing more attention won't change anything in this election. I don't want the elders putting themselves at risk on my behalf."

She held out her arms. "Come here." I stepped close and she embraced me, resting her chin on my shoulder. It made me ache because I wished my Amma would do this for me.

"It's all confusing, Nida, but none of us here are going to let Wilson pretend he wasn't complicit in frisking a girl. Maybe we'll end up voting for him, but that doesn't matter. It doesn't mean I can't criticize him or absolve him of accountability."

"But would that make a difference? No one cares about what we say. Even at school when classmates discuss the election or progressive politics, their talk always excludes the people who don't fit their picture of liberalism. And that's all of us."

"Stop thinking, Nida. That man *hurt* you. You're *allowed* to feel hurt."

I stilled in her arms. Her words—so small—felt heavy for

just a moment. And I felt small—but heard—for just that moment.

"Thanks, Aunty." I buried my face into her chest.

"Mama?"

Over Aunty Aamiina's shoulder, I saw Jawad walk up the sidewalk. "Baba told me to get you before you're late for teaching tonight's Quran. . . ." Jawad's voice trailed. "Nida? Is that you? You haven't answered any of my texts."

Aunty Aamiina pulled away and placed her fists on her hips. "Oh, so you were texting her?"

Jawad blanched. "No, Mama. It's not like that, it was about the MIST competition."

She looked unimpressed by his explanation, which was clearly a lie.

"Is it cool if I speak to Nida for a few minutes? Tell Baba I'll see him in half an hour for Hifz lessons."

Aamiina took the both of us in. "I better see you a good five steps away from her then."

I withheld a snort. "You don't have to worry, we have a halal gap here, Aunty."

"He could be your damn honorary brother; I better still see that gap."

Thankfully, Aunty Aamiina left us, while Jawad looked mortified.

"Let's go talk at the garden," he finally suggested.

I nodded and trailed him to the "community garden"—a generous title. Really, it was a fence of weeds around mint plants tangled into each other. At the heart of it, two patches were dotted with the last of the surviving tomatoes, cucumber, and chilies. We called it a community garden because most of us—the uncles, really—leeched off the fruits of Aunty Sobia's labor. She didn't mind though. Widowed and all, she named us her true brothers and sisters.

Standing there felt like a betrayal after my failures. I was not fit for this neighborhood's generosity.

When Jawad paused at the tomato patch, I waited, expecting him to be partially disappointed. We carried a mutual respect, the way you respected anyone who you thought was better at the things you cherished most. He must have heard from Aunty Farooqi that I was with Mr. Wilson's team. I wondered if he finally realized I was lacking the backbone the rest of Al-Rasheed seemed to possess.

But Jawad's next words were much softer than I'd ever heard him, surprising me.

"Are you okay?"

"Great," I answered as my stomach turned. "The world thinks I'm a terrorist sympathizer."

"This city isn't the world," he said, but there was a hitch to his answer. I only picked up on it from years of watching him in performances. Jawad never carried a hitch to his tone. Ever.

"You're bad at lying."

"Make me understand before I get angry. Aunty Farooqi said you were with Mitchell Wilson's team."

"Damn Aunty Farooqi, she can't keep her mouth shut—"

"And I didn't believe it but you're not denying it."

My hands clenched. "Have you seen what they've been saying on the news? All the accusations put against my family?"

He stayed silent but his eyes were sympathetic, so I looked away.

"I had a choice, Jawad. Either I let it happen, or I make a statement and rescind my accusations. I couldn't sit by and let them tear my family to bits, especially Mamou. It's affecting his legal case."

"You had more than one choice," he retorted, and I huffed.

"I don't want to hear a lecture."

"Well, you're going to hear it. You had more than those choices. A lot more. But instead, you wanted to cover for the man who brought these problems instead of the people trying to help you?"

"That's not fair. I thought you'd understand. You almost had this happen to you. You were forced to back down because your uncle is in prison too. Anything I do affects Mamou and his legal aid. I can't stand it! I was so close, Jawad." My voice cracked. "The legal aid team was on board before my family was accused of supporting violence. And the worst part is, it wasn't even my choice. The poetry contest was a mistake. And now I can't even wri—"

I tried to tell Jawad more, about the curse that had banned my ability to write. But the blue string sprang from thin air, slithering heavily along my throat until I bit down a gasp of pain.

My lips were stitched together, like the curse was warning me against speaking more.

His glare morphed to confusion. He stepped forward, hand hanging in the air. "Are you okay?"

I wheezed out a small breath and nodded. The blue string disappeared. I prayed that he assumed it was anxiety.

Jawad took my silence in stride. "Nida, I don't understand you. All these years, when you and I hung around the Poet's Block, I'd rant to you about feeling helpless when it came to my uncle's arrest. It wasn't for nothing."

Dread coiled through me. "I know it wasn't for nothing," I said.

But he wasn't having it. He raised his hands to shield the sun's glare. "I confided in you because I thought you understood. The difference between what happened to me versus you is that I had the news agencies against me because they thought my uncle was affiliated with militant groups. I didn't have poetry that went viral. But you have people supporting you, you just don't see it. When our uncles were arrested, we couldn't help them, we didn't know how to raise any attention to their cause because no one besides other Muslims believed in their innocence. It's like that disgusting term 'Lady Al-Qaeda' all over again—no one talks about Dr. Aafia except Muslims. They catch wind of the words *radical* and *terrorism* and *Muslim* and they turn the other way. It takes a stroke of luck to get any attention around here. And now . . ."

"Now what?" I whispered thickly.

"If I had the attention you have, I'd be on TV. I'd perform the poetry I wrote about my uncle. All these Muslims and immigrants around here, who are stuck in run-down schools, over-policed, and told to be thankful—I'd make the state listen. But mostly, I wouldn't be silent and cover for the man who contributed to this mess. You know, Mitchell Wilson is having a press conference right outside Al-Rasheed. The damage you're doing by covering his name makes it worse for every other Muslim who might face the same frisking you did."

"He *what?*"

Jawad continued impassively. "It's like a big show to him, talking to the press."

"He's having a press conference right now? *Without me?*"

"You didn't know? I thought you were with his team," he said slowly.

"We were tricked."

At my request, Jawad took me to the outskirts of the neighborhood where the press conference was taking place. We heard the noise before we saw the crowd, arriving in time to catch the end. Mr. Wilson's deep, smooth voice was a familiar and permanent stain ingrained in my memories.

"I don't know who Nida Siddiqui is." The politician spoke into the reporters' mics. "My team informed me that she's a volunteer from this neighborhood, but I've never contacted, spoken to, or seen this girl. If her accusations held any weight, then volunteering for my campaign contradicts her statements. She has ties to an alleged terrorist sympathizer, a man by the name of Abdul-Hafeedh who is being held in federal prison. That erases any shred of her credibility."

I ducked behind a cluster of pine trees. My heart was a drum in my chest. Out of my own paranoia, I glanced at Jawad to see if he could hear it. But he was too busy staring coldly at Mr. Wilson's back.

Suddenly, I was transported to that day of the frisking, alone, cornered, and unable to do anything about it. Thankfully, I couldn't see the politician's assured face, comfortable in front of the dozen microphones thrust beneath his chin.

"This wasn't what we agreed to," I said.

Jawad turned. "What do you mean *agreed?*"

After a moment of hesitation and filled with shame, I told him about the meeting with the lawyer.

"And he made you sign an NDA? Without your attorney present?"

"It happened so fast; I had less than an hour to think about it," I protested. "We agreed that when Mr. Wilson and I made a media statement, we'd call it a misunderstanding. He promised that my uncle wouldn't be mentioned again. He'd apologize for any offense he'd caused, and I'd accept his apology, publicly."

Jawad's eyes narrowed in skepticism. "Was that on paper?"

My voice was small. "It was agreed . . . orally."

"Nida." His hands clenched and unclenched as if he wanted to throttle my shoulders. "How did Zaynab let you do this? She's going to make a terrible lawyer."

"What was I supposed to do? And Zaynab was at school. It was Amma and me. We had no leverage. Wilson is the one paying analysts under his PR team to slander my family on the news. He has connections to journalists. His voice matters. Not mine. If you were in my place, and your uncle was mentioned in a media frenzy all over again, you would've done the same thing."

"Nida," he repeated with more force.

Oh, there it was, the disappointment.

"Nida, you haven't contacted any of us at the Poet's Block. Not once. If there's anyone who would have had your back, it's every single person in this neighborhood, including me. Instead, you turned to Wilson, who made this scandal worse for you."

I flinched. If cold hard truth were water, it was poured all over me.

I glanced at Wilson's back, then looked at my wrists banded by the curse of the blue string. I recalled Amma and her disappointment. I made my choice.

"Since we're on topic, Jawad," I said, "I can't compete in MIST. I probably won't be at the Block. I'm done with poetry for a while."

Stunned, Jawad's mouth opened and closed. When he finally found his words, he was colder. "You're giving in, Nida."

There must have been something in the air because I felt numb. It was like I was there next to Jawad, but also not. Even his words sounded slurred and far away.

"They *want* us to distrust each other so much that we end up hating our own ummah—our community. You're accomplishing everything they want. You're giving up poetry because of *them*? After your uncle's sacrifices? What would he have done?"

I couldn't tell him about the curse, but I was beginning to think, even if the curse didn't exist, would I want to return to poetry? Maybe the curse was a blessing in disguise. It would save me a world's worth of trouble.

"I am not my Mamou. My Mamou fought and it ruined his life and family." I was strangely echoing my Amma's justifications. For all my fight against her, we were startlingly alike.

"Really? My uncle never ruined my life. That's why the mosque continues to rally behind the Al-Rasheed Five. Your uncle never gave up on speaking for us and he never turned his back. Muslims aren't only in Al-Rasheed; there are millions in America. And something Muslims do well in the ummah is when one of our own is hurt, we come running to help. But it's a shame you never gave us the chance."

"I can't care about everyone else! I don't know what justice is!" I burst out before reeling it in, half-afraid the riff of our argument would carry above the crowd. "I'm just myself, I'm just me. I'm just a girl. I'm not some poster child for advocacy. That's something that you may want, but not me. I want my Mamou back. I want my family to be left alone."

His body shook from bitter laughter. "It's not like we have a lot of choices around here, not with our uncles, our jobs, our families. It's because of those tragedies that we're forced into it. I just wanted to play ball. No one does advocacy for fun. Everything we do is political, including our art. If that wasn't true, then why'd poetry speak to you? Something about it resonated when your uncle introduced you to the Poet's Block. If you won't take my word for it, go ask him." After another hard stare, Jawad shouldered past me, returning to the mosque.

I pressed against the foliage, my vision blurring.

Where do you go when the only home you've known for eighteen years wants to kick you out of its front door?

Dear Islamophobia,

My mosque was shot up.
Boom, boom.
Who knew ten seconds
was enough to take out ten bodies?
Don't know your name.
Don't deserve a name,
or I'd be inviting murder as your claim to fame.

You're Islamophobic: you fear Muslims, a popular world-
  view.
Islamophobia is the fear of walking by a Muslim child
thinking they will hurt you.
Fear morphing to hatred
from a game of peekaboo.
Peek: I wear a niqaab.
Boo: it scares you.

The hate festers into a torrent that wipes away
all the empathy, washing away lands that were green,
until it's bereft of life in an empty scenery.
Afghanistan, Waziristan, Balochistan, Pakistan.

Progressives and conservatives find common ground in rage
until unanimously, they agree to invade;

that fear feeds and feeds, from their unflinching greed,
making the saintly bleed
so the youth sign up
to salute and clasp guns,
marching forward in rows obsessed by Hollywood,
where movies praise how many of us they can snipe,
then be named heroes.

Thirteen

Back home, Zaynab had informed Amma about the disastrous press conference. By then, we'd unplugged the television, fearful of the conference's ramifications.

"I think I should speak to Mamou," I told Amma. "He's been through this. And I have to tell him that his legal case has been affected."

"Are you crazy?" Amma turned on me. "You want to go see your uncle? After how our izzat has been destroyed?"

I recoiled at her frank words. *Izzat, izzat, izzat.* It's the same justification. To Amma, her honor was more important than her own blood.

Izzat poked the first hole in our family quilt. After the Al-Rasheed Five, the neighborhood was suffocating under its own mourning, streets congested in grief. You couldn't find a family around here that wasn't weeping.

Instead of joining them in mourning the injustice against her brother, she'd tried to erase the incident. Amma had rifled through drawers, straining her back from hunching over for so long, tossing out every heirloom sent from Pakistan.

First was a replicated Mughal dagger, passed down from her

paternal grandfather. Next were the ajrak shawls, woodblock textiles from Sindh. Photos of Mamou on the media showcased him in the same maroon ajrak. To save our izzat, Amma was determined to distance us from that imagery. Even Mamou's old notebooks weren't spared. Those were tossed into the fireplace.

But why, Amma? This is going too far, I remembered arguing.

We're loyal here, she answered. As if this was a war zone and we'd shook hands across enemy lines. But I'd learned that patriotism requires speaking the right language and wearing the right uniform.

Amma was in survival mode. Even if her version of protecting hurt.

Looking at her now, the past was mixing into the present. The frown lines marring her forehead had deepened. Her eyes were outlined in purple bruises. She looked as if she'd aged five years.

It pained me.

"Amma," I said quietly.

"I said no, Nida."

"But—"

"*That's enough.*" There was no anger behind her tone. Her eyes glistened. I realized that she didn't enjoy any of this. To her it was simply a cruel necessity.

"Okay, Amma-ji. I'm sorry."

Her eyes softened before she opened the refrigerator. I was reminded of the canceled client orders and another pang of guilt shot through me.

"What will you do about this month's rent?" I forced the question.

"I asked the committee for this month's earnings, which will help us for the next three months of rent," she replied.

Many Muslim families refused to deposit their savings in banks for fear of involving themselves with usury and interest.

They either hoarded their earnings in safe boxes, or they deposited them into committees where people distributed part of their income into a neighborhood pool of money. Since no one had enough of an income to open a savings account nor any desire to do so, one person every month would take turns inheriting the big sum. It was informal lending, an interest-free community credit system, a tradition among Pakistanis to bypass banks.

"Aunty Aamiina told me our turn is next month for the committee so I'll inherit almost twelve thousand dollars at once," Amma explained as she threw the old atta into the compost bin to feed to the birds later. "By the way, she called. She's worried about you missing your Quran lessons. Which reminds me, where is your brother? He's late for his classes."

I pointed down the hall. "Still in his room."

She cursed, went to his room, and pounded on the door before disappearing inside. "Oi, Mohamed! Your Qari Saab is waiting, you have your lessons!"

"I'm not going!" I heard my brother shout.

"My slipper is so loose on my foot right now, *Moha-med*."

My brother ran from his room, Amma at his heels, her left slipper missing. "Amma, I can't, I hurt my ankle from basketball."

I rolled my eyes. "He's faking it."

"Liar!"

Mohamed had the audacity to limp in exaggeration.

Amma glared, but he tugged at the hem of her kameez. "Ammaaaaa." He dragged out her name. He was the youngest and, by default, Amma's favorite. Which was unfair because if I'd pulled something like this when I was young, Amma would've killed me for the disrespect alone.

"*Mohamed . . .*"

"Amma, my limp is so bad, I think I'm going to die if I step out that door."

She stared.

He didn't dare break it.

"Fine, no Quran lesson."

She snatched her phone off the counter and messaged the Qari Saab before returning to the kitchen. From behind her, Mohamed winked at me.

"You dirty liar. You're avoiding your Qari Saab. Go pray, you need all the holy you can get," I hissed.

Meanwhile Amma pulled out a cutting board. "If he wasn't so bad at his tajweed lessons, he wouldn't be so scared of his Qari Saab."

"You're not strict about his lessons. When we were little, you would threaten to cut our tongues out if we didn't learn."

"Oho, no I didn't," Amma said without glancing up from chopping onions. "Our little Mohamed is only slow. You and Zaynab are smarter. The youngest are always the dumbest. That's okay."

"I can hear you, Amma." Mohamed was in the living room, searching for the TV remote. "You both are backbiting. That's haram."

"Since when did you become the haram police, hypocrite?"

"You're the hypocrite. You didn't go to your lessons this weekend!"

"Because my world was ending!"

"Now who's dramatic?"

My mouth dropped open. "You piece of manhoos—" I paused and Amma raised a brow. "Aloo. You piece of overcooked aloo."

"Amma, tell her I'm not an aloo. She called me an aloo!"

"You're my little aloo," she said to him as if that wouldn't hurt his ego even more.

I laughed, and for a moment, it was easy to pretend everything was normal. As I helped Amma prepare chicken karahi by chopping the tomatoes, her phone buzzed.

"Jaanu, my hands are greasy, check the message."

I picked up her phone, reading, "*I will du'a shifa for little Mohamed, may Allah make his sudden injury, that was not there earlier—that was not told to me until Subhanallah five minutes before his scheduled class—disappear as quick as it came,*" I read aloud. "Damn, Mohamed, you got exposed by an old man."

"Amma." Mohamed shot to his feet. "I got exposed by my Qari Saab because you couldn't explain I was really sick!"

"I don't see you limping." Amma pointed at him with her extra-sharp cutting knife.

Mohamed's eyes widened. Before he could think of a clever comeback, the Qari Saab texted again, requesting a catering order of two veal pulao trays to be sent to the mosque for next week's Brothers Quran Reading Halaqa Marathon.

A few minutes later, Amma's phone rang. In the next hour, it rang two more times. And the hour after, and the hour after. Each call was a catering order.

I glanced at Amma in confusion. After my news scandal, catering orders were canceled. But suddenly today, people were booking Amma for the next three months. We even got orders from as far away as two hours, for a dinner party.

But Jawad's words pressed at my memories. *Something Muslims do well in the ummah is when one of our own is hurt, we come running to help.* Aunty Aamiina and Jawad must have had something to do with this.

Islam was not a religion of uniformity. It didn't matter if you were black, brown, or white Muslim—it was an ummah. A religion of mercy. That's something Imam Abdullah always reminded us of in his weekly sermons.

As the calls came, Amma repeated *Subhanallah* over and over in a mantra. She couldn't believe it either.

It wouldn't solve our problems, not by a long shot. Most of

these Muslims were lower- and middle-class people; they couldn't support us forever, not with their own families to feed.

But if complete strangers could stand up for our family, couldn't we do it too?

I pushed away from the counter, facing my Amma.

"I need to see Mamou," I told her firmly. "I have to talk to him about his legal aid case. We shouldn't give up on him. I know seeing him is risky, but we met with Mr. Wilson, and he deceived us. We have to try something else. I need to see him," I insisted.

Surprisingly, Amma did not yell at me. "Listen, jaanu, all we can do is say *inshallah*." She pointed up.

I sighed and stopped her hand before she grabbed her Quran. Anytime I wanted something, she always pointed up and said *inshallah* because it meant *by God's will*. But really, it was code for *no, and you better not question it*.

"Saying *inshallah* isn't an answer," I reminded her.

"Nida, we have so many things to worry about. And I won't have you interrupt my recitation time. I have a test next week at the masjid, on Surah Mulk. Ask me later." She yanked the Quran from the shelf and sat down in the living room.

But I knew better: it was another tactic. Whenever Amma refused me something, she'd grab the holy book and recite verses aloud, the blessed words like their own warning crammed into my ear.

"*Tabaarakal lazee biyadihil mulku wa huwa 'alaa kulli shai-in qadeer*," she began to recite. If she was going to use Islamic parables to convince me, I could do the same.

"Amma, remember the hadith where God says trust Him but never be idle? Like that story where the man should've tied his camel instead of leaving it unleashed. It means, say *inshallah* but also be proactive."

That cracked her. She stopped her recitation and even pushed her glasses down. I think Imam Abdullah and Aunty Aamiina would've been proud of my explanation.

"Where did you learn that hadith?"

"Easy, Friday sermons. I pay attention."

The doorbell suddenly rang.

"Go open it. Or will you disobey this too?" Amma raised a brow.

Before I could go, a voice rang out. "Oho, it's me. I'm letting myself in!" Aunty Farooqi shoved open the door, coming to the living room. She carried with her the sharp scent of paan and mint. "I am dropping off taza taza saag and bajra roti. I even have ass cream! I know my Nida had a terrible day with that Kilson. I saw them hurting her!"

Ass cream in Punjabi was actually *ice cream*.

"Wilson, not Kilson," I corrected with a wince. "Also, no one touched me. No one hurt me."

"And yet she is begging me to see her Mamou." Amma ignored my correction. "Please talk some sense into her."

Aunty Farooqi made fists with her hands. "I think your daughter is correct."

Amma sat up. "Farooqi baji!"

"Tell me, Zuha, when Nida was born, didn't I bound the ajwa dates myself, distributing them at the mosque straight after my Hajj with a big pot of suji halwa to ward away the evil eye? Didn't I open my safe box with my precious gold jewelry and gift my childhood bangles to her?"

"Of course! And I haven't forgotten!" Amma defended.

"I have no daughter," Aunty Farooqi said. "Nida is like my daughter. Aren't you, my sweet gulāb?" She pinched the meat of my face.

I scrubbed my reddened cheek.

She faced my Amma. "Since Nida is like my daughter, I

would never advise you to do anything that would bring more problems to your family. But Zuha, listen to me. Nida must see her Mamou. You are hurting her. You are hurting him. They are your blood, are they not?"

Amma did not answer but her eyes dropped to the Quran in her hands.

"You are making a mistake. You have driven your brother away from you. Do not drive your daughter away too."

With that, the aunty drifted into the kitchen, stacking the container of curry and aluminum foils of roti into the fridge.

Amma released a deep, exaggerated sigh. "I'll think about it. Maybe you can see him later in the week, after school."

She went back to reciting, but this time, with a deeper scowl. That was perfectly understandable. I decided not to push it. As I tiptoed back toward my room, Amma gestured to the shelf without looking up.

"Don't think I forgot you skipped your Quran tafseer on the weekend. Go study! Then, after, run to Aunty Nadia's shop to get milk and suji. I need to do your sadaqa. Who knows what types of nazar has tainted my house," Amma muttered.

It's like Allah gave mothers some special intuition where they knew when their kids missed their scripture readings.

After grabbing my books from the Islamic studies shelf, I sat at her feet on the Persian kilim. My phone buzzed on the carpet. In bold words it read, *BABA*.

One time, back in our village in Sindh, I saw a crow scoop up one of our baby chicks with its pointed beak. And the way the mother hen shrieked, flapping around, back and forth, reminded me of the alarm stitched across Amma's face. A mix of rage and sadness, and overprotectiveness.

"I could answer him later?" I said quietly.

Amma tried to keep her tone level, but she was practically grinding her teeth. "Talk to your Baba."

I wondered, was she mad at me or herself? But who am I kidding, the woman still hadn't forgiven herself for a divorce she didn't even want.

Dear Baba,

Summers in Pakistan dripped like honey,
slow, sweet, and sticky hot.
You would take me to visit
the old sandy forts of dynastic empires
or trips north, into the protruding ice-capped mountains up
    higher
into the greater Himalayan chains.
My favorite were the three days of Qurbani Eid
when the streets boiled red beneath the sweltering sun,
ripe in freshly spilled goats' blood,
the meat distributed to our old village and the city poor.
At night, we'd skitter through the small bazaar
fencing my father's old village,
snacking on messy falooda.

Pakistan . . .
a land of fallen empires and a mismatch of tribes,
    the clash of the Turco-Persianate world,
    vibrant in boasting arts.
    If only the rest of the world
    understood its beauty too . . .

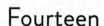

Fourteen

B aba?" I greeted into the phone.

"Jaanuuuu!" Baba stretched the endearment. "Your Dado told me what happened. Why didn't you call me?"

"I haven't had any time, I'm sorry."

"Nida, I'm booking your flight. You stay with me in Karachi and finish your schooling here. I keep telling your Amma, Amreeka is no good for you, not for your health, not from the way she's raising you."

"Baba." I groaned. Not this again. Baba called every other day. Even divorced, my Baba was never stingy on checking up on me. And during school breaks, for three months out of the year, I was down in Karachi, living with him and his mother, my Dado.

As much as I loved Pakistan, I wouldn't abandon Amma here, in America, in a mess I created.

"Nida?" Baba urged. "I will book your flight tonight—"

"No," I cut in. "I'm not leaving Amma alone."

"But Dado told me that your Amma threw away your journal!"

My heart sank. "Who told her?"

"Your sister. She blames herself. I told her, nonsense! Your Amma is to blame for all of this."

"Well, Zaynab didn't exactly stop Amma," I muttered.

"*Nida*," Baba said. "You are sisters. You should not be fighting. It's your Amma's mistakes that have brought you here."

"Baba, don't say that!"

"Your Dado is angry, and your mother isn't picking up her phone calls. But that's how Zuha is. She'll do anything to fit in with them, she'll even hate Pakistan if they ask her to. That's why she never visits."

"For us," I said, before realizing what I'd admitted.

"For who?" Baba said.

A rush of protectiveness flooded my veins. "Baba, Amma doesn't hate Pakistan. If she visits, what if she gets the same accusations that Mamou did, of being recruited to jihad groups? She's not visiting Pakistan for our well-being. She's also on the no-fly list. The government's blacklisted her from leaving because of her ties to Mamou. As for the poetry, Amma got rid of it for our safety."

At first, I wasn't sure why I was defending her. But Amma was my Amma, and my Baba had no right to judge her actions. Amma sacrificed her own identity to stay in America, to give us the chance at a better education. Amma grew up believing the American dream was the only road to success, the same way my Baba made love to that dream in a marriage more sacred than his own wedding vows.

Over the phone, Baba emitted a noise of disagreement. "Enough with this, Nida."

Easy for you to judge. But he was my Baba. It was the problem of my parents. In every conversation, they had this habit of putting each other down because it was the only way they could battle their own guilt.

Baba continued, "When you come down to Karachi, I'll buy you a new journal. And you will write for us."

"Yes, Baba." But I wasn't so sure that would be happening

anymore, not with the curse of the blue string. "You shouldn't be surprised though. It was only a matter of time until she would take away my journal. She hates poetry."

Baba suddenly laughed. "Your Amma can never hate poetry. That's why I'm surprised she took your notebook."

My words were stifled in my throat. "What do you mean?"

"Jaanu, when I met Zuha, she performed a poetry letter for me on the night of our shaadi. She inspired your Mamou. She's the elder sister, after all."

"What?"

Amma performed at her own wedding? And she never told me?

"You should ask her," he said after a moment. "She'll tell you."

No, she won't. As Baba went on to update me about how our family was doing in Karachi, all I could think of was that I was living with a stranger.

———

By the time I hung up, my mind had quieted, and as if on cue, I had another call.

"Hello?" I answered.

"Is this Nida Siddiqui?" a male voice asked.

"Yes."

"This is Eric, I'm a publicist at TNS *Fifteen Minutes*, where we break down news stories into fifteen minutes." He paused.

"Okay," I said, to show him I was listening.

"Originally, we were scheduled to interview the winners of NSPL. But with NSPL revoking their awards, we canceled the interviews in hopes that *you* would be interested in an exclusive showing with our host, Michelle, live Wednesday morning to cover your piece about the election."

An interview? This week?

At my hesitation, Eric said, "Michelle hopes to do a deep

dive into what prompted the accusations in your letter. To help America understand your family, especially your uncle."

I was silent for a long moment.

"Hello? Are you still there?" Eric prompted.

"Sorry, can I return your call tomorrow? I'll have to think on this."

"Sure thing. If you have any questions, here's my number!" After rattling off the digits, he ended the call.

I thought I had the power to reverse all the damage caused by my letter, only for that to be twisted against me. All they wanted were statements, but Mr. Wilson proved to me statements could easily be cut apart and restitched into a whole other meaning.

But was this interview my chance to undo all of the accusations?

Dear Izzat,

I ran to the grocery store
and overheard local aunties gossiping about me.

Poor Zuha. First her brother and now her daughter,
always causing trouble. Nida should be more like Zay-
    nab, the eldest daughter. Caring for the izzat of her
    house.
I crouched behind
a shelf of spices, making a home between the stinging itch of
    chili powder
and the sour tang of dried methi.
And Zuha is alone. I always said she should've married
    again after her divorce. Who can run a household in
    this day and age without a man?

The burn of shame
heated my spleen.
The salt of tears
stinging my eyes.
Which aunty was speaking—I was not sure.

Oho! Do not say a word against my baji . . . *Aunty Nadia*
    interjected.
But was this the izzat

Amma seemed to worship?
Did she absorb these jabs
left, right, and left,
unable to pivot away?
First about her husband and divorce,
then about her brother, and now her daughter
debasing the family name.

Izzat.

I was beginning to understand its rotting presence.

Dear Prayer,

I grabbed my tasbih from my bedside table.
Amma gifted it upon returning
from her Hajj pilgrimage in Saudi Arabia.
A necklace of beads to recite the praises of Allah.
Religion became the string
connecting Amma and me,
like those prayer beads.

I found myself reciting the ritual
Subhanallahs, Alhamdullilahs, Allahuakbars on the tasbih.
Amma did this a lot,
abating that thick temper.

When Amma and Baba got divorced,
I threw myself into the arms of prayer;
I saw it as an embrace that cradled me in its warmth
while brown men were arrested and veiled women were
*   threatened, torn from the arms of that warmth.*
It must have been some spiteful streak in me
that was determined to understand
my religion and all its peculiarities,
just in case someone questioned my beliefs.
They wanted me to hate my religion
but I only fell more in love with it.

It was the beauty of prayer
—that musky scent permeating the walls of the mosque, that
    softness of the indigo carpets with
gold embellishing, those walls of flesh pressed up against you
as hundreds performed the same worship in perfect unison.

Tonight, I bowed in tahajjad nafl for guidance.
My head was telling me
to accept the interview;
I know Amma and Zaynab
would agree too.
But my heart
clenched in protest.

Oh Allah, please guide me, I recited,
kneeling in sajood du'a.
After prayer, in answer, the blue string blinked into view,
slithering up my wrists,
my shoulders rounding and straining
from the immense weight.
I stared at it, transfixed.

I wish I knew in the rips and tears of the pages
making up the Book of my Fate,
scribed by Allah
before the creation of time,
Allah's plan for me in this.

Dear School,

My school district was overwhelmingly white,
a sprinkle of brown and Black students who were granted
    admission
through an open enrollment program.
Fifteen Muslims in an almost
1,500 student body.

It was Monday, the worst day,
I was met with stares from the senior class,
murmurs cascading down corridors
like a broken tune,
rumors were a plague, skipping from one person to the
    next,
worming contagion into people's heads.

Her uncle was a terrorist, didn't you hear? It was all over
    the news.
She defended jihad in that contest.
Her uncle stowed bombs at the mosque and Nida defended
    him!
Even Sharon, my chemistry partner, requested a switch,
because why tinker with chemical solutions with a girl
    whose uncle could bomb the school.

The urge to muffle those sounds was tempting,
but I'd look crazy, with my hands slapped to my ears.
I felt so small with my head bowed.
I was well aware they feared the idea of people like me.
I also understood that when they got to know me.
I was an exception in their eyes,
one of the better Muslims.
But this was different.

After first period, I was called down to the office,
Mrs. Alexandria, the secretary, told me:
"Nida, I think we're all aware of the . . .
sensitive situation at hand.
It's important for the school's safety for us to think of a
    plan moving forward.
The principal, Mr. Malcolm, wishes to have a word with
    you."

I'd been to the principal's office once before . . .
in elementary school
when I'd spoken to my friends about the mosque shooting, on
    the day of Eid.
My teacher, a nice lady named Miss Kristy,
overheard and went to Mrs. Davis,
who told the principal, Mr. Williams,
who, after tugging at his peppered hair in aggravation,
sat me down and reprimanded me for spreading graphic
    stories to the other children.
Now, don't go telling such stories Nida, he said, more
    annoyed than concerned.
You see, my actions had interrupted his lunch break.

He was one example in a long list of authorities who saw us
as nothing but problems.

I'd never gotten detention, suspended, or expelled.
My grades weren't top; but they were average.
I'd never screwed up to make my teachers overtly dislike me,
never "too political" to scare them into hating me.
I was the model of a quiet student, but maybe that was just
part of the bigger problem.

———

The principal, Mr. Malcolm, was seated in his swivel chair behind a wide desk, hands folded in front of him. "Nida, how are you doing?"

"Good," I mumbled as I sat on the chair across from him. I hated that question. No one ever answered it honestly.

Mrs. Sophia, my old English teacher and the after-school supervisor for the Muslim Student Association and Friday prayers, sat beside me on the other available seat.

"Mrs. Sophia is here to provide some perspective as well," Mr. Malcolm began. "I'll cut right to the chase. With the media attention from the election, the matter of your poetry ended up reaching the district board."

My jaw dropped. "How? This has nothing to do with the school."

"Videos of your poetry, including a performance at MIST—a competition where you represented our school, that Mrs. Sophia supervised—went viral with millions of views across social media because of the negative media attention. We were emailed the clips from local parents who were concerned about their children's safety."

"What's unsafe about poetry?"

He cleared his throat. "Not poetry but an environment supporting radicalism."

"But that's not true."

Mr. Malcolm continued with a thinly concealed grimace. "The board has decided to investigate the matter, and after an emergency vote, they've mandated that all related after-school activities, including the Muslim Friday prayers and any poetry club must go through new regulations. This doesn't mean they're canceled; it seems the board will now require Muslim Student Association events, the MIST competition, and poetry to be scripted and vetted by the board. And during the recitation of a sermon, it must be filmed for transparency. The policy will be revealed in a school-wide assembly this week. The board also voted to suspend you from class until the election's end for your safety. The official notice should be emailed tonight."

I bolted out of my chair, seeing red. "Is this even legal? You want to *censor* Muslim students? A bunch of children? Are you sure it's for my safety? It sounds like it's for *yours* and the rest of the school!"

I thought the ramifications of my actions were felt only by me. But Jawad was right. Even if I wanted this to be only about me, I didn't have a choice. I wasn't just a girl in their eyes. Every Muslim was considered a monolith. If one of us messed up, the rest of us would pay.

Mr. Malcolm began tugging at the gray locks of his hair. "I'm doing everything in my power to advocate on your behalf with the board, Nida. Between you and me, the accusations against you are ridiculous exaggerations."

"What about my education? Mr. Malcolm, it's my senior year. I can't afford a suspension. What about college applications?"

"I've emailed your teachers, and we'll set up a plan to make sure you don't fall behind in your classes. We'll make sure you graduate on time."

Tears sprung from my eyes. "But NSPL isn't even a school-affiliated competition. It's independent; how does it affect the school?" I blubbered. "What about MIST? It's tomorrow. You can't stop those students from going the night before, they've prepared for weeks, that's not fair! That's equivalent to canceling all extracurriculars. Imagine if our basketball team was disqualified from their championship the night before its occurrence because of the mistakes of one player. How is this any different?"

"The policy will go into effect by the end of the month, which means this year's MIST cohort will still be able to attend the competition." He tried to smile encouragingly, but it looked more like he was in pain. "I'm sorry, Nida."

I didn't dislike Mr. Malcolm. These ideas weren't his, he was only the bearer of bad news. But I couldn't help the threads of frustration. I was hearing *sorry* instead of a concrete way to solve this.

"The school board is hiding behind overexaggerating parents. Why hasn't the school defended me? I've done nothing that justifies this."

"I understand the need to lash out. But believe me, I'll do whatever I can to advocate on your behalf," he said, trying to reassure me.

"I'm not lashing out," I snapped.

"What Mr. Malcolm means," Mrs. Sophia cut in finally, "is that it's important we address this matter thoroughly. That also means we should not isolate you from your school peers. MIST is tomorrow, and you've been a vital part of the team for the past three years. You were supposed to be a spoken word representative. Of course, you shouldn't participate for your own safety, but if you would still like to attend as a non-competitor, you're welcome to. Mr. Malcom and I decided on this after the board meeting. I think your presence is important and reassuring to the team."

"But I'm suspended."

"The parameters of the suspension are applicable once the letter is sent, which is tonight, but we could . . . consider that maybe you'll see the suspension letter a day after it arrives."

But I was already shaking my head.

"I don't think I'll be attending MIST, not anymore."

While Mrs. Sophia's disappointment was clear as day, I swear I saw a flash of relief in Mr. Malcolm's gaze.

Dear Classmates,

A group of boys from the National Honor Society mur-
    mured,
Unpatriotic
Traitor
I shut my eyes and plugged my ears
Angry
Aggressive
to cover the noise.
Terrorist
Paki
Wow the world is beautifully silent
Liar
Attention-seeker
when you've overcome
all the senseless hum.

Dear Origami,

In the sixth grade,
Mrs. Hansen taught the class origami.
As a new student, I was a clean slate,
like the blank, uncreased paper.

Mrs. Hansen said,
Class, bend the paper like this, make it fold in and fit this
    shape.

I had no friends.

Nida honey, just make yourself fit.
Okay, *I replied, as if I am pieces of paper,*
hard edges,
made to bend, twist, and fold,
to fit imagined molds.

I saw the shape
as the landscape of the world.

I am paper.
I tuck my arm against my chest,
bend my knees,
crease my skin,

fold my legs,
flatten myself into the paper walls,
bent like origami,
shaped by the hands of an artist.

I am origami. I did it.
I hope I fit.

Dear Max,

Max, a boy from geography,
president of the Young Republicans Club,
invited me to join their meeting after school.
"I heard the news, I'm so sorry," Max said.
"It's a political agenda from Mitchell Wilson, just dirty
     politics."
The irony of his words
when we'd never even spoken
until today, when he asked me to help canvass
for the Republican candidate against Mr. Wilson.

But I'm not a piece on a political game board,
walking the path between enemy lines,
trying to choose sides.
If I had it my way,
I'd swipe that game board,
and break those pieces,
never partial to any side.

Instead, I answered, "Why would I help the Republican
     candidate,
an anti-immigration racist
who's supported the Muslim travel ban,

who's supported terror against brown and Black men.
My vote is not your business."

Max had a reputation for instigating controversial debates,
acting like the smartest in the class,
refuting whatever our geography teacher claimed, with his
    hands innocently raised.
I have a comment not a question, he'd say
before he went on and on in political tirades.

"At the time, the Muslim travel ban made sense," Max
    argued. "It upheld American secular values.
I believe in religious rights, but we can't ignore the dangers.
Just look outside America, the threat from Middle Eastern
    men.
Look at France and the Paris bombings. My father fought in
    the war in Afghanistan,
he saw how religion comes in extremes."

Max's father passed away in Afghanistan
in the outskirts of Kabul,
but that wasn't our fault. That was America's fault.
If my tongue could spin a story, it would go . . .
Once upon a time,
America installed military regimes
funding all kinds of terror groups,
forcing people
from Asia, Africa, and the Middle East to immigrate overseas;
how my family lived through coups and dictatorships
funded by this country
they call a democracy.

Death was a tragedy,
but what was equally tragic
was the way Americans were coerced into giving their lives
    to wars
they had no business being involved in,
lied to by politicians who simplified conflict into ideological
    battles
by dehumanizing the people they called the enemy.

There were many surviving war veterans
who realized they were lied to about Iraq and Afghanistan,
protesting outside of Washington.
But what about the millions of Afghans, Syrians, Pakistanis,
    Yeminis, Iraqis, Somalis, and more
left dead from these wars?
Just a series of glossed-over tragedies
under the guise of liberation, that we were told to be thankful
    for.

Max awaited my answer.
In that moment, my thoughts clashed,
an invisible battle of wits, the blue string wrestling for control
    over my soul.
If I had my pen,
    If I could speak poetry,
        If I could write a letter to Max I'd say . . .

Dear Max,
Equality in the West was a ruse for chains
to encircle wrists and ankles,
guidelines with a dress code.
Any violation to this memo

was a criminal charge;
handcuffs and a stain to your record.
But the same state charging us
turns a blind eye to other religious symbols:
    crosses around necks,
    bibles in court,
    the Gregorian calendar,
    Christmas,
    prayers in politics,
    churches and *Amens*.

We didn't live in the secular utopia they claimed it to
    be . . . just a culturally Christian, Western society
    brainwashed to hate us.

Dear Who Are You Voting For?

Every day,
at school the eighteen-year-old kids would say,
who are you voting for?
Vote Red!
Vote Blue!
Vote for somebody but make sure you did your research and
*   know who!*
I tell them . . .
I did my research,
I liked none of them.
They said,
You're against progressiveness.
You're against conservativeness.
She's probably for extremists. Or she's an idealist.
Are you a Democrat or a Republican?
I say, But that candidate supports increasing the police
*   budget!*
Okay, but are you a Republican?
But that candidate supports stop and frisk policies!
Okay, but are you a Democrat?
But that candidate doesn't have gun reform. My mosque was
*   shot up!*
Okay, but are you a Republican?
But that candidate supports a travel ban!

Okay, but are you a Democrat?

But that candidate's healthcare plan . . . my family can't
    afford it!

Okay, but are you a Republican?

They kept asking and asking,
until my problems went zip
and my protests went hush.

Only two problems really mattered:
        voting
        and which party was winning.
Two colors, blue and red.
The same people hurting me
were playing these games of politics,
until I switched from worrying about policies to asking
        myself

Am I Republican or a Democrat?

Fifteen

During lunch break, Mrs. Sophia found me packing up my textbooks at my locker. "I know it's a stressful time, Nida. You're always welcome to come talk in my office."

"Thanks for the offer." Mrs. Sophia meant well, but looking at her reminded me of Alexis, and how trustworthy she had seemed.

She caught my shoulder before I left. "Nida, I hope you reconsider coming to MIST. I think you could use the safe space of the competition."

"I'm not sure it's a safe space," I said. "They used my videos from MIST. Besides, I've disappointed my own community."

Mrs. Sophia emitted a noise of disagreement. "I'm not Muslim. But while supervising you and hearing you practice after school with the rest of the team all these years, I was so moved. It's rare to see kids proud of their religion despite the risks. It put a lot of things into perspective."

"Really?"

She nodded. "I took my own kids to the poetry festival downtown. If you can inspire others through your art, you are not a disappointment. Be proud of winning a national poetry contest, regardless of what's happening around you. You deserved that accomplishment."

My teacher was inspired? Suddenly, I wanted to confess everything to her: that despite the pain it caused me, I *missed* writing. And despite missing it, I would never be able to recite a verse again.

As if to remind me, the blue string manifested from thin air, thickening into a solid rod around my throat. My throat clenched from a choked breath. I forced the words out, "I can't even perform at MIST."

"Watch as a visitor. You already paid for the ticket."

"I'll think about it."

"I hope you do."

Before I left, I stammered, "Thanks, Mrs. Sophia. I really needed to hear that."

She waved and let me know that her office doors were always open for me as a safe space. But what was a safe space anymore?

Dear Safe Spaces,

It was supposed to be a room
to speak my mind without regrets
without another deciding for me.

Someone should show this to Alexis,
if only I wasn't so scared to answer her messages,
because what if that was turned into a weapon against me
  too?
She's made a coward out of me—
    quiet and stammering,
    eyes down, and body hunching,
    a wilting sunflower trapped in a shadow,
    one with no warmth to grow in
        —that's no good. At this rate, that flower will be so
      silent
          and so very alone.

Dear My Weak Ankles,

A familiar voice shouted, "Nida!"
just as Amma came to pick me up from school.
I spotted big blue eyes and sleek blond hair. Alexis.
"Wait up, Nida!"
I noped so fast, my left ankle rolled.

I should've been angry at her
like gasoline poured over flames,
enough to demand, Why? Why'd you do it?
So why was I running with my weak ankles?

I didn't talk to Mr. Wilson and the cops when they were
*   frisking,*
I didn't talk to the attorney when he was threatening,
I didn't talk to the news when they were accusing,
because I wasn't good at talking.
I was good at writing,
I was good at making words sound pretty, as long as I
*   rehearsed.*
All I had was a mouth once used for spoken word,
now just an idle tongue I'd never use.

Sixteen

cursed at myself for having the weakest of ankles—that's why I quit competitive basketball. With my rolled ankle, I had no choice but to lean against the school doors long enough for Alexis to catch up to me.

"Nida, I've been messaging you, but you blocked me." Alexis bent over to catch her breath. "Why are you ignoring me? You're still mad?"

Her words gave me whiplash. "Still mad?"

Alexis began twisting then untwisting the long strand of her ponytail. "I know I entered the poetry contest without telling you, but I texted you my apology days ago, and . . . you're still ignoring me. Even after the poetry went viral? It sounds like it did more good than bad."

"More good than bad?"

She dropped her hands. "Quit repeating what I'm saying!"

"I have to repeat what you're saying because I can't believe someone can be that tone deaf!"

"Tone deaf? About what? Have you seen the comments below your videos? So many people love it, not just Muslims. And why would you turn down the chance to win a couple thousand dollars? Even if the contest revoked your entry, there are so many others that would love to book you. You're controversial, in a good way! They want that attention. I'd want my friend to do something about it—"

"This isn't about the money!" I spat. "This was never about money. This was about . . ."

Privacy. My own safety.

"You cried to me about your financial issues. If you were in my shoes hearing your friend rant, then turning down the chance to win cash, you'd feel helpless too."

I flinched. "I didn't cry to anyone. I didn't want to talk about my uncle. Putting myself out there was hard."

Her gaze softened. "Okay, that came out wrong. I didn't mean it like that."

No, she did. The realization slithered through my mind. She wasn't even apologizing. My anger flared but if I yelled, the teachers would hear.

"Have you seen what they're saying about my family on the news?"

"I've seen some of it, but I've seen the good side too. Nida, some of those videos about jihad . . . can you blame them?"

"What?"

"It was alarming. All that talk about jihad in that MIST video, that was crazy. And with your uncle in prison, of course it makes you look guilty. Why would you say words like *jihad*?"

This was the thing with white guilt: they had a funny way of flipping the problem and turning it against you. My anger reached its threshold. "Do you even know what jihad is?"

"Of course I do."

"No, you don't. No one in this country understands what it is. You like to assume everything about us."

She gaped. "I've never assumed anything about you! I've defended you, that's how we became friends!"

"That doesn't excuse what you said right now. Jihad is translated to *struggle*. I'm allowed to use and own a word in my religion! Jihad isn't about terrorism; it's literally about how a Muslim responds to hardship. It's a beautiful concept but it's been stolen and turned against us. Like this conversation with you, it's *my* jihad."

Maybe it was fruitless to educate Alexis on jihad. During the war on terror, politicians bastardized the religion. But that's the truth of racism, it makes you fear the things that make us different.

I was so comfortable with people getting my religion wrong that the fight to tell them what was right seemed unwinnable. But if we didn't take the time to clarify all the myths about Muslims, then who would? An internet search couldn't. The government certainly wouldn't. People like Mr. Wilson, who'd fought wars that imploded the Middle East, reserved only one idea of who a Muslim could be. But maybe I could try to clear up the biases that Alexis harbored.

As soon as the thought crossed my mind, Alexis said, "That's not true. Why do most terrorists scream 'jihad' before they kill Americans?"

And like that, any hope vanished like the warmth of our friendship.

Across the parking lot, Amma's van honked two times.

"I can't deal with this."

I turned my back as she cried out, "You can't just blame the contest on me! There's more to it—"

Amma honked again, Alhamdullilah. The Lord saved me before I could say something else that I would come to regret.

Dear Allah,

What is forgiveness?
It comes after an apology,
but Alexis hit fast-forward and skipped the apologizing.

I beg you to pull the mercy from me,
to extend the hand of grace
and plead away the disgrace,
but if mercy was there,
why did I dread seeing her face-to-face?

Dear World,

Ever wish to run away?
I didn't. I wanted to fly away
from the looks and whispers
and the broken world
more malicious than the jinn brought to life,
from whispered stories behind the flame, at the dead of night,
I wished . . .
To
    Fly
        So
            High
                Up
                to a Heaven
                Amma promised me exists,
                so I promised in belief, hands
                    stretching out for
                eternal bliss.

Seventeen

Amma kept her promise. She scheduled an appointment to see Mamou and drove me to the prison.

In the visitation room, Mamou appeared paler than when I last saw him, the rich brown sheen of his skin a sickly yellow-brown.

"Mamou?" I greeted into the pay phone.

"Jaanu," he said quietly.

"How are you doing?" I asked gently.

"It's always the same answer, Nida. But your Amma and I had a long call."

"Uh-oh."

"Don't worry," he reassured me. "She told me about the poetry contest."

"I was hoping to tell you myself, Mamou."

His sigh came. "Have you been crying, jaanu?"

I pinched my thumb and finger together. "Just a little, wallahi."

"Just a little?"

I grinned. "Yeah."

"This isn't a time to joke. Tell me what happened."

"Really? I thought we came here to laugh."

"*Nid-a*," he warned in that *don't you dare disrespect me* tone like Amma used.

My gaze found my lap. I couldn't bear to look him in the eye. "It's Amma. Because of the scandal, she got rid of my journal."

"I know. She told me."

I blinked hard, worried about crying in front of him. "I don't understand why she did it. She's paranoid. She's afraid. But Zaynab told me that Amma has regrets. She said . . ." My voice broke.

"She said what?" he urged.

His gaze felt as fragile as my thoughts, like at any moment, I'd lose him too, the way I'd lost Amma. "Did Amma write poetry as a child?"

He blinked. "What kind of question is this?"

"Baba mentioned something. He said Amma wrote letters too, that she carried the family tradition?"

Mamou's eyes caught in a faraway look. "Yes, she did."

"And I'm only just finding out?"

Hip lips curved. "What's the use in speaking of the dead? That Zuha doesn't exist anymore. She's passed and moved on." I flinched at the cold frankness.

"When we were young," he continued, "we performed together during chaand raat on the nights before Eid, writing poetry about the beauty of the moon." His smile grew from reminiscing at some memory. If only I could dip my hand into the pool of his mind and sort through the images, plucking the one he was seeing. Maybe then I'd understand my Amma better.

He suddenly straightened. "But I'm shocked you never told me about the frisking."

"I didn't want to worry you unnecessarily."

"Nida," he admonished. I sank lower in my seat. "Tell me everything from the beginning."

I explained about the frisking, the unveiling of my hijab, the contest, and finally, about Alexis taking my letters and entering the contest. I even told him about how Mr. Wilson tricked us with his canvassing team.

Instead of reacting in anger, Mamou Abdul-Hafeedh simply stared at the shiny prison posters tacked against the wall, full of smiles and promises. He looked unsurprised. He didn't force a smile and tell me that I would be okay, or that he felt sorry for me. He knew eventually I'd be okay.

The issue was the anxiety of knowing it'd happen again. And again. And he was helpless to stop it.

After squirming in silence, I asked, "What are you thinking, Mamou?"

His eyes never left the posters. "How this country is full of lies."

"What do you think I should do? Amma is saying our izzat is ruined."

"Your izzat is not ruined. Your poetry is also your izzat. You know how proud your relatives back home are of your art? Most native Pakistanis in the West have forgotten these old traditions, but you haven't, despite living here. This poetry is your honor. Hang on to it."

For some reason, his words hurt as much as Amma's. Was that all they saw in me? Amma saw the poetry I carried as a family curse. Mamou saw the poetry I wielded as a family honor. But what about me—Nida—a high school girl unsure about anything? Why couldn't I decide who I was, on my own terms?

"I got a call from a news channel for an exclusive interview. I think that could help me clean this mess up," I eventually said.

His brows shot up. "I hope you said no. With the canvassing, you played right into that politician's hands. It's like what they did to me. They want you either silent, or they want to manipulate you. You need to use your voice with your own microphone, not theirs."

The shame heated my face. "What microphone? I don't have one, except for this interview. I can use it to clarify the poetry. There's no point in trying to defend it. If you saw how they took those lines and repurposed them against Islam . . . I have a responsibility. If I buckle down on the words, Mr. Wilson will just keep coming after us until the election."

"Nida, that's not what I taught you. You have to stand behind your words."

"Mamou, didn't you just hear me? It doesn't matter if I do or don't!"

"Then don't do this interview. Don't put yourself in that position."

"But I have to! Because—"

"I'm not against *any* interview," Mamou corrected. "I'm against *this* interview. They want an exclusive with you to stir more controversy. They want you to think you'll have control, but remember, they contacted you. You don't know what questions they'll be asking."

"Mamou, I have to do *something*. Especially with your appeal coming up. JBB is reevaluating your case because of the controversy." Guilt clenched my throat like a noose. "It's my fault. It's affecting our entire family!"

"Nida," he repeated, more sternly. "Forget about me. Forget about the case. If I've made peace with it, so can you."

"No!" My heart was breaking into brittle pieces. How could Mamou say that after always telling me to fight? How could *he* give up?

He continued, "If people's reactions scare you, including what they say about me, that's shameful. How is my own niece unable to stand behind her words? You're telling me you want to forget our family art, our traditions? When was the last time you stepped foot in the Poet's Block?"

My silence gave him the answer.

He bowed his head like the sight of me hurt him. "You don't go to the Poet's Block, you refuse to participate in any slams, poetry mobs, or competitions. I know you've stopped writing. That's not what I taught you."

"Mamou," I protested, but he wasn't having it.

"Just when you need your community most, you're letting yourself be isolated. Think about how if you were to continue speaking, people, including Muslims who are doubting you, would listen. They would realize the power behind your words. And Mitchell Wilson would regret what he did. The community's attention is on you, and if it's anything like what happened to me, the news takes what they can get. Our stories aren't always prewritten, Nida. But in this instance, you're letting Islamophobes write it for you, for their own agendas."

"Because Mitchell Wilson has more influence and connections than any of us!"

Mamou leaned against the partition until we were eye to eye. "Maybe. But the attention is still centered on you. If you perform anywhere, people will listen, including journalists. I learned the hard way, *Nida always has something to say.*"

I stuffed my free hand under my thighs so he wouldn't see it shaking. "How did you tolerate people speaking bad about you whenever you performed? How did you cope?"

He grinned. "That's easy. I had my community behind my back. I had you. I had Allah." Mamou released my gaze. "Do you remember when the Paris attacks happened, and all those laws started being passed to ban the hijab and niqab?"

I nodded.

"Muslims have always been politicians' distractions to cover the lost promises they were unable to keep," he said. "They used the war on terror and justified invasions that bled bodies stretching from Yemen to Pakistan. Because they wanted to create fear. Fear about us. So much so that they passed laws forcing Muslim women to uncover their bodies because it went against their definition of liberalism."

"What's your point, Mamou?"

He pinched the bridge of his nose. "They'll try to take a lot from you, including the rights over your own body. It's scary to speak up, but Muslims, especially women, have always been viewed as strange. One of the most beautiful things about poetry is that it's an art they can't steal from us. My Mamou, he would tell me about his Mamou, and his Mamou's Mamou being threatened over their poetry. Back then, the British Raj censored all kinds of art. Later, the military charged them with sedition. But they never stood down. My grandfather, and my Mamou, they would never let anyone manipulate their voices. They understood the responsibility in our family. It's our legacy."

"A legacy that sounds like a burden."

His features narrowed. "You sound like your Amma. Nida, this is for your betterment. No matter what happens, don't let them steal your tongue."

My fingers curled in. He was wrong and I wished I could tell him. Poetry was stolen from me the day Alexis broke my consent and the blue string cursed me. What tongue did I possess? That was stolen from me too.

"If I do what you're saying, no legal aid service will help you."

Mamou shrugged. "I told you not to get your hopes up."

I flinched. *That stung.* "You can't say that. I'm doing this for your sake. Helping you is *my* version of hope."

Mamou's features twisted into something bitter and dark. "Hope ran out a long time ago. If I had the opportunity you have—"

"You did," I said quietly. "But eventually it backfired against you."

He rolled his eyes. "You're not sounding like the girl I helped raise."

"Well then, Mamou, call me a coward, or naïve. Poetry isn't the same when you're stuck here! You keep pushing me to speak and it's hurting me. I don't care if you or Jawad or the others think I'm a coward. I *am* scared. I just want you back! I want you with *us*. I don't want you to—to deteriorate here. You're dying. Not physically, but I can see it in you. You fake your laughs and smiles as much as I do. And no one can blame you for it. I just want *my* Mamou back!"

He sat back, almost stunned. "Nida, jaanu, you won't get me back even if we win my court case. I'm not the same Mamou from before. This place"—he gestured around the prison—"it changes you. But what I can't bear is seeing you lose the parts that made you so talented. You're killing yourself to cover for your family even if it means you stay quiet. It makes you a shell of who you could be."

"Not who I *could* be," I snapped. "Who you *want* me to be."

I didn't even realize how true the words rang until I admitted them. I was either what Amma wanted me to be or what Mamou thought I should be. Nothing in between.

I would stand forever in Mamou's shadow.

"Nida, none of this is your fault or the fault of your poetry letter. It was inevitable." He inhaled deeply as if reeling himself back in. I hated that he did that. Like he had to hide his emotions from me. Like he wasn't allowed to be tired in front of me.

"Listen to your Mamou," he said. "You think it's your fault that JBB let you down? No, Nida, if that were true—if justice in this dunya were real—I wouldn't be stuck here. Your poetry didn't cause it. These aid organizations are always choosy—they want digestible narratives, not controversial ones. They want cases ripe for a documentary deal, things easy to sell . . . not the ones about people who have suspicious criminal records."

"That doesn't mean I shouldn't try. And I won't compromise your case no matter what you say."

"There's nothing to compromise," he insisted. "Don't be like your Amma, don't sacrifice your gift."

I gripped the pay phone hard. "You keep saying I'm like Amma, but you never answered my question! Amma was a poet, so why did she stop?"

He ignored my words, again. It was funny. He insisted I find my voice, but my voice was right *there*—across that partition wall in the prison and . . .

He. Couldn't. Seem. To. Hear. Me.

"You are stuck in the past," Mamou droned. "You focus on your mother's past. You focus on my legal case. You focus on everything except your opportunities."

"Opportunity? You went down this path and look where it got you." The words left my mouth before I could stop them.

I tried to apologize—he was still my elder after all—but Mamou turned away on his chair. "This is not my Nida. You sound just like your Amma. Go. Only come back when some sense has entered you." He slammed his pay phone back into its slot. The chains from his wrist rattled as the guards stepped forward to escort him. I flinched.

"Mamou, wait, I didn't mean that."

But I was too late. He was led back to his cell.

Amma always thought I was too similar to Mamou, but in

moments like this, we were never further apart. To Mamou, I was too much Amma. To Amma, I was too much Mamou. Caught in the middle with no way to turn, what half was Nida?

Why even bother asking. . . .

I had no fraction to myself.

Dear Puppet Shows,

A Kathputli Tamasha
is a type of drama
popular in Pakistan's String Puppetry Festival.
Puppets dance,
strings attached to wrists,
guided by the hands of a puppeteer
twisting and dancing at wrist bend.
That puppet plays an infinite role, sharing our folk
*   tales,*
nothing left to free will.

Puppets are dressed in thematic finery,
hand-stitched handicrafts
hailing from the village women.
The female puppet glitters,
in gharara dresses,
trimmed silk and net dupatta
crowning her small head.
She's the lady of the hour.

The male puppet wears threaded shalwar kameez
poised sweetly like toffee candy.
Who would have known chiffon could be suffocating?

Mamou is trapped in a drama,
a myth reenacted,
an entertainment repeated for onlookers
to feel a torrent of emotions
but never close enough
to snip the puppet strings, freeing him.

Dear Puppet Master,

Puppets tell stories,
strings pulling
                            this way
                then that way,
a master toying with its prize.

Remember that puppets tell stories
but never their own.
Only a person dressed prettily,
following the strings that control them.

Amma enjoys her puppet shows,
but here, she is the puppet master,
guiding blue strings as she pleases,
or snipping them to dismiss.

Dear Puppet,

I am the puppet.
Trapped in chiffon and silk,
wrists held imposter,
dangling above me,
yanked whichever way my master orders.
One day those blue strings will be loose.
I will dance across the show.
I will speak my own words,
but never to another's tune.

Dear Hope,

Mamou thought I abandoned poetry,
but didn't poetry also abandon me?
He didn't see the blue string
shadowing my steps,
reminding me of the curse.

Mamou thought I abandoned my community.
His reprimands had burrowed like a worm into my mind,
reminding me I once had a MIST team
who wouldn't forgive me so easily.

When I asked Amma if I could attend the competition,
she began her pacing, tasbih dangling from her fingertips,
whispering her Alhamdullilahs, and Subhanallahs,
and at that point . . . all of Allah's ninety-nine names.

Little Mohamed huddled on the sofa
watching us argue like we were a basketball game
composed of one-man teams.
Back and forth,
    back and
            forth, his gaze swung to me
                and then to Amma.
"I hate when they argue," I heard him mutter.

He'd snatched Amma's phone
and FaceTimed Zaynab, who was stuck on campus.
"Look at them argue," he said. "If I'm experiencing it, you
    should too."
"Shh!" Zaynab quieted him,
watching us from the phone screen.

"What if you perform? I can't risk that."
Amma's words had a point.
But was I a dog tied to a leash,
led where my owner wanted me,
all because the authorities found my poetry?
It was just poetry! Just some clever rhymes on a beat,
tied together loosely.

"I won't perform, I wouldn't risk that."
And I'm cursed! I wanted to scream.
My hope was a firefly,
flickering its wings,
scared to light the darkness of the bleak night.
Amma stared and stared before she nodded.
Then the hope was a star ablaze,
warming my blood,
shining me with its rays.

Eighteen

S o, you won't be performing?"

I shook my head at Jawad and my twenty other teammates. It was the day of MIST, and our school was one of the smallest cohorts in the all-Muslim regional competition. "I'm not allowed."

"Wallah on that?" Jawad made sure.

I snorted. "Wallahi Jawad. Call my Amma if you don't believe me. I'll be watching and cheering you on instead," I told them.

"But we're going to lose points for a competitor being a no-show," Ahmer said, a freshman.

Bushra, the vice president of our MSA, elbowed him in the gut. "Shut up and read the room."

During the opening ceremony, the MIST executives announced a new policy where filming was to be banned in all oratory competitions. They didn't state the reasoning but from my teammates exchanging long looks, it was obvious that it had to do with the video of my performance last year going viral.

After the ceremony, our team huddled together outside under the gray sky, propping up our school banners like umbrellas, same as the dozens of schools crowded around us boasting school colors.

MIST was the rare day when hundreds of hijabis of all skin colors gathered in one place. For once, I didn't stick out like a sore thumb. Muslim girls were clad in the latest sneaker fits and oversized long-sleeves, their hijabs colored in every shade of nude. It was easy to blend in within the sea of Muslims.

Before the competitions began, Mrs. Sophia took me aside. "Remember, I'm here if anyone gives you trouble, Nida. Just a phone call away."

I nodded. "Thanks, Mrs. Sophia. But I've only had a couple stares. With so many hijabis here, it's hard to recognize me as 'that Muslim on TV.'"

———

The day began smoothly. I tagged behind my teammates, watching the different categories, keeping to the back of the room, away from sight. Safa, the Muslim Student Association president, competed in oratory speech. Afterward, I attended extemporaneous speaking as moral support for Bushra.

At lunch break, a rap battle drew in a crowd between the competing schools. I took it in from afar until suddenly, my skin prickled like I was being watched.

I glanced to the side. A girl from an opposing arts school stared at me.

"You were that poet on the news, right?" she said.

I froze, my stomach churning.

"I recognize you! My sister mentioned that she knows you from MIST's spoken word category. Are you competing today?"

At the mention of spoken word, the blue string manifested from thin air. My left foot staggered back.

"Sorry, did I scare you?" the girl asked, but I couldn't speak. The blue string tied knots around my tongue, squeezing my ability to answer.

I shoved myself behind my teammates before she could follow and ask more questions. My lungs ached. For some reason, I found it so difficult to breathe.

I had to get out of there.

"Hey, Nida." A warm hand grabbed my elbow. It was Jawad intercepting me. I looked up at his tall figure, the sun throwing contrast on his face. "Where are you going? Ahmer's about to compete in a rap battle."

My thumb pointed to the campus entrance. "I don't feel well; it's cramps." Which wasn't technically a lie. "I'll meet you at the next competition." I jogged off before he could reply.

Instead of the bathroom, I ducked behind the halal hot dog stands. *No crying, Nida*, I reminded myself. *You're here to support your teammates, not drown in self-pity.*

At one o'clock, the time slot in which Jawad was scheduled to perform, I forced myself to slide into the back row of the spoken word theater. Seated ahead of me, headphones on, Jawad bobbed his head.

"Hey, how are you feeling?" I whispered over his shoulder.

He turned and his eyes lit up. "I didn't expect you to come." He glanced at his notebook. "It feels weird to not see you competing."

"It doesn't matter if I'm not up there. I can't miss a chance at seeing your performance."

He passed an earbud. I leaned down, but instead of hearing the expected J. Cole playlist, a routine of his before any performance . . .

"Is this a nasheed? Why aren't you listening to J. Cole?"

"I made a Ramadan resolution a while ago to give up music."

"How am I only finding out about this now?"

"I haven't really told anyone. But I listen to some nasheeds when the temptation gets to me. It puts me in the mood before a performance, you know?"

I was shocked. "But why'd you give up music?"

He shrugged. "It's been on my mind ever since Ramadan. And giving it up really cleared my mind, helped with my ADHD. It's forced me to just chill alone with my thoughts, to be okay with silence and not freak out."

"That's respectable," I said. "I kind of wish I had the willpower to do that."

"You can though," he suggested after a moment. "I started out by only letting myself listen to music on Tuesdays and Saturdays. And then slowly my reliance faded."

Smart boy. He must get all that will from his father.

"Maybe I'll try that."

"My Baba said that we can all find the willpower to get over our fears if we remember that it's all in our head. Usually he says this with some parable."

"You sound ridiculous."

He raised his brow and suddenly, it didn't seem like we were talking about music at all.

The loudspeaker cut in. "Now announcing number 34128 to the podium."

"That's my cue," Jawad said.

He nudged his way through the rows, our teammates clapping his back. The room quieted. I was fearful of exhaling too loud because every scuffle was audible, down to our whispering.

Jawad cleared his throat into the microphone on the podium. He wore a dark button-down, almost as dark as his skin, with a maroon shawl dangling from his shoulders. It was our team accessory to coordinate with our school colors. Jawad looped and unlooped the scarf, the only telltale sign of his nerves. With a deep breath, he began.

Over the years, I'd become accustomed to watching him perform. We'd spent years at the Poet's Block, in front of Muslim audiences. But every time he spoke, it was fresh air, like the room had been limited in oxygen and through his words we could finally breathe.

Poets can make people laugh, they can make people cry, or they can do both. And Jawad was an expert. He knew when to pause and gesture with his hands at the right moment, building up his verses into an orchestra before shattering the tension with clever one-liners.

Today was no exception. Of their own accord, my hands were up and snapping at the crux of each stanza.

Jawad pulled no punches. He spoke first about his experience as a Somali artist in America, reminiscing about home. He took us through the image of Somalia, how his home was shattered by drones, and about the lies of the media, his words speeding up, the brunt of his rage weaving through in a quick cadence. The reminder weighed heavily on my mind. He sounded so angry, my own blood roared through my veins.

Around the room, the audience's faces mirrored my own. Jawad's words carried us into that rage, painting the room black and red.

Then he spoke about his dreams; about the subjectivity of art and the way words can be twisted. Suddenly, his eyes swept the room until they pinned me in place. He wasn't talking about himself anymore, I realized. No, he was referencing what had happened to me. He was so emotive; his hands were balled tight and the veins carving his neck were popping.

Shame curdled in my gut. *This could've been you*, it reminded me. *But you were a coward. You threw your pen away.*

Jawad released my gaze.

He's reminding you of what you've lost.

Finally, Jawad finished, his chest rising and falling. The audience stood up and cheered, snapping and clapping. But me, I backed out of my seat and hurried down the aisle.

I felt exposed. I felt like a coward.

"Now announcing number 34136 to the podium."

I froze at the exit.

"Number 34136," the presenter repeated. "We're calling 34136 to the podium."

That's right. I couldn't formally cancel my registration, so they still had me down as a competitor.

The audience searched but I didn't step forward. My nails dug into flesh. Jawad made his way back to our team but when he caught my gaze, he pointed to the podium mouthing, *Last chance.*

Instead, I shoved open the theater doors.

In my hurry to escape, I bumped into the same girl from earlier, the one from the arts school. She was leaving the theater too. Her gray eyes squinted at me. "Oh, it's you!" Oblivious to my anxiety, she continued, "You left before I could tell you that I saw your spoken word video from last year. The one on the news."

"You did?"

"Yeah, I thought you'd come through and perform today too."

The words rattled me. I glanced at her expression, but her face blurred. I felt only the blue string stitching across my lips as if to mock me.

Behind her, a voice called out: "Rayan, aren't you coming for prayer?" She turned at the mention of her name, so I took the split second of distraction and left. Amma was right: there was no place for me here anymore.

"Nida!" Jawad's voice echoed from behind me. "You can't just leave."

I whirled around. "I told you, I feel sick." Technically not a lie.

"I didn't want to overstep before, but now I'll say it. This is ridiculous."

"What?"

"You heard me. You keep running away, it's ridiculous."

"I just had a girl recognize me. This is exactly what Amma warned me about. The last thing I want to do is bring our team unwanted attention."

"Unwanted attention?" he scoffed. "Because you tried to cover for Mitchell Wilson to back out of your accusations? Or because he said all that stuff about you in a press conference? You want to leave because you were recognized from a video going viral? Or because you screwed up by trusting an Islamophobe? Which one is it?"

My ears burned. "You have no right to say that."

"*Right?* My uncle is in prison too, Nida. I could understand some semblance of what you're going through, but the difference is, I won't conform myself to please people who'll never accept Islam for what it is."

"How am I the one conforming? This all happened because we never conformed!" My hands clenched. "It's because of the Poet's Block. It's because of everything we're doing."

"You're blaming our Block?" He looked bewildered. "You decided to help someone who treats Muslims like dirt while hiding behind his party instead of doing the right thing. If I were you, I would've performed today. I would've showed up every day at the Poet's Block and continued speaking my truth no matter what they accused me of. I would've brought the Block more attention—I would've made crowds come and talk shit about that politician. I'd make the Block known so well, artists from all over the state would come to us. Wallahi, I'd be doing it on TV. But you didn't even do that. You've been absent. Did you know, ever since they dragged your name through the news, we've had feds visit the Block, questioning all the poets? But no one stopped coming, except you. We're not going to let the authorities intimidate us into silence."

"You guys were interrogated?"

Jawad ignored the question. "You're being a coward."

My ire rose. "Did I tell you that I didn't want to enter NSPL? Does that make me a bigger coward? It was Alexis who entered the contest, not me."

He paused. "That's messed up."

But now it was my turn. "Everything that happened, happened because of that stupid contest. I didn't have the courage to share my letters for exactly the reasons around us. There were journalists stalking us right outside our house; Mamou's legal aid organization is reevaluating his case—"

His eyes blazed black. "What Alexis did is messed up, but you can't take it back. Open your gaze. You think everyone is against you? Your poetry went viral, Nida. *For a reason.* I've had people here at MIST coming up to me asking about you, wondering where you are. Because your spoken word and the letter resonated with them. They told me your performance comforted them. If you weren't so busy hiding, you'd see those people. You aren't the only Muslim who was frisked."

The blood drained from my face. "Who asked about me? Who else was frisked?"

But he shrugged. "Forget it. There's no helping someone who doesn't want to be helped." He turned on his heel, making his way back to the theater toward our teammates.

I kneeled down beside the water fountain, confused and angry at myself. Because the truth hurt. Jawad was right. I knew it the second I saw my name on the news. I couldn't admit it to myself then, but I was admitting it now.

I wanted to be silent because I was scared. I didn't know how to get past my own nerves.

Eventually, I dragged myself to the Sisters' Praying Room—a fancy name for an empty classroom.

Zhuhr prayer was almost over. There was just one girl. She was praying on a turbah, arms down—finishing up. She was Shia Muslim. I drummed my fingers against my thigh, hoping she'd finish fast so I could cry alone. Really, it was a new low, even by my nonexistent standards.

Finally, the girl finished praying and said, "Oh salaam, it's you again. You left before I could talk to you. You *are* Nida, right? Now I'm thinking I've confused you, so maybe that's why you keep running off."

I lifted my head. It was Rayan. She looked younger than me and her Jordans were crisp and fresh, not a smidge of dirt on them.

"Yeah, I'm Nida. Sorry about running off," I said sheepishly. "It's been a long day."

"I was so excited. I thought I'd see you perform today."

"Sorry," I muttered. "I'm kind of good at never meeting people's expectations."

"Expectations? You've already surpassed them! My sister and I are fans."

"Fans?" I repeated, dumbfounded. "Of what?"

Now, Rayan looked confused. "Of your spoken word. I saw it online and then found out you'd be at MIST. Last week, my mom came home because she was frisked by a bunch of cops at a rally downtown—I'm pretty sure it was for the same reasons you were frisked. It's been happening to a bunch of hijabis all over the state. They did it to my friend too. So, when I saw your letter online, I realized it had happened to a lot of us. It was brave of you to publish it."

I wasn't brave. I was the one hiding in a classroom.

"I also saw your teammate's performance," she said. "Jawad was *really* good. I wish I got to see you too."

"I can't perform for a while," I said. "Not with the media frenzy. I'm sorry."

The apology weighed heavy on my tongue. For a second, I pretended I was apologizing to everyone, not just her. I wished Jawad were here.

"Oh." She frowned. "I didn't realize you were banned from competing."

"Not exactly banned," I answered. My instinct told me to end the conversation, but this felt like a fragile moment. As if she were glass and if I stepped wrong, I would crush her under my sneakers. "So, you like poetry?" I asked.

Rayan nodded as she adjusted her hijab. "I write some too. I tried out for my school's spoken word team with an Iraqi-inspired piece, but I didn't make the final cut."

"Who cares? Just try out next year," I felt obligated to say.

She paused, her eyes darting up then down. "Can I give you my number? My teammates mentioned that you and Jawad know the poetry scene well because of the Block. I just moved here. Maybe you know people in my area? I don't know who else to talk to about this. Maybe you have an idea of some slams I can go to. When I heard your work, it was really good, and—"

"Of course," I cut off her rambling. "I think it'd be dope to hear your pieces." Her eyes lit up. "Rayan, right?" My fingers fiddled with my phone, scrolling into my contacts section, eyes landing on Alexis's name. I hesitated before pressing my contact list and exchanging numbers with Rayan.

"Since you're here, we can go eat some halal poutine, the stands have it," she offered.

"Wait, there's halal poutine? I thought it only existed in Canada."

"Yeah, finally! Thank God for the aunty running the halal hot dog booth."

My mouth opened to say *hells yes*, but I paused.

She sensed my hesitation. "Or if you're busy . . ."

"Not busy," I quickly said, overthinking it. "I just have to go, and my team . . . well, my Amma is scared about you know . . ."

She slowly nodded in pretend understanding.

"I'll text you though and connect you to the others at the Poet's Block."

She grinned. "Awesome. See you around." Then, she excused herself to go practice for her nasheed competition.

My smile disappeared because I remembered my argument with Jawad. Would any of the poets even want me around anymore?

———

In the bathroom, I undid my scarf and splashed cold water on my face. The stall opened and out walked Mrs. Sophia just as I was redoing my hijab.

"Nida!" She clutched her chest. "We were wondering where you ran off to."

"Well, I'm right here." I gave her a tight smile.

"Are you okay? I was told you were feeling sick?"

I nod my head. "I'm better now, but thanks for asking. Where is everyone?"

"Outside for the rap battle." She began washing her hands. Through the wall-length mirror, she watched me pin my hijab.

"Excuse my question, but you can take that off?" she asked.

"Come again?"

She reached out to touch the fabric, but I moved back. "You can take it off? Don't you wear your headscarf all the time?"

"You don't need to feel it, it's not a creature or a pet. It's just a piece of fabric," I said.

She recoiled at that. "I didn't mean—"

"Yes, I can take it off in front of women, for security purposes, in the bathroom, to shower, to sleep. See?" I unclipped it and her eyes widened at seeing my hair—like I was a completely different person with my loose curls.

"Wow," she said. Something about her tone made me pause, but I brushed it off.

As we walked out to the hall, she said, "Did you hear Jawad's performance? It was beautiful."

A twinge of jealousy ate at me, but I couldn't help but agree.

Dear Rap Battles,

Rap battles weren't my thing,
they were Jawad's game.
Spoken word battles were a rich Arabic oral tradition
—dating from pre-Islamic Arabia
down to Muslims even to this day.
Maybe that's why on the football fields, the rain paused for
    the Muslims,
where dozens of schools gathered in a circle,
banners like bloated gray clouds,
and below their cover were Jawad and Ahmer,
finishing a rap battle.

"Oh, Nida's here!" Bushra yanked me inside the circle.
"She'll go next, poet versus poet!"
My eyes went wide. "No!"
I couldn't do battles; not on the spot.
All I did was compare myself to everyone else.
But the rest of the crew cooed, ohhhhh.
"Bring the heat!"
"A poet battle!"
Jawad rubbed his hands together.
"Sounds fine by me. Let's do this." He pointed at Bushra
pretending this was 8 Mile shouting, "DJ spin that shit!"

I tried to protest,
but the crowd's chant
swallowed my cries,
until the hundred students yelled, "Battle! Battle! Battle!"
The energy infected the air,
Ahmer bouncing on his feet, snapping,
"The crowd wants to see
why you went viral."
Bushra shoved him. "Man, I told you to read the room. You
　　can't just say that to her."
Ahmer shrugged. "Everyone saw the videos. She has to battle."
My gaze ran through the crowd,
my ears ringing from their chant.
"Still feeling sick?" Jawad had the nerve to ask, but his eyes
　　went dark.
I met his gaze head on. "Shut up."

From the determined expression on Jawad's face,
my nerves shook.
He jammed his hands in his pockets.
"Heads or tails?" Bushra rolled a nickel onto her knuckles.
"Heads," I said.
She flicked the coin.
The Lord was trying to tell me something
because the nickel landed on heads.
"Your game," Jawad conceded.
"Nida goes first!" Bushra announced, and
the crowd cheered.

A sharp ache speared through my body.
The blue string unspooled from my wrists,

diving into the ground, and I withheld a grimace,
my shoulders caving from the heavier weight.
The crowd's silence
urging me to begin.

Can I even rap?
Rap is poetry. No, rap isn't poetry.
Maybe I could trick my mind into thinking it wasn't poetry
—then maybe the curse wouldn't manifest.

Mentally, I rolled through some bars, straightened my
    shoulders,
sunk into the crowd's rhythm.
"Just run with it," I muttered to hype myself up.
After a quick bismillah, I opened my mouth and . . .
the string clenched around my throat.
I bit my lips to withhold a whimper.
It grew tighter and tighter
until my tongue was paralyzed.
The blue string strangled me.

Jawad's eyes narrowed. The crowd rose in a chant,
jeers, and guffaws,
laughing and laughing,
thinking I chickened out.
Oh no. No, no, no.
Jawad stepped in. "I'll go first to ease up your nerves,
    yeah?"
His lips tugged into a pretty smile.
The blue string eased along my throat.
Bushra shrugged. "Fine, just someone go already."
Jawad nodded along to an imaginary beat.

I spit my rhymes in two-beat syllables,
Nerf myself to make this game more
Acc-
     ess-
         ible.
It's child's play, been at this for longer days
Count your blessings my words convey, to a
less-
     than-suspecting
         audience,
     not ready for the heat
the minute I unpause,
accelerate,
spitting words to this beat.

She watches and prays
Hands up to God
saying oh Allah
I want mercy,
to escape the fray.
'Cause she dropped the pen.
She's caught in her web,
those lips sealed wholly
drifting astray, slowly.
Someone call the cops,
we got an imposter here trollin'
Where's the real Nida? I don't see no poet.
Just a scared girl with gifted words
but unable to show it.

"Ohhhhh!" *the crowd went wild.*
Jawad's honesty was boom

a thunderclap,
but his eyes were bright
like the eye of that storm.

I compared myself to him,
the passion behind his voice,
and the dryness in mine.
What was the point in running through different verses in
    my head,
piecing together potential rhymes?
What was the point of even being here
to be humiliated?
It served me right. If my own pen rejected me,
shouldn't my people too?

My chest tightened and
a fourth blue string grew out of my heart,
a small flower under a cold frost.

First the humiliation of Wilson
and his guards frisking you.
Then, this curse.
Wilson's press conference and the aunties' disappoint-
    ment in you.
Now even MIST?
What else are you going to let them steal from you?

Jawad watched me.
The slow anger drummed inside my chest,
pounding up,
raw and naked until the blue string shriveled against my throat,
overwhelmed by the rage.

No, Nida. You'll figure this out like you've always done.
You're not leaving until you spit something.
Anything. Doesn't matter if it's a nursery rhyme.

I prayed that the knots in my tongue would loosen,
I prayed to Allah the blue string would let me speak this one
*   moment,*
I prayed that I would have an answer.
The crowd felt uneasy. I pretended they were empty.

"Come on, Nida.
You always talked big at the Poet's Block," Jawad tried to
*   goad me.*

It worked. The anger drowned my senses.
Imagine they're not there.
I shut my eyes,
welcoming the darkness behind my eyelids.
You're in your bedroom. You're alone. You have the pen
    and paper.

I bobbed my head.
You're alone. It's just you and the four cramped walls of
    that room.

My mouth opened.
The string
*   dragging like a torn noose from my throat to the ground,*
*   began*
*   lifting*
*   up.*
But I imagined snipping that one string and—

Miss me with your empty words to an imaginary beat.
Wasn't it you
back
   there
         begging me to 3-peat?
To win a competition,
   I have the receipts,
I recall some boy at my feet,
sad and reminiscing about my poetic beats.

Jawad couldn't admit it,
it was him who missed me.
Angry at me
for giving up poetry?
But why try
when the competition's empty?

The words spitting out of my mouth
felt like my tongue was whole again
and nothing was cursed.
Like I was on the top of the world
ready to unleash a torrent.
My tone was cool,
like a lash of wind.
My body pivoted to the onlookers,
arms jerking from the weight of the two blue strings encir-
   cling my wrists,
but I forced myself to move, hyping the crowd.

—Can't be topped,
Don't

need
    a
        pen,
        ability's in the talk,
pen and paper? I ain't a casualty,
when a gifted tongue
becomes my symbolic decree,
born from a beat-down legacy
to become its raging heir
lighting fire to my opponent's paper,
they're in shambles, they're in despair.
My flow rate too fast,
    this is poetic warfare.

You wanted this, Jawad?
Alhamdullilah, I got my
prac
   -tice.
When the true competition awaits me
    I'm ready to attack it.
Call me weak with no bars?
Man, I didn't invite you to this battle,
I'm the poetic murderer.
    I'll see you on Judgment Day,
    when you complain to God,
    testifying against me . . .
    for leading your words astray,
    before snatching your life away.

The world went pin-drop silent.
My face was beet red from the way it burned,

but it was the good kind of rush
only felt after a performance.
Around me, awe shone in the crowd's faces.

"That was sick, Nida!" Ahmer cried.
"That hurt." Jawad smiled, looking almost relieved.
It was just a rap battle. But my shoulders felt lighter.
I rapped? No. I spoke poetry. *Ridiculous poetry but*
poetry all the same.
I grasped at my throat, absent of blue string.
Did that mean the curse had broken free?

When the crowd moved on to another rap battle,
I sat on the bleachers and uncapped a pen.
Pressing it to the notebook,
I attempted to scrawl the bars from the rap battle,
but like before, the pen ripped a hole in the sheet and the ink
    dried up.
What—

On cue, the blue string erupted from my wrists.
I couldn't believe it. The string was here. It was still here.
I sat back on my heels, stumped.
It tightened around my wrists like I was a girl
chained at the bottom of the ocean,
drowning in her own misery.
What is the curse? And why hasn't it broken?

Nineteen

At home, I prepared for my live interview on the *Fifteen Minutes* national news segment.

Zaynab tried to help. "Here, this will keep your mind sharp," she said, holding out a green drink sprinkled with crushed almonds.

Pakistanis held this belief that almonds in any drink—especially warm milk—would cure the diseases of the body, including the evil eye. They also believed applying surmeh to the eye would sharpen one's sight and mind.

"Why is the drink green?"

"It's a smoothie. Taste it," she urged.

"Get that *thing* away from me."

"I swear it tastes better than it looks. I mixed frozen mangos with discount kale I found at Walmart, and some almonds and cacao."

"That's a crime. You lost me at cacao." I shoved it away. "May Allah guide the healthy folks onto the straight path. And may He especially save us from mixing precious Pakistani mangos with cacao powder. Ameen."

She shrugged and sipped the drink. She was braver than me.

But she also had better skin, so maybe she was doing something right.

For the next hour, Zaynab quizzed me with interview questions. When we stopped for a break, this time, she did the right thing by warming leftover jalebis to snack on, before oiling our hair. It was another Pakistani belief that by massaging black seed and mustard seed oil into our hair, somehow, the grievances of the mind would subside.

I plopped down between Zaynab's legs. It was a familiar position, practically a rite of passage. When you're a Pakistani girl, you sit between the legs of your wizened grandmother, then your Amma, then, if you had a sister like mine, her, as each massaged oil into your hair.

Zaynab began yanking her prized denman brush through my curls.

"*Ow!* Easy, easy."

She softened her strokes. "Did you end up talking to Alexis when you went to school?"

"She said some uncool things."

Her hand paused. "What did she say?"

"She said sorry but then she turned it on me. She made it sound like my poetry was a problem, like I deserved the backlash. She thought she did me a favor."

"What?" Zaynab almost dropped the hairbrush. "That doesn't make sense. Alexis has always defended you. She helped you in school against your own gym teacher. How could she turn against you?" Zaynab's anger bled into her brush strokes.

"I was shocked too," I answered in a small voice. "I don't know how to salvage our friendship."

"*Salvage?* You didn't do anything wrong. The most you can do is decide if you'll give her a chance to be listened to."

I moved my head up. "But if I don't do something, then I won't have Alexis. Which means I'll have no one."

Senior year, and I'd have to start from the beginning. It was always the same routine. You meet someone, maybe a classmate, greet each other with the usual pleasantries, crack a few jokes, smile and exchange numbers, go through the preliminary texting stages, see if your banter meshes, have a few deep talks to test the waters. Friendships were an exhausting cycle.

"You're not even in college, you'll make new friends. Why are you holding on to Alexis?"

"Because she felt safe," I realized. "She knew more people than me at school, everyone liked her, including the teachers, and they listened to her. She said the things I was too scared to say. She defended me against the gym teacher. She pushed me to do things I didn't want to do, she helped me stand up for myself. I didn't think she'd go this far though."

"She's not the only person who cares about you. You have the aunties, you have the Poet's Block, the MSA, you even have Jawad and his family. And you have me."

"But family isn't the same. Also Jawad doesn't count, we're not thirteen anymore. And I don't know if the Poet's Block will accept me after how I've abandoned them."

"Don't be so dramatic," Zaynab said. "People screw up when they're emotional. My best friend, Aliyah, was once jealous of me because the man she was almost engaged to turned out to be in love with me."

I laughed at that. "This sounds like a Pakistani drama."

Zaynab shrugged. "It was dramatic," she agreed. "And she almost ruined our friendship. But her father was sick, and the one reliable thing she had going on in her life turned out to be a lie. In the end, she groveled and apologized."

"But I don't know if I could forgive Alexis like you forgave Aliyah."

Zaynab shook her head. "You're missing the point. Just because you give someone the dignity of being listened to, it doesn't mean you embrace them back into your life. You could be the better person and move on. It's a mercy." Zaynab's words were muffled from shoving hair clips between her teeth as she parted my hair into four sections.

"Besides, Nida, I've been careful about who I let into my life. It's just the reality of who we are. Which is also a good lesson for you. You have to be more careful about who you trust. Maybe all your friends will turn out to be Muslim; it's not bad. You are who you surround yourself with."

She had a point. In fact, I preferred it if all my friends were Muslims because everything flowed easier. I would never be scared about saying Arabic words out loud, fearful of misinterpretation. I would never be embarrassed about dressing modestly, praying five times a day, fasting on Mondays, going to the mosque for Jummah—Muslim friends automatically understood even if they weren't religious.

I just wished non-Muslims would understand and not judge me for it. I wished they understood why honor was such a big deal in Pakistani culture and why having my words plastered in a magazine was dangerous.

But maybe I had to give more people the chance to understand me.

As if reading my mind, Zaynab said, "You know, you have all this attention on you. All you have to do is use it. Not everyone is an Alexis. If you spoke *your way*, without anyone trying to control your voice, wallah, more than Muslims would listen. When I began prepping for law school, I was intimidated. None of the students looked like me. But I only had to find the right mentors to make me believe I had a chance."

"And family expectations," I muttered. "It's easy to find your voice when it's for law school. How could Amma ever be against you?"

"What?"

I pushed away from her lap. "Did you even have a choice? Amma supports you in your studies and career because, in her eyes, it's safe. I feel like I can never measure up to you. I can't imagine a day where Amma ever expressed disappointment in you. Not once."

"That's not fair. What about Mamou? He was always disappointed in me for leaving poetry. He paid attention to you. He saw my actions as a disgrace. Working in the legal system, the same system imprisoning him."

I blinked. "No, he sees you working in a broken system to *improve* it. He loves you. He always tells me. He would never see you as a disgrace."

"Amma loves you too, in her own way. Her anger is her protectiveness."

My shoulders slumped. "Of course Amma loves me. She has to, the way you have to take on burdens even if you don't want to. But Amma admires your actions in a way that she doesn't mine. Your degree and your near-perfect SAT score are even framed on our walls. She went to the dollar store to get it. That takes effort! She has a trophy shelf for you. But for my spoken word awards from MIST, she would rather hide them."

"That's because of her own shame. She has regrets, and she doesn't want to face them, Nida. Ask her instead of assuming she's against you."

"But that doesn't change the truth. Every aunty knows you

because you're the child she brags about. I even heard them at the grocery store. Amma can never brag about my poetry."

Zaynab put down the hairbrush. "What did the aunties say at the store?" she demanded.

A knock jarred us from the conversation.

"What's going on here?" Amma poked her head into our room. I wondered how much she'd overheard.

"Salaam, Amma," Zaynab said.

I still didn't know how to behave around Amma. "Zaynab's about to massage oil into my hair," I stated before standing up, accidentally spewing jalebi crumbs all over the carpet.

"Oho, I'll bring the new amla hair oil that your Nano sent from Pakistan." Amma disappeared before reappearing a moment later with a plastic jug full of amla and onion oil, and a biscuit tin in her other hand. It broke the tension of the room.

I licked my lips. "Is that bakarkhani?"

Zaynab snatched the tin from me. So much for her healthy diet. She tore open the biscuit tin . . . only to discover threads and a sewing kit, and *more* hair oil.

"*Stoopad kids,*" Amma snapped, taking the tin back.

"I hate when you do this, I thought this was bakarkhani!"

Amma whacked my head. "Tobah! Tobah! Where else will I put my sewing kit! These tins are perfect storage."

This woman. Unbelievable.

I uncapped the hair oils so Amma could make her scalp-stimulating concoction, while Zaynab opened her laptop and hit unpause on a Pakistani drama. "Now we can watch reruns of *Khuda Aur Mohabbat.*"

That night, Amma massaged oil into our hair. In the background, Zaynab bickered with Amma about the P-drama. I shut my eyes and listened.

No one talked about poetry or the news or the election. No

one asked about how we would vote or what I would say in my interview. It was just messy oil, Pakistani dramas, sticky jalebi, and lots of hair. I'd missed this.

At the mirror, I wrapped a silk hijab bonnet around my head to plop my hair. In my reflection, I saw me but not me. A different version through a stranger's eyes. Light brown skin depending on the season, beauty spots freckling my cheeks, a deep widow's peak, and hooded eyes just like Amma's. And the scarf, smooth and soft, a plate of armor.

At home, I felt safe.

When Zaynab left to finish a paper, it was just Amma and me. She pointed to my closet.

"Do you know what you're wearing tomorrow, jaanu?"

"Not really, I was going to pick my outfit tomorrow. . . ." My voice trailed off as she stared me down with that *you're useless* expression of hers. I think it was the other power Allah gave mothers: the power of speaking through glaring.

My legs jittered from nerves. It was so very funny. I was supposed to be good at words, but when an audience stared at me and I didn't have the rehearsed words of my journal tucked into my hands, my voice stayed stuck in my throat.

I overthink and become hyperaware of how I look and sound. And if I don't hear reassurance, my thoughts become worse.

As Amma began sifting through my closet, I wished she would reassure me about tomorrow.

"Blue? Yes, blue is good," Amma muttered into my clothes.

"Amma, can I ask you something?"

"Mm-hmm." She squinted her eyes.

"Baba told me you used to write poetry, is that true?" I was not sure where my bout of bravery came from but it was too late to take the question back. Maybe it was Zaynab's conversation rubbing off on me.

Amma froze. After a moment, she answered with a tightly measured voice. "Your grandfather was a poet, so of course he inspired all his children to write. I even performed a piece to your Baba on our wedding."

"Do you still have the letter?"

"No, I got rid of it. For good."

What was Amma not telling me that had her avoiding my gaze? My fingers dug into my T-shirt. I wished for once we could talk openly. That we could forget honor and izzat and legacies.

Amma brushed back her loose, oily hair. "Do you think I am a coward, beta? Because I am not like your Mamou?"

"Does it matter if you're like Mamou?"

"Your elder asked you a question first."

"My opinion shouldn't matter."

She blanched. "Of course your opinion matters."

I realized that our fears were the same: Amma would never think she was good enough in anyone's eyes, fighting against outsiders' expectations, just as I thought I would never be good enough in her eyes. For all of our worries, they were only as real as the importance we gave them, I decided.

"You don't need to be like Mamou," I said.

Usually, Amma seemed firm and unwavering, but she clenched her hands together before wrenching them apart.

I wasn't good at heart-to-hearts with anyone. But I forced myself to be honest, because if anyone needed to hear reassurances, it was Amma, a woman who was still ashamed for being divorced.

"You're the bravest woman I know. I can't imagine packing up my things and leaving my home to go to another country or working alone and taking care of three kids. Mamou did incredible things, but so did you. We give you a lot of trouble, and I know my poetry definitely has."

She appeared surprised. "You think I was brave even when I stopped wearing the hijab? My own daughter wears it, but her Amma doesn't."

I shrugged. "I wish you would wear it again. But I can't force you to."

She gave me a sidelong glance. "Maybe one day. May He give me the courage."

To Amma, it was about necessity, to keep her job and give her children a better life. It didn't make Amma's decision right. It was just her logic.

I'd never considered how much the sacrifices had hurt her. But I was beginning to see that just because actions weren't loud, it didn't mean you weren't resisting. I kept comparing Amma to Mamou, someone who was vocal in his resistance. But my Amma was pragmatic. And my uncle wasn't the only one who knew resistance.

There was resistance written into how Amma raised me. She may not wear the hijab, but her daughters did—her living, breathing children. She made me love my religion regardless of how it was criticized by the outside; she encouraged me to go to the mosque despite the shootings around our country, to learn about the holy Quran and not miss a Jummah sermon.

I couldn't find it in me to say any of this aloud to Amma, but I handed her the last jalebi like an offering. Her lips turned up. It hurt to never be able to tell my mother's fake smile from her real one.

I didn't ask her why she'd said those hurtful things about me to Zaynab. She didn't ask me why or how I entered the poetry competition. I didn't ask her why she destroyed my journals— and what about our past made her give up the art of letter writing. She didn't ask me what actions led me to write those letters in the first place.

I didn't ask if she regretted her choices, or if she resented me. I didn't ask any questions because I didn't know if I was ready to face the hard truths her answers would present me.

We were good at this—not asking. We circled around each other like diplomats on opposite sides, unable to wave the flag of truce. We were good at fighting, then ignoring the hurt, pretending it never happened.

I still held out the jalebi, nails digging into the sugary crust, reminding myself to *just let go*. But it was hard to unclench my hand from the pastry.

Let go, I told myself. If only I could.

Amma nibbled on the jalebi as she walked away. Before she left my room, she squeezed my shoulder.

How sad was it that the woman I wanted to be closest to was the one who stood furthest away?

Dear Baba . . .

  I asked Amma about the poetry. I wish I knew more about the both of you. I miss you.

Love,
Nida

Dear Amma . . .

I wish I could understand you.

Love,
Nida

Fifteen years ago

Dear Zaynab and Nida . . .

~~Here is a hukum from my mother and her mother and her~~
~~mother:~~
~~One mother can care for ten children but ten children can~~
~~never care for their one mother.~~
~~For the lengths a mother would go~~
~~to protect her children~~
~~meant that what a mother did well~~
~~was trade that child's pain for another,~~
~~as long as the second pain was less than the first.~~
~~I wish you knew what went on inside of me . . .~~
~~I wish I could tell you everything so you could understand.~~

~~Love,~~

~~Amma~~

Dear Fifteen Minutes,

Backstage at TNS news,
interns spoke into mics and scribbled onto clipboards.
I shifted on my seat, uncomfortable,
my clothes didn't fit right.
Like my baggy jeans, long-sleeved blouse, and sneakers were
    rejecting me.
Like they would rather
        nose-dive
        and free-fall
      to dress the floor
      than my brown skin.

Amma smoothed my hijab,
adjusted the fabric,
stabbing it in place
with an army of hijab pins.
They always shifted and poked my skull,
but Amma explained that for a televised appearance,
it would be worse if my hijab came undone.

"I feel sick," I whispered.
Amma sighed. "We can make nihari tonight."
I immediately perked up.

Tender beef stewed in a warmed blend of spices dipped
    with Afghan sesame naan . . .
"I think I should feel sick
more often," I suggested.
Amma whacked the back of my head.

The backstage manager arrived. It was time.
Amma pinched the baby fat of my cheek.
"You're shining, Nida," she said.
"I think that's my sweat."
I was whacked again.

Onstage and mic'd up, the host Michelle greeted me
with a ruby-red-lipstick smile,
wearing a fitted gray suit.
"Hi, Nida," Michelle said.
"Hi," I managed, sinking into the dark cushioned chair.
The overhead lights were unforgiving,
making me see black spots.

I wondered if this was the beginning
of the end of this nightmare.
I whispered, Bismillah.

Twenty

Michelle faced the camera. "Nida has taken the country by storm in the lead-up to a polarizing Senate race. She penned a damning statement in *American People* magazine. Her letter addressed Mitchell Wilson, accusing him of allowing an illegal frisking.

"But her poetry has raised concerns and questions about women in Islam," Michelle continued. "So tonight, in fifteen minutes, we present a deep dive into the girl behind the letter."

I swear my ears bled from the way she pronounced the religion, calling it *Iz-laam*, instead of *Is-lam*.

"Now, Nida." She turned, crossing her legs. "Tell us about yourself. Where is your family from and how did you arrive in America?"

"I was born here," I clarified. "But my parents emigrated from Pakistan two decades ago to give us, their children, better opportunities."

"And your mother is here with you today?"

I nodded.

"And your uncle, when did he immigrate?"

"He immigrated long after, when my mother sponsored him."

"I see. According to your letter, your uncle is incarcerated at a federal prison under terrorism charges. Yet, your letter speaks about how your uncle inspired your art. You even detail the scrutiny directed toward Muslim women and how it goes against human rights. What are your thoughts about how much a woman should cover up here in the West?"

"Cover what?" I sputtered.

"How do you reconcile the notion of strong women with your beliefs? Wearing the hijab is only required of women, right? You said it yourself. Your mother left Pakistan. She emigrated because of the oppression she faced from jihad campaigns. That's why she doesn't wear the hijab. So, tell us, what goes into the decision behind the hijab? For your mother, what was that liberating decision like for her, to leave a country that forced it? What inspired her empowerment after she immigrated?"

My gaze darted behind Michelle as if Amma was standing there, but I couldn't see anything past the glare of studio lights.

"My mother is the strongest woman I know," I finally answered. "She loves the hijab."

"Loves the hijab?" Michelle tilted her head to the side. "But did she not take the headscarf off after immigrating to the United States? The normalcy must have been a relief, she wanted something *better*—something *normal* and freeing—for herself in America, like all immigrants."

She was the better one. The normal one, a demeaning phrase without anyone even realizing. It was exactly what my friends in middle school would call me when I shared the same interests and hobbies. They would say, *Thank God you're a chill Muslim*—like I was some kind of an exception in their eyes.

The minute you classified a person with a label, you created a spectrum. It was no longer, *you are a Muslim*. You became either *a radical Muslim* or a *moderate Muslim*. I wished to be neither.

I was a Muslim, and so was my mother. It didn't matter if you wore the veil or how you dressed. Religion couldn't be quantified by other humans. It was up to Allah.

"I'm not a spokesperson for all Muslim women, I'm just a spokesperson for me, that's why I agreed to this interview," I answered honestly.

Michelle pretended to look apologetic. "You talked about your family in that poetry letter."

"But that letter was written for . . ."

Even as the words left my mouth, I knew it didn't matter. Jawad had said as much, that to the rest of the world, Islam and everyone in it was a monolith. If one of us acted in a certain way, it would be applied to the entire religion.

Michelle's cool stare burned into me, choking off my will to conjure a reply. Why have a cursed blue string steal my voice when Michelle's words accomplished as much?

"Your family has a history with jihad, correct? As you said yourself, your uncle is in federal prison because he was convicted of terrorism."

"That's a misunderstanding."

She arched a brow. "But it was a conviction. There was hard evidence." She glanced down at her notes. "He was a poet too, using his words to criticize American values. You claimed to be inspired by him. Can you elaborate? Like him, you perform at the notorious Poet's Block, a radical poetry hub which many view as the match that sparked the Al-Rasheed Five."

"American values?" I repeated. "What even are American values?"

"The promotion of liberty, and democracy, something your uncle seemed to detest. We couldn't help but notice the parallels between your poetry and your convicted uncle's. You both mentioned the Koran, hijab, jihad, and American wars."

The realization swept over me. It was strange how the journalist wasn't mentioning the accusations I made about Mr. Wilson, even though that was the subject of my letter, as if it was a topic Michelle didn't wish to engage with.

Wasn't my original plan to clarify my accusations and poetry? I was prepared to reject my letter, but Mamou was right. They would always criticize Islam, our clothes, our scriptures, and our values. Even my own body didn't belong to me. All I had was my religion and art. I couldn't let them take that too.

I forced the words out. "My poetry parallels my uncle's writing because, like him, I'm a victim of Islamophobia. People like Mitchell Wilson hide behind liberal agendas to deflect their own bigotry and problematic foreign policies. My letter was an attempt to show that—"

She cut me off with a wave of her hand. "A victim? Bigotry? Pictures surfaced of you volunteering for Mitchell Wilson's election campaign, mere days after your letter was published in the magazine. Is that not inconsistent with your accusations? If he was really a racist, why support his electoral campaign?"

This felt like a trial. The fear returned. I was underwater, drowning. I knew I had a choice to defend myself and my family, but if I did, it would only open me up to more attacks. If I told the truth about my poetry letter, it would only confirm that my words were inspired by my uncle, making the audience perceive my family as problematic. If I shut my mouth and pretended what she was saying was okay, I would be seen as a conforming liar.

There was no winning. At the end of the day, this host had accomplished her mission: to alienate me from not only America, but my own Muslim community.

I gripped the rails of the seat tightly. "You have it all wrong. I was frisked illegally and Mitchell Wilson supported it. My uncle is not a terrorist, he was wrongfully incarcerated. I wouldn't be a poet if it wasn't for my uncle. And I'm proud of that."

"But it's a known fact that your uncle used his poetry to spread a jihad agenda. He founded the Poet's Block. And he was proud of yelling jihad."

"No, he was wrongly incarcerated with the four others arrested alongside him."

The panic threading my words must have been hilarious because she emitted a low chuckle. "Wrongly incarcerated? The evidence was clear. According to the police report, explosives were discovered at the site where he performed his recruitment propaganda. The Al-Rasheed Five were guilty of taking funds overseas to Pakistan and Somalia, funding militant groups. The reports confirm your uncle visited Waziristan. It's jihad."

"There was no funding overseas," I snapped back. "The money was sent to non-profits in Waziristan, where my uncle's friends live! It's one of the most beautiful places in Pakistan. But what would you know? It's so hypocritical that Americans can donate to overseas militaries in Eastern Europe, yet if we try to send money back to our own country, we're put under suspicion. Besides, jihad is misunderstood."

"Misunderstood? Are you apologizing for jihad?"

"No!"

She faced the camera. "Jihad is the single biggest factor that increased terrorist attacks against innocent Americans. The same attack that resulted in 9/11 and the Paris bombings. What about it is misunderstood?"

There was that buzzword—*9/11*. Like every Muslim was responsible for it.

At my shocked silence, false worry settled across her frowning lips. "We've talked about your uncle and your mother. But your father is out of the picture as well."

"What does my father have to do with this?"

"An absent father made you view your uncle like a paternal

figure. Is this what inspired you to turn to your uncle's fundamentalist traditions?"

"Why am I being questioned for something that has nothing
to do with my letter?" I demanded, as if having an absent father
made me more vulnerable to the influences of my uncle. What
was the American media's obsession with assumptions and sob
stories? It's like nothing could be delivered straight, it had to be
paired with tragedy.

"You made daring accusations mere weeks before the election. America has a right to understand the girl behind them,
and which side to believe. Has your family voted before?"

"I'll vote whichever way I want," I forced out. "It isn't supposed to be anyone's business. Not yours or all of America's. Isn't
that in our fifteenth amendment?"

"You're eighteen. It's your first election, and we're curious if
your family ever partook in exercising their democratic rights in
a democratic country. You were a volunteer for the Democrats;
it seems like you'll be voting for Mitchell Wilson, yes?" Her
smile was the final nail in my coffin. She was painting a deft but
twisted picture.

My eyes burned and my wrists tingled. The blue string reap-
peared, but it wasn't just one. Several sprang forward, eclipsing
my limbs, climbing up my chest, clamping around my throat and
hands.

"Nida?" she had the audacity to repeat.

I.
　　Couldn't.
　　Breathe.

My fingers clawed at the cushion beneath me, grasping for
something—*anything*—to get me through the interview. I was

aware that I wasn't speaking, that I *couldn't* speak—from Michelle or the cursed string, I couldn't tell, they were equally binding. The cameras were pointed our way and the thousands of people watching on their screens had probably made up their minds about me.

No matter what I stated, they believed the one who was called a hero for fighting in American wars. A man who had powerful connections. A man who clung tightly to his bright image and hoped to keep it that way.

It didn't matter what a Muslim girl had to say against him. It was times like this that exposed the rotten nature of American politics, full of cyclical name-calling and finger wagging.

I was tired of the assumptions. Of being hurt but still the expectation was to vote blue. People thought the Democrats were on the *good side*, without realizing both political parties could be racist and complicit in the dehumanizing of brown bodies, domestically and overseas.

My long silence must have frustrated Michelle because she touched her earpiece. "This just in, we have Mitchell Wilson's attorney, Benjamin McCarthy, on the line in the *Fifteen Minutes* newsroom to join this debate."

On the large screen, a staticky image appeared. The same attorney who had sat at my breakfast table and made me sign the NDA.

"Mr. McCarthy, we're so glad you can join us in this debate on the nature of jihad."

In the camera reflection, I was beet-faced with terror. The TSN team hadn't even *informed* me before I agreed to the interview.

My eyes stung. *Don't cry, don't cry*, I kept chanting.

As Michelle turned to address the attorney, I spoke up.

"I thought this was an interview to discuss my story. But all I hear is you weaponizing my words and refusing to acknowledge the frisking incident! Weren't my rights violated when I was forced to strip from my hijab for no reason? When I was racially targeted?"

Michelle waved a hand dismissively. "We've debated your encounter. The hijab is a threat to security; when women wear it, it's a coerced choice."

I blinked at her and for the first time in the interview, I no longer cared.

"Hijab isn't my choice," I blurted. "It's my submission. In fact, Muslim men have a hijab too. But America monopolized that conversation. You're focused on the women's hijab instead of how men have a hijab. All you do is focus on women's rights in Islam, ignoring your own country's poison."

"So, you didn't have a choice. You were forced to wear it?" She conveniently ignored my explanation.

"No, I'm not forced," I said, calmly. "That's where you get it wrong. It's submission, there's a difference. I choose to submit to the God I believe in by wearing my hijab, but it isn't a choice. The same way Christians go to church or wear a cross; Muslims pray and some wear their hijab. That's part of our rulings. Is that a choice? No. We don't have a choice in praying. It's a commandment, just as we're commanded to pay a charity tax and donate to the poor annually. We're told to submit through religious practices, and hijab just happens to be one of them for men *and* women. Hijab isn't just a fabric, it's a veil. Veils are manifested in different ways; men have their own and women do too. I don't understand why it's a big deal: a woman's headscarf is a damn piece of fabric.

"America likes putting other cultures in the dichotomy of choice, and if it's not American values, they call it oppression. I'm not oppressed because I'm not obsessed with trying to convince people that a piece of fabric oppresses me. It's how I practice my religiosity. I'm proud of wearing it because now people know I'm Muslim. I look different. I'm proud of that difference. But no one should be forced to wear hijab. I was not forced."

I could tell any nuance of my words was lost on her. "You said you have to submit. To me, that sounds like oppression."

My teeth gritted but I recited zikhr in my mind to let the faith quell my anger. I prayed I could draw on my knowledge to defend myself. My lips parted and I felt possessed, like I was channeling the energy of every Muslim scholar and paper I'd ever read.

"Submission isn't what you think it is; in an Islamic context, it's the pinnacle of the religion. The contradiction of your own criticisms is that you are guilty of something worse: in the West you practice submission to your own society. You wear these clothes. You come to work wearing high heels, a skirt, and makeup. How is that different from my hijab? Do I enjoy the hijab? What a stupid question. Do I hate the hijab? Another stupid question. Might as well ask if I enjoy having hair, if I enjoy wearing pants or shoes. It's an article of clothing. How the hell does that oppress me when I decided to wear hijab by my own volition? And who cares? People are dying because of wars, and because of your hurtful rhetoric; because all of you are obsessed with being right about your values without understanding mine."

I stood up from the chair. "Let me ask you, Michelle, aren't *you* oppressed for wearing those shoes? Oh wait, your shoes are just shoes. My hijab is just a scarf. I guess your shoes oppress you. Yes, there are countries where the hijab is forced, but I beg you to take a history lesson into how corrupt regimes, funded or isolated by the West, manipulate religion against people by warping its messaging. The West has a history of warping Christianity to voters, taking away people's rights. It doesn't make the religion poisonous. It's only power-hungry people who commit poisonous acts."

Michelle's laugh was tight but nothing in my sentence was a joke. "My shoes aren't forced on me."

"Please," I said. "That's such a lie. Why don't you spend the rest of your life not wearing shoes or your dress suit, then? You can't because it's a societal expectation—it's a normative construct. Isn't that just as imprisoning? My hijab protects and veils me, just as your shoes protect you. The difference is I believe in God. And I'd rather submit to Him than a society and its expectations that choose to demonize my people."

I couldn't stop now that I'd started, my tongue loose.

"And I'm not oppressed because I believe in my religion. The only person oppressing me is you. You all harbor warped perceptions of lands outside this country. Pakistan is not a dangerous wasteland full of oppression and conflict. We refuse to be defined as inferior, or defined by the drones, invasions, and military dictatorships you funded. Like any normal country, Pakistan has its issues—problems that were compounded by America. But it's a land with provinces, cultures, ethnicities—*human beings*. It's living, it's breathing. It exists and it's not a symbol of oppression or war. It's flawed like any other country."

"Then why do all Muslim women in Pakistan and Afghanistan wear hijab? You said men have hijab, why aren't they wearing a headscarf?"

"I will not be your mouthpiece to analyze policies in lands far away from this country," I snapped. "I am one person. My identity and experiences cannot speak for or represent an entire country of dozens of ethnic groups. Just because I am Muslim does not mean my experiences can represent every Muslim out there. For God's sake, how can you see me and pretend to understand everything about a country or religion? I don't see one Christian and generalize the entire religion. I don't see one American and assume I know the entire country either.

"Besides, your questions about Pakistan, about Afghanistan, make no sense. Religious principles are separate from the actions of corrupt regimes, especially regimes that were supported by Washington, D.C. It just shows how America is *so* obsessed with brown women from 'the poor little Middle East,'" I said, using air quotes. "You make women the objects of your liberal values, and it's weird. You talk about the Middle East, but the only people you pretend to care about are the mothers and children. As if our men and elders don't deserve any sympathy.

"As if America had no role in their demise: stealing their money and resources, bombing civilians and then calling it an accident. Shame on you. I have neighbors who fled those bombings, people who saw their neighbors bombed to bits out of *nowhere* because America's missiles were aimed wrong. I don't know how many times you can *accidentally* kill civilians, but America's apparently perfected the art. You dehumanize us and pretend to care by trying to liberate us; the hijab and burqa are your excuses. You're obsessed with how women are oppressed instead of how an entire country was deprived of basic human rights because America invaded them."

Her cheeks flamed red. "Human rights organizations don't lie when they show examples of women beaten and bruised, unable to access education because of sharia law—"

"If we're going to talk about human rights organizations, then let me tell you about Iraq." I began rattling off facts I didn't even know were in my head as if I was possessed by an anger from decades past of people who'd been hurt far more than I could fathom.

History took ahold of my tongue:

"What about the evidence of the US military's war crimes against Iraqis in Abu Ghraib prison? The US government, military, and private contractors hid these crimes with total impunity.

Hundreds of leaked photos showed US soldiers torturing and sexually assaulting detainees at the US-run prison for fun. Most of those Iraqis were mistakenly detained. Interrogators humiliated male and female Iraqi detainees; soldiers laughed and posed next to corpses who were tortured to death by the CIA. US soldiers took pictures of corpses, laughing and giving a thumbs-up.

"Thousands of leaked photos of female detainees showed them being assaulted and forced to ingest human waste. Many Iraqi women were put into prisons because the Americans couldn't find their husbands or fathers to arrest instead. These US soldiers weren't heroes, they were animals. The Iraqis who live with this trauma found no justice; the dead deserve more dignity than politicians reducing them to a stereotype. Tell me who truly needs to be saved? Call me a terrorist again. I'd rather be depicted as a terrorist than be subjected to an interview by you. I'm done here."

I tossed aside the small microphone before shoving my way to the back of the stage where Amma was standing, staring at the screens, in utter shock.

On the video call, Mr. McCarthy looked aghast. *Good*, he must be thinking, *for showing the American audience exactly how angry you Muslims can be.*

Good, good, everyone must have been thinking. They could all shove it.

"Let's go, Amma."

———

The security guard ushered us out of the studio. He was a pale older man with a wrinkled blue security shirt. Smudges of finger grease stained the front—probably from fries.

"We can walk," I said after he pushed us through the corridors.

"Well, no shit," he said.

My hands wouldn't stop quivering from the adrenaline. "Will I be sued for what I said in the studio?" I wondered to Amma.

Surprisingly the guard answered, a little flicker in his stone eyes. He'd probably seen all sorts of guests.

"Nah. If it makes for good views, you did your job, kid." He surprised me again when he asked us at the exit, "You got all your belongings?"

I nodded.

He seemed alright. He probably had kids. Before he left, he said, "You spoke a lot of smart things, lady. Things Americans should realize. Be proud of that instead of sulking." He walked back toward the studio.

Wordlessly, Amma and I left. I half-expected Michelle to call us back, but maybe my tantrum just made good TV.

Twenty-one

For once, Amma meant to defend me when she cursed the interview in Urdu under her breath. Amma went on and on, muttering about that liar Michelle, and dirty politics. Then she vented her anger out on the kitchen knife, expertly chopping tomatoes to whip up the spiciest nihari.

We played back my horrible interview on the TV.

The segment began with Michelle's voice-over narrating the life of Mitchell Wilson, a war veteran who'd served in numerous American wars. He was a man who'd *helped America liberate the turmoil of the Middle East.*

An old clip played of the president saying, *We will make those terrorists pay,* with snapshots of tanks in dusty streets and marching soldiers carrying sniper rifles. The same secondhand catchphrases, the same old rhetoric. It was funny how Americans thought they were saving the world when really it was the world who needed saving from them. But when you blindly believed your government was fundamentally just, then its people would overlook the unjustness of their own actions.

Amma puffed out a small sigh at the screen before pulling out the roti atta from the fridge. "This is why these public shows are dangerous. You shouldn't have done the interview."

"You didn't exactly stop me," I said.

Amma's eyes morphed to a glare. "I have been. This wouldn't have happened if it wasn't for your letters."

A disappointment as always. Look at Zaynab, be more like her, I imagined her thinking. That was the true nickname that people should have called me by. Not Mamou's legacy but the girl who could never measure up to anything her family wanted her to be. Not her sister, not her mother, and not even her uncle. I was a soul attempting to fit into other bodies because I didn't have my own flesh.

She seemed to read my silence. "I know you think I am wrong." She patted the dingy pot full of atta. "But I am in a foreign country. I cannot speak its language. I have no degree. But I raised my three kids. I cook their favorite dishes to remind them of my home. And that is enough for me. Surely, I have learned something, some kind of wisdom. Yet you think you know better. But there is a difference between being right and surviving here, Nida." She looked at me. "I survived. I want my children to survive too."

I backed away, unsure of a response. Our relationship would forever be defined by the words left unspoken.

Dear Congress,

*All I hear are politicians
declaring their intentions
to civilize the Middle East.
Tell that to the man
who found the charred remains
of his mother in his ruined neighborhood streets.*

*Tell that to the boy
who gazed at the clear skies
on a school day until
he spotted drones circling overhead,
streaking the clouds like fireballs.
Tell that to the girl who
was collecting okra
with her grandmother
when the bombs blew her to bits
and all she heard of her grandmother
were bloodied screams.
Normal nine-year-old kids sketch pretty pictures but
that Pakistani sketched the imagery
of the US drone strike killing their relative,
in a desperate attempt to evoke an ounce of empathy
from the US Congress.*

Veterans who returned from fighting overseas in Iraq
were immediately asked to write important memoirs,
   —the same accounts that would later become book club
      picks and bestsellers.
But what about our stories?
The ones marred by devastation and arrests?
The stories of angry American veterans protesting
that their own government be held accountable
for senseless invasions?

But if I were to say any of this,
I'd be declared an unpatriotic citizen.
If I called their leaders true war criminals,
I'd be called disloyal.
I couldn't do anything about how the American media
   dehumanizes Muslims.
All I could do was watch
as my humiliating Fifteen Minutes interview played,
with Michelle's voice-over reaffirming
all the misconceptions harbored about my religion.

I'd doused my problems in gasoline
instead of putting out the flames.
My tears flowed out,
an endless river that could
not extinguish the fire I'd created.

Amma paused while crushing the garlic cloves.
She dropped her mortar and pestle. She realized her mistake.
   "Oh, Nida."
I needed to get out of the kitchen, bolt to my room
and curl into a ball. Instead . . .

"Amma," I hiccupped into my quivering fingers.
"You were right. I made everything so much worse.
It's all I'm good at."

Amma nudged me to sit
at the dining table. After bringing a plate and knife,
Amma placed a mango in my hands.
"I-Is it Mexican or Pakistani?" I stammered through my
    tears.
No way could a mango this late in the season
be from Pakistan.
Amma feigned shock. "It's a Pakistani mango, of course,
the last shipment from the shop.
Now focus on cutting it."

Slowly I sliced the mango into five orange wedges.
"Now eat it," she ordered.
I bit into the mango like it was a slice of watermelon—
a true art of sticky hands
and splattered juice.

Amma nodded at the plate. "Finish it."
Slowly, I ate away my pain
into crookedly cut,
sour mango until only
one wedge was splayed on the table.
"This was your solution," I mumbled,
through strings of mango caught between my teeth.
Amma sighed. "Inshallah."
She pointed up. By Allah's will.

Twenty-two

Zaynab returned home from campus, shoving her phone into my watery face. "Nida, you're Twitter famous!"

"I don't want to look online." I tried to push the device away.

"But Nida, Muslim Twitter is retweeting clips of that woman who interviewed you. People are spamming the account because of her Islamophobia."

"Wait." I sat up. "They're calling her Islamophobic?"

Zaynab sat beside me, scooping up the last mango wedge. "Yeah," she said through a mouthful.

From the kitchen, Amma eyed Zaynab. "Eat with your mouth closed, don't break the sunnah!"

Zaynab gulped hard. "Sorry, Amma-ji." She turned back to me. "Don't even get me started on Pakistani Twitter. Those brown uncles are going crazy, but secretly, I think Uncle Jihad is leading the charge. He's definitely using his fifteen burner accounts to target Afghan cricket fans, and now he's going after the news channel. They're tagging *Fifteen Minutes* and demanding an apology. After I quote-retweeted and said you were my sister, my comments went viral."

"You did that?"

She wiped her mango hands on my shirt. "Of course!"

"I can't believe people are defending my interview."

"Well, the host basically bullied a high school girl on national television. And you saying, 'Call me a terrorist again,' that was classic!"

When she framed it that way, she made it sound so simple.

Zaynab went to freshen up, so I scrolled through my phone. After a moment of hesitation, I reactivated my social media.

My inbox was congested with messages.

Some said I was exaggerating my letter to cover up my own people's faults. Others claimed I was avoiding the hard questions that Muslims couldn't answer. Some were debating the jargon of my poetry like it was an academic article and I was their next subject to clinically analyze. Another said I accepted the interview as a way to fame, for more people to find my spoken word.

I clicked exit, nauseous. I felt like I'd finished running a marathon only to realize I'd merely crossed the halfway point in a race that seemed to never end.

I was too scared to peek at my follower count, but I did click on Zaynab's profile and retweeted everything she'd posted before logging out for the day.

Baby steps, I knew that. But it was still a step past my anxiety. For once, I felt like some semblance of control had returned.

"Oho, Nida," Amma said without glancing up from stirring the degchi full of gosht. "If you are Twitter famous, we must update my WhatsApp status. I can't let Uncle Jihad take all the credit!"

Her and her damn WhatsApp, I swear. The world could be burning, and she'd still ask me to update her status.

Amma ordered me to snap a picture of the Quran shelf stacked with ajwa date fruit and a liter bottle of zamzam water.

She told me to be creative since an uncle had just returned from Saudi Arabia and brought the dates as a gift. The caption was the hard part, but I thought I nailed it.

Thank you, Hamza Bhai for the ajwa dates and zamzam. We could use the holy water after our family got the evil eye in Nida's interview. May Allah curse Michelle, the devil's host. #Blessed #Spiritual #Dates #UmrahandHajj #AllahIsAlmighty #ByeEvilEye

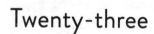

Twenty-three

'd scheduled a visitation appointment to see my Mamou after my interview. Amma offered to drive me as her way of an apology.

As we drove past downtown, the streets were blocked for another political rally. In a stroke of bad luck, police were stationed on the road in the name of checkpoints.

"Maybe we should go back. . . ."

Amma shook her head. "We just drove thirty minutes."

My hands gripped the door as if any moment, I'd leap out of the car.

"Beta, are you okay?" Amma glanced away from the road to have a good look at me.

"Yeah." I tried to breathe, recalling the cops who'd cornered me. I wondered about the likelihood of it happening again.

"Nida, it's just a checkpoint before the rally. Okay?"

I forced myself to nod so she knew I could hear her. My self-deprecation was back in full force. *Why can't I act normal? It's just a checkpoint.*

But checkpoints weren't just checkpoints. I couldn't remember ever passing through one successfully. Not without my Amma being forced out of the car and felt up by security.

Which was exactly what happened. A cop standing outside his patrol car gestured for Amma to roll down her window.

"Can I see an ID?"

Amma nodded and pointed at her purse. The cop nodded impatiently. Amma rummaged through her bag as I counted the seconds.

"Here is," Amma said in English before handing over her license. Behind the cop, volunteers were setting up signs for the evening rally.

The cop stared at Amma's ID, his brows scrunching together. "Zuha Siddiqui?"

"Yes, sir," Amma answered, but the cop stared at me. I wondered if he recognized me. I gulped hard, trying to fix my expression into something neutral.

"We're going to have to ask you to step out of the vehicle. Just a standard search."

From a glance around, the only ones being stopped and frisked were Black and brown people. Somehow—even though it seemed statistically impossible despite this being a "randomized" search—these were the only standout colors in a white stream.

After pulling us over, the cop rummaged through the Toyota van, making a mess until old McDonald's receipts scattered across the dashboard. He turned to us.

"For security protocol, I'll have to search you too."

"What reason?" Amma pressed in broken English. Which made it worse. The cop realized my Amma was *foreign*.

"It's okay, Amma," I murmured. "Let's just do what he says."

"What'd you say?" the cop snapped.

"Nothing, sir. My mom can't understand English well, I was just translating."

His eyes narrowed to blue slits. "I see." But it sounded more like, *I don't believe you.*

The cop patted down Amma, starting with her head. He went down, up, and back down, all while volunteers continued to put up political yard signs, and onlookers were trying not to stare. It was humiliating.

Then he shifted to me. I shut my eyes as his hands patted my head aggressively, his fingers poking around my hijab. But he didn't try to rip it off. Only made a mess of the wrapped fabric. His hands went down, up, and back down. A minute later, he nodded, and we were sent off.

In the car, Amma didn't start the engine. I let her take a moment to shut her eyes, fingertips gripping the steering wheel so hard they edged white.

"Are you okay, jaanu?" she asked.

"Yeah, are you?"

She nodded and that was the end of the conversation.

It took another half hour to reach the federal prison before visitation hours ended. Amma's jaw remained clenched the entire trip.

———

In the visitation room, Mamou wheezed through the pay phone. "Beta."

"I'm sorry, Mamou!" I said immediately. "I'm sorry about our argument, I shouldn't have said those things to you. It was disrespectful."

"Me too. Me too." He waved his hands, his smile growing. "Forget it now, my beta. I don't even remember what we argued about."

"You're in a good mood."

His features relaxed. "Subhanallah, the prison chaplaincy finally hired an imam. He gave a lecture today, it put me at ease."

"Oh, he gave a lecture to the prisoners?"

"The imam gave dawah," he corrected. "He discussed justice and peace in Islam. Three brothers even converted and took their shahada. They said it would keep them grounded on the right path. They said the concept of judgment and order in Allah's divine plan drew them to Islam."

Shahada was the Muslim testimony of faith. Back when Mamou was granted visitation rights, he'd told me how surprised he was to learn that 10 to 15 percent of prisoners in America were Muslim—the majority being Black and brown. The highest growth of conversions amongst inmates was to Islam.

"Why did the chaplaincy wait so long to hire an imam?"

"Because of a lawsuit," Mamou said. "Prison policies began barring Muslims from congregating for Friday prayers. If the prisoners tried to pray, they'd be penalized for missing prison labor. Incarcerated Muslims are underserved by the chaplaincy, hence the lawsuits. It was good of the prisoners to organize together and win the case." Mamou looked pointedly at me. "Even behind bars and struck with a hardship like prison, they still advocated for their religion."

"What kinds of dawah did the imam give?" I asked him.

"He gave us reminders. He said, in an isolated prison, there is no human who will hear you—no one who will accompany or understand you. But you have faith. It reminded me that though I feel alone, I am not alone. You must remember this too, Nida."

"At home Amma and I have been arguing," I admitted. "We're okay now but she doesn't understand anything I do. I wish you were with me."

He leaned his head against the partition glass. His gaze looked heavy. "I am, Nida. And if not in this world, then in the afterlife."

"Please, don't speak like that." I brushed my cheek, surprised at a stray tear. "Did I mention, I had the interview?" I blurted, "With *Fifteen Minutes*."

I rattled off details about the humiliating comments from the interviewer. When I was done, I expected rage to dance in Mamou's eyes or force to reverberate in his tone, but all I saw was a dim light.

"What else can you expect from them, beta?" He shrugged his entire body. "The state is violent; they target us and there's no use trying to please them. But I'm proud of you for owning your art, defending Islam, and not regretting the letter." He paused. "Does this mean you're writing again?"

I couldn't tell him the truth, so I tried to pivot with a vague answer. "I can't for now. I think Amma is relieved. And if I'm being honest . . . I think this is for the best. I don't want more trouble."

He looked away. "Because your Amma always plays it safer."

"Amma has good reason to. She told me she survived. And we can't ignore that."

"Not this again, Nida."

My grip on the pay phone hardened and my cheeks flushed. "Mamou, I'm not like Amma, but I also can't be you. It's taken me a while to realize that and . . . you've always inspired me. But that doesn't mean I have to *be* you, Mamou."

His brows bunched together. I realized his eyes weren't hazy. They were glazed over. Almost feverish. "Everyone criticizes my past, your Amma included, and now you. That host in your interview criticized me because I didn't have a squeaky-clean past, so she thought I deserved this? I wasn't the picture of a successful immigrant, so I deserved prison.

"Nida, listen to me carefully. Don't let them brainwash you into thinking we deserve this, that we should police each other's behavior. You go to any rich neighborhood, and you'll see those kids breaking the laws while the authorities turn a blind eye. It doesn't matter what we do, they'll find an excuse to blame us anyway. Or they'll make Muslims target other Muslims, so we fit their image of a good citizen. That's what your Amma did, she wants to be more American without realizing that she's turning her back on her own family. But I guess this is part of our legacy. And our blood," Mamou finished. "It's a curse."

"A curse?" I sat forward. "What do you mean?"

He stared into my eyes intensely. "I wasn't the first to be imprisoned for poetry. Remember what I said in your last visit? My grandfather died during the resistance movements under British occupation. And my Mamou was imprisoned during a poet symposium speech on his campus, which led to a union crackdown in Pakistan. Even his Mamou was imprisoned before partition, when the British passed laws and arrested a number of writers under sedition. They claimed our art was an incitement of violence. Even after jail, my great-grandfather and great-uncle spent months under house arrest. The British banned anyone who tried to employ them, so their entire family went hungry for months. There were all kinds of famines that wiped out millions. Many artists were jailed, not just our relatives. But they kept their faith."

My mind spun in circles, completely stunned. "I didn't know. No one's ever told me."

"Our family's history is complex and bloody. Sometimes I think that history is repeating itself in funny ways. But when I heard about you winning that contest, I was so proud. Because I knew no matter what had happened to me, our family would never let its legacy of letters die." He clutched at the pay phone with both hands, trying to hide the tremors. "Allah guided me, kept me with sabr—*patience*—in this prison. Sometimes you cannot fix a system that's been broken for too long, but you can have faith that there is a plan, there is order, that the events around you happen for a reason. You must draw on that patience, you need to turn to Him."

"But how, Mamou?"

Mamou scrubbed his jaw. "In Islam, do you know about Allah's first creation?"

"The universe?"

"The first creation by God was the pen," he answered, "because words hold the greatest power. We can think, speak, and write, that's why the tongue is the sharpest sword to exist. The pen is not a tool. And the words are not actions. The writer is simply the conduit for justice. Don't fight that truth. Become it."

"Become it?"

"Become it." He nodded with a small smile. "Come on, nod too, Nida." So, I nodded along with him.

But there was something else that was bothering me, an inkling I was scared to confirm. "Mamou, you tell me to speak and write. But it's been years since I've heard you recite poetry."

His grip loosened on the pay phone. "I wish I could, beta."

"But why?"

He sucked in a breath.

It was silent.

Then . . .

"Because I haven't made poetry in years. I haven't since I received my prison sentence."

"Because you don't want to?"

He shut his eyes. He didn't answer.

I waited for surprise to settle in me, but it didn't. My heart was already shattered.

A part of me always knew that my Mamou had given up on

his writing. Maybe all this time he'd insisted that I continue so I wouldn't repeat his mistakes. But I guess his efforts were for nothing. I had rejected the pen too.

We were the same. We were humans. We were weak-minded. We were quick to give up the things we loved.

"Mamou, why?"

"Because I didn't want to, beta. I just . . . couldn't. I can't explain it."

His frankness stung. I studied him as another cough wrung his body like he was a wet cloth being squeezed between the universe's hands. Was it that he gave up writing or that he couldn't think of any verses? Or was it both?

"Mamou, remember one of the first verses you showed me by Faiz Ahmed Faiz?"

His eyes lit up in remembrance. "*Victory is to return/Alive after death . . .*" Mamou replied with a nostalgic grin.

I nodded. "Remember your explanation of the verse? You said, we have won because we're here smiling."

"Surviving death while living, smiling after hardship," he said.

I felt relieved. He was still my Mamou.

I still had him. *Right?*

"Mamou, we'll make a deal. You promise to think of some verses and say them to me next time. If you do, I will too."

I held out my fist for a bump of solidarity against the glass partition, but the guard began walking forward, our time together expiring.

With that, Mamou's smile disappeared, as if seeing the guards reminded him again of this dark reality. Mamou didn't promise or even fist-bump against the glass. But, at first, I believed that silently he did. Because the miraculous happened.

The blue string at my wrists manifested, lifting up and slithering through the glass. Another blue string appeared, dangling from Mamou's chest before it connected with mine like two puzzle pieces fitting together.

My eyes widened.

Mamou has a blue string too? He's had it this entire time?

I wondered why I'd never seen it before. Or maybe the blue string never wanted to show itself until now.

I kept staring in awe at the blue string stretched taut between us like it was a lifeline.

Was this what stopped Mamou from reciting poetry? Was Mamou cursed too? Was he like me? Or was I like him?

Who else was cursed in our family? Did my great-great-grandfather have a blue string? Did my great-uncle? And his uncle? How many poets in other families faced this curse? How many arrested artists were cursed by the pen for abandoning their art?

The questions whirled through my brain. But my longing shattered when the last words Mamou said were, "Oh, and Nida?"

"Yeah?"

"Don't keep coming here with all your hopes about me. You're better than that. My life is done, but you have yet to live. I have Allah, He is all I need."

The guards took the phone, slotting it back in place.

What?

My feet moved forward without thinking. So fast my knees strained. I pressed against the partition, trying to make Mamou look at me.

Look at me, Mamou. Just look me in the eye.

But he looked remorseful as he was ushered away.

Where is his hope? Where is the fight from the infamous Abdul-Hafeedh? Weren't we reminiscing over poetry?

"Mamou!" I tried again. "Mamou! *Please look at me*," I cried, and an unexplainable dread pounded in my chest. But he didn't glance over his shoulder.

The blue string connecting us snapped.

The door shut with a resounding boom, leaving me alone in the empty room. *How could Mamou switch so fast? From bonding over verses to looking so vacant?*

Mentally, I flung away the image of his sullen stare, so cold and tired. All the hope bleeding out.

He was my Mamou. Right?

Still

   My

         Mamou?

Dear Lies,

Lies are a pretty rose
dressed in thorns.
Lies I keep telling myself
because roses are pretty,
but all pretty things eventually wilt.
Like the dead rose . . .
    in the glass
    vase.

Dear Confrontations,

Confrontation was like dodging invisible bullets,
whizzing through the air to find their target.
When you're hit
you feel the pain but you can't identify it.
Unable to see but only feel, as anxiety rises.
You're drowning but the pain can't be subdued,
so you struggle in your panic,
letting it strangle you.

Mamou looked tired,
he stopped fighting the curse,
but I wouldn't stop,
I would fight for us both.

After my visit, I decided to stop running and start
*   confronting.*
I swallowed the sick in my throat,
and took the first bus to school.
In the yard, Alexis's eyes locked with mine.
"Nida?"
That was all it took.

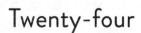

Twenty-four

'm angry." The words poured out, raw and hurt. "I'm so angry; I avoided you because I could barely look you in the eyes without feeling all this anger."

Alexis dropped her bag. "Nida, why are you still angry when you won? Because of that, now people hear you. I saw your interview yesterday. You're not just saying your poetry to your bedroom walls or the Poet's Block, people outside of the community *know you.*"

"The Poet's Block was my home and it was enough. But it was never enough for you," I immediately argued. "It was my safety. It was the only place I felt like I belonged, and you took that from me. You did it because you had this ignorant assumption—"

"Ignorant?" She looked hurt. "I've always defended you. I was proud to be your friend. How am I ignorant when I've always stood by you?"

That was a low blow. "Was our friendship a charity case?"

She threw her hands up. "Nida, I can't keep explaining myself. All I know is that my instincts were right. You won! Besides, you needed the money! I don't know what else you want."

"What else *I* want from *you?* A simple apology. Is that so hard?"

"An apology?" she repeated. "An apology when you were so afraid to enter a contest? I can't apologize for doing what was right. I was trying to help you, Nida. Besides, entering the contest wasn't even my idea, you can't just blame the whole thing on me!"

"What?"

Understanding dawned in her eyes before she sputtered a laugh. "You don't know. You *really* don't know."

"Know what?"

"Entering NSPL was Mrs. Sophia's idea. When I saw the application, it required an academic reference. I went to her because I remembered she'd emailed you. She wrote the reference, thinking the submission could be a surprise. She thought you had a good chance at placing. She knew we were applying without your permission. So, if you're blaming me, go blame her too. But if you do, everyone in our grade will know. She's the staff supervisor for the MSA. People will know you reported her."

"Mrs. Sophia?" I repeated.

"Yeah. Your *own* supervisor."

This couldn't be true. This wasn't just wrong. This broke all kinds of ethical codes. My own teacher did that? Mrs. Sophia? She'd told me her office was a safe space.

Outrage flared in me, burning from my feet to my head. I felt like my entire body was on fire.

How dare she? How dare they all?

I stepped back, intending to go to the principal's office. Alexis read the intent on my face, panic leaking into her tone. "If you report Mrs. Sophia, she'll be suspended from her job. Why would you do that over a contest? She meant well. Just like I did."

I paused. "I have to report her."

"No, you don't. She has a family. She entered for you out of goodwill. She's been the only teacher willing to supervise the Muslim Student Association and your MIST trips and you want to report her? If she's gone, who would support the MSA?"

"But . . ."

Alexis's face swam out of focus. My emotions felt like they were sawed into pieces, and I was giving them all away.

"You know how much attention this will bring to you? In your last year during college applications? I thought you wanted to move on from the controversy?"

What did I want? I did want to move on. If I reported Mrs. Sophia and Alexis, wouldn't it bring more attention? More than I already should have in my last year of school. And what about the other teachers? They'd find out. They'd resent me. Would the MSA support my decision—reporting their only supervisor?

My teacher and my friend exposed my letters, but the letters and the words were mine.

What did I want?

I wanted closure. I never got that.

That simple realization made me blink at Alexis, clearing the fog in my brain. Why was she pinning this on me? As if Mrs. Sophia wasn't an adult who'd submitted my private journal letters. What about the pain it caused me and my family? What about how it affected our livelihood?

"You keep telling me to care about Mrs. Sophia, and her family, emotions, and job. None of you cared about mine. I want an apology from you first," I demanded. "For all that stuff you said about jihad and my poetry. It was wrong and racist."

"Racist?" Her hands rose like the dreaded word *racist* was worse than actually being it.

"Yeah, it was racist."

Her voice dropped. "How am *I* the racist? Go call Mrs. Sophia that too then. I tried to help you. Sometimes we have to confront the things we're afraid to do to realize the good stuff in the end."

"Are you serious?"

"Girls? What's going on here?" a familiar voice interrupted from a distance.

We turned.

Mrs. Sophia cut across the school field. Our gazes locked. I didn't know what she saw. The betrayal? The rage? The exhaustion? All of it?

It didn't matter. By the time she reached us, her expression had dropped. She knew that I knew the truth. She'd had all this time to admit her actions, but she never did. Maybe she thought that there was still good in me winning the contest—maybe to her it was my chance to gain an audience. But she saw the damage it had caused me. And she still didn't say anything.

"How could you—" I began.

"Nida," Mrs. Sophia interrupted.

"I trusted you! Our entire MSA trusted you. And you exploited it!"

She winced. "Nida, I promise you, I meant well. I'll answer all of your questions, but let's talk about this inside my office."

"*No.* I don't want to go anywhere with you. You stole my words, and you thought you were helping. Even if none of this trouble ever happened, it doesn't make anything you did right. You both thought I was incapable of making my own decisions."

I thought back to the day at the principal's office and then MIST, and all the years Mrs. Sophia had supervised the MSA. Her actions, like Alexis's, came from a good place, but unlike Alexis, I knew Mrs. Sophia had never believed all the assumptions about me. Somehow, it made this hurt more.

"Do you even realize how my family has been harassed? We had journalists find our address and harass our neighbors. Feds interrogated kids at the Poet's Block, our only safe space. Then, Mr. Wilson and his lawyer tricked me, making me look like a liar when he took pictures of me with his team. And the televised interview was a nightmare. The host accused my family of radicalism, insulted my uncle, and humiliated me. Don't you see? This is about *my* rights. This is about *you* violating them. Just like how the cops and Mr. Wilson did to me. You're no different from them."

Alexis flinched. "I'm not some cop sticking their fingers through your hijab."

But Mrs. Sophia was rooted to the spot, horror stretching across her face. "Nida. I didn't realize it had gone so far. I'm sorry. Really. I'm so sorry."

I wanted my words to poke and poke until Mrs. Sophia's composure cracked. "Are you though? You've had all this time to tell me. You only seem sorry that I finally found out."

Her tears surfaced. She got to cry. But I didn't. *I couldn't.*

Mrs. Sophia reached out to me. "We can go right now to report my actions to the board. I'm sorry I waited this long and never told you. I didn't realize the extent of the damage. I only saw other Muslims supporting you, and I thought it was good you had the attention. I wanted to tell you, but I panicked. It was wrong. I wasn't thinking enough about your family. I'm sorry."

My hands uncurled. That's all I wanted. An apology. It was laughable that my standards were so low, but in all this time . . . no one had properly apologized to me.

Alexis shook her head in disbelief. "So, you can forgive her but not me?"

"What forgiveness? I'm not forgiving anyone," I said.

I wasn't sure what I expected, certainly not Alexis to bow at my feet and apologize for her ancestors. But I did think, for one heart-pounding second, that maybe, just maybe, I would be able to get my friend back. I was stuck between the fear of losing my old comforts and braving new frontiers.

Alexis wasn't just *anyone*. She was supposed to understand, because in the past she always had. It's what set her apart from every other classmate I knew. She'd understood my position from the start. But it didn't excuse the mistakes she'd made now. Because she liked the feeling of always being right rather than being explained to how she might be wrong. When I tried explaining the consequences, Alexis brushed right past them.

"I won't take back what I said, and I can't just forgive you," I answered. "You and Mr. Wilson are the same to me. You both violated my privacy. It makes you just as ignorant as him."

With the three of us together, I didn't realize we'd started a commotion in the schoolyard until another teacher approached us. "What's going on here?" asked Mr. Peterson, a staff supervisor. "Nida, why would you call your teacher and classmate ignorant?"

I faced him. "Mr. Peterson, respectfully, you don't know the full story."

The teacher's face scrunched up. "Nida, you shouldn't even be on school grounds because of your suspension. And you're certainly not allowed to be here starting fights."

Mrs. Sophia put up her hands. "Mr. Peterson, I'm handling this."

"Handling what? She's violated her suspension and fighting with another student. She should be at the principal's office."

In front of me, Alexis frowned but she didn't speak up to clarify the situation.

"Mr. Peterson, I didn't come here to violate my suspension," I explained. "I was hurt by—"

"You can tell the front office," he cut in.

"If you'd only hear me out—"

"Front office. Now," he ordered.

Helplessly, I glared at Alexis. I was being dragged away by a teacher before I could let all the words loose.

"Nida, we'll text about this later," Alexis had the audacity to say.

I didn't want this. I didn't want the teachers to handle anything. I didn't want to receive any text messages from Alexis. I didn't want to act like everything could be patched up.

I didn't want to talk. I didn't want to act calm.

I wanted to yell. To beat my fists and *scream*.

No regular words would articulate all the feelings bundled inside me, somersaulting and flipping, trying to break free.

The blue string snapped to attention from my wrists, thinning into a hair's width.

My mouth opened. I knew what to say.

What I expected wasn't what I saw,
but illusions can only support us for so long.
My friend wasn't ever my friend;
I was just a broken case
she was trying to mend.

The poetry trapped inside,
erupted into waves of agony.
Alexis spoke excuses and justified her actions.
Mrs. Sophia was a coward who chose silence.
I let the verses unravel,
murmuring their lilts,
until the words climbed higher and higher
up the shaft,
into a volcanic cadence.

"Nida? I said follow me," Mr. Peterson repeated impatiently.

This is a spoken word battle
The words are my claws.
The pages my armor.
The ink my war paint.

They all reeled back.
My words rose above the three of them.

My soul bends worlds, accomplishing things that shouldn't be
possible,
full of blue string and curses and magical capabilities.
With the way my flesh and this world are set up,
I'm learning that my mouth is
something to be reckoned with.
To the friend who cast me away,
and a teacher who stole my rights away
without acknowledging their parts in
how my family's been torn apart.

I did you a favor with the prize, *Alexis argued.*

Who cares about money?

People can't stop speaking about
your poetry, *Mrs. Sophia said.*

I didn't ask for your help.
I wanted someone to confide in.
I wanted someone who could be my safety.

You act like the money doesn't matter, but it does!
Your uncle is in jail, so I saw your journal,
knowing your Mamou's court case,
and I knew I had to enter the contest for you, *Alexis*
    defended.

All my Amma speaks about is honor
but no one could buy back honor
for a pretty dollar.

I knew because of the names in that letter,
controversies win contests, *she said.*

You liked my poetry, so hear out my letter:

They paused—

Dear Alexis and Mrs. Sophia,
In the subject of history,
we learned the Western empires colonized
unsuspecting countries,
invaded and devastated many,
unveiling Muslim populations
before abolishing previous governments
in their version of legislation.

They were the litigator,
they dictated laws and morality,
they raved about freedom and waved their flags in paternity,
they manipulated history,
their first project was Rumi.
They tried to divorce Islam from his poetry
but what they forget was Rumi was Muslim.

Throughout history, people tried to decide what was good for us.
They had light skin and claimed to be the paragon of justice
without considering that our religion
was already morally praiseworthy.
So, don't try to instruct us.
Don't try to instruct me
on my own capabilities
especially

in
my
poetry.
You are not my justice.

Sincerely,
Nida

Dear Hijab,

When I first decided to wear you at the ripe age of sixteen,
after talking to God,
aunties on the block said,

> You are too young to wear this.
>
> You will get no job
>
> or marriage proposal.

Amma said, You will look ugly, hiding your beautiful hair.
I ignored my own Amma,
and my aunties.
I went to you, cradling your veil close to my chest,
murmuring, Remember this is for Allah

> Subhanahu wa ta'ala.

A veil that is not a choice,
but my submission.
I am lucky to wear you
as my private and public decision, without coercion.
I only wish ...
the rest of the world
understood the burden of responsibility
that came with the veil too.

Twenty-five

In the end, Mr. Peterson reported me for *strange*, aggressive behavior while violating my suspension. But the satisfaction of speaking my mind overrode the disappointment of my punishment.

In Mr. Malcolm's office, I explained the revelation of Mrs. Sophia's actions—and the consequences I hoped would reach the school board.

Mr. Malcolm rubbed his temples but promised he would ensure the board investigated the matter. I hoped I would never see Mrs. Sophia's face again.

As I approached home, I took a detour to Aunty Farooqi's house. After ringing the doorbell, I discovered her standing outside in the small shared green space next to our townhome. She paced with a container of roti in her hand.

"Oho, Nida baby." She waved me over. "I saw that interview. Wow, I was like, *go baby. You tell that gori.* I sent it to my sisters back in Kashmir. I think *Geo News* is going to cover it."

"Thanks, Aunty," I said, but I didn't know how to feel about it. "I saw Mamou actually. And I came because I wanted to ask you something that's been on my mind. It's about Amma's family."

A wrinkle formed between Aunty Farooqi's brows. "I don't know your Amma's family well."

"But you knew Amma well. Baba told me that Amma was a poet. Mamou confirmed it. But Amma also threw away all his old poetry notebooks a long time ago. And I think she got rid of her own too."

Aunty Farooqi mulled over my words as she broke apart the roti. Ahead of us, a small raccoon was eyeing the bread. "Your Amma couldn't burn all the notebooks," she told me.

"What?"

She dangled a piece of roti at the raccoon. "I remember the day she was tossing out the journals. I took a notebook before she could burn it because it was a damn shame she was doing that, especially when I was a fan of your Mamou's ghazal. I meant to return it to your uncle when he was released from prison. The notebook was old. It's not even in English. But you should be asking your Amma about this."

"Oho, Aunty, if I asked Amma, she'd never tell me!"

She harrumphed. "I could try to find the notebook. But first help me toss these old roti and kebabs. We need to feed the animals!"

"Aunty, no." I groaned. "Stop that. You're fattening the raccoons and squirrels."

"Oho, shut up, my jaan. These animals will testify for me on the Day of Judgment before the Almighty," she yapped.

"Aunty, with all due respect, those animals are going to argue for you to go to hell!"

Aunty gasped. "Nida! Don't say that to your elder. You want me to burn!"

"No, I mean this in the kindest way possible, but Aunty, when the Lord is going through the witnesses to argue if you've done them good, the raccoons and squirrels will be right there in the crowd of souls and they'll say, '*Oh Allah, this is Aunty Farooqi who gave me diabetes and that's why I died two years too early. Those naan, roti, and kebabs she kept feeding the backyard animals gave us IBS and destroyed our stomachs. Send her to hell!*"

"We'll see about that, Nida. God's on my side. Allahuakbar." She blew on the roti and threw out more before the racoons nose-dived right into it.

After she was done feeding animals so the food wouldn't go to waste, she gestured for me to follow her.

Inside her house, she made a beeline for her closet. After half an hour of searching, she unearthed an old cardboard spice box. Rummaging through it, we found books, CDs, and finally, a dark blue journal embossed in red and gold geometric designs. I recognized it.

"I think this is it," she said. "Some of this is in the Arabic-Urdu script. You're only literate in Quranic Arabic," she said.

"Can you translate?" I asked. Because of the curse, I couldn't translate any poetry letters, even if I knew how. But Aunty Farooqi could.

Her eyes darkened. "These letters are written from your family's oral traditions. Translation won't do it justice. After all, Urdu is a language of poetry, and the best stories are the ones in their original script."

"Aunty, I can't learn how to read perfect Urdu that soon. I need to know what the letters say."

She sighed. "First, I need chai."

"I thought the doctor said take it easy with the dairy."

"Kasam se, you want to kill me!" she complained.

Aunty's living room had a traditional manqaal setup with decorated pillows and carpets covering the hard, cold flooring, and a low wooden table at the center, a tradition from the mountainous regions. I sat on my knees, silently pouring us Peshawari qahwah into her copper teacups. She began reading the letters silently.

"Nida, most of this isn't legible. The script is very faded. Pages are torn out. The language is so sophisticated. I wasn't educated like your uncle!"

My heart sank. "Maybe the letters at the end?"

She tried again. I waited, but as the minutes passed, I noticed her eyes becoming misty.

"Aunty?" I asked softly. "Is everything okay?"

"Of course," she snapped. "But these . . . these aren't your Mamou's letters. They're your Amma's. I remember now, she also had a journal like your Mamou. She took it with her when she emigrated to America. This was her notebook. It's a record of family stories."

"What?" I placed my teacup down. "That's impossible. I never remembered her having it."

"Oho! You were a baby. Barely a toddler."

Aunty Farooqi had emigrated with my Amma; she'd seen Amma through before and after her marriage. They'd been friends as children in Karachi. Aunty had heard all the stories, even those of my grandparents.

"There are two letters that are legible. They're the last ones in this book," Aunty warned me. "They are incomplete letters, the pages are torn, so you won't find the stories complete. But that's the beauty in family stories, you hear bits and pieces and the rest is lost to history."

An awe at Aunty's wisdom overtook my frustration. Maybe this was the journey to any family history and I was simply the observer. A deep regret stabbed my gut for never asking Aunty about my family before.

"I will say the letters in Urdu and then English, so listen carefully. Stories are like a journey; the unprepared traveler will get lost in the translation." Clearing her throat, Aunty Farooqi began. The pages were faded and ripped like an anxious hand had once dealt them.

Dear Omar,

Before I met Omar
in Karachi, I wondered if entering college
was a goal worth pursuing.
I first saw him at an Eid gathering,
this man who hailed from Sindh's rural lands—
a landless peasant who managed to escape feudal bondage,
before moving to Karachi.

Omar found managerial work in a textile factory to afford
    his degree,
before he was sponsored to the United States and married me.
My Amma told me emigrating was a blessing
—a chance to live in America! You must take it, it's a
    dream!

Omar was soft-spoken, he was kind, and I knew
eventually we could come to care for each other too.
Our relationship was a marriage of convenience.
He would bring me to the United States, chasing the dream
    of liberty,
but I wondered,
if a land gluttonized with so many promises
would eventually vomit?

Arriving in a one-bedroom apartment.
anxious at the possibilities,
Omar swore up and down
he would do this, he would do that,
so many false promises
I lost count.
The curtain of those desires had dropped before his eyes,
separating their dreams on different planes
in another partition.

I remembered the feeling of hope and opportunity
blossoming like a gulāb.
I remembered our march to the bank,
in a newly bought Toyota car,
and the loan signed to afford a house on rent.
I remembered he'd worn his best suit,
gelled his hair until it was slicked left.
I remembered that I'd argued and warned him
but he'd cried and tittered, What is it? Everyone is doing
    it; everyone is getting a house and credit cards and
    loans. It's America!
At all my concerns, Omar brushed them aside.
It's free money, like toffee, *he'd crowed.*
And he hadn't thought about earning it all back,
not the sky-high interest,
not the mistakes everyone was making during the impending
    recessions.

I'd remembered at the time,
this was why usury was outlawed in my religion.
This was why I worshipped my Allah.

This kind of life, of hustling and then shackling yourself with
  more debt,
and then hustling some more,
and then gazing out at the future and realizing the expenses
  would never stop:
inflation, groceries, rent, interest, credit cards, healthcare,
  children, and eventually university tuition . . .
none of it made sense. Hadn't we come for a better life?
Perhaps the sacrifices would be enough,
for the sake of our children.

But Omar began realizing it too,
only many years too late,
when he'd already been snowed in by an avalanche of debt.
He knew he worked just as hard in Karachi,
but in America for jobs that had little to do with his
  education
in a land where he didn't speak the language.
Leaving seemed more appealing.
At least he had work experience from America,
so when he returned to Pakistan,
he could attach America onto his name,
like a patchwork stitched crooked: Pakistani-American
  businessman.

Years grew into more years.
Omar hadn't imagined America quite like this.
You have a bachelor's in business management and
  engineering?
employers would muse,
squinting and looking down their noses
right into the brown of his eyes. From Pakistan?

Pakistan—that realization would make employers squirm
*   and question*
every credibility Omar claimed to have.
Job after job, he wore the successes of his old life
like a weathered badge.
His jobs were rejected until he found himself . . .
working in a factory again
tugging at a collared uniform which
almost seemed to choke him.
Only this time with a family and rent to pay.
He took a second job:
*   driving delivery trucks on the weekends.*

I was supposed to feel joy in this American dream.
But we were both resentful:
him at a family he couldn't look in the eye and
me at a country that I was supposed to worship more than
*   my God.*

Omar stopped coming home at all during the day
—choosing to work long hard nights.
He would visit his friends
who reminded him of a home across the seas,
more than we—his family—ever could.
The quiet was a great blanket smothering me,
and Omar never quite saw me suffocating,
but how could he
when he never looked?

I was not fluent in English. I was not educated.
I smiled about my new life
on phone calls back home. I wore that same grin

for my neighbors,
while preparing for community dinners,
and a laugh on my daily walks
to the community mosque.

When I was pregnant with my first daughter,
the early contractions arrived.
I remembered the local aunties remaining throughout the night.
I realized, maybe I could make my own community.
During the birth of my second daughter
I remembered calling her mushkil
while her Mamou called her his naqal.

But three children, and twelve years total, my marriage
    ended
to the great embarrassment of my aunties.
A Pakistani woman divorcing?
Oh, the shame to her izzat.
I laugh because the decision was not mine. It was Omar.
Omar had overestimated the great hurdles of America.
He arrived, one foot in this country,
while the other remained in Karachi,
begging to return home.

He wasn't a monster. He was a simple man
tempted by the jeers of the American dream
only to be thrown under
the bloodied pennant of the othering.
He tried to love his family
more than his country, but he could not.
A different home called him across the seas.
One without me.

Dear Zaynab and Nida,

Food is my answer.
When Omar left, Zaynab and Nida stopped eating.
Abdul-Hafeedh worked
driving delivery trucks late into the night,
to help me with the rent.
Aunties rang my phone,
demanding answers about the divorce.
Little Mohamed was the only quiet one, never crying as a
    baby,
never wondering when his father would return,
unlike his two sisters.
My Baba was concerned, claiming I must return with the
    children to Pakistan.
Divorce was a great blow
to my reputation—
    I was the gossip of the relatives.
    Abdul-Hafeedh was arrested again in a protest.
    I worry about our life here,
    and the mess I've landed myself in.

My two daughters are at the age
where they are wise enough
to understand something terrible has happened
but could not reason the what and the why.

They screamed and screamed at the sight
of their Baba departing for good,
even when he promised to call every night.

My brother distracted my daughters,
drawing calligraphy,
but the girls were in a fit,
refusing to see past this family rift.

Sometimes I saw Nida sobbing as she scribbled in the
      journal her uncle gifted her,
tears ruining the ink,
rivers of blue running down the pages.
She had every right to cry.
Her Baba had taken a machete,
severing the thin strings of flesh
between himself and his family. All they had left was me.
I had no degree nor any credentials
for a job with protections that people like us needed.
How would I survive in a land
with no honor or dignity to my name?

One day, I snatched Nida's journal
before tearing through the pages
to make sense of my daughter's scribbled gibberish.
All I saw were the words biryani and fish curry
—Nida missed her Baba's food.

The journal reminded me of when I was a little girl
and my Baba had introduced me to poetry
—but I'd forgotten the innocence of this art

because now my letters are nothing more than silly musings.
My daughter was able to scribble in abandon while
I had let that freedom slip from my fingertips.

I stared at Nida's gibberish,
as if her wishes would make her Baba return to this country.
In this, I had my answer.

I cooked an aroma of turmeric and fried onions,
  fish curry, and heaping plates of veal biryani.
I applied to work at a Pak grocer,
and alongside the help of my brother,
the next week I advertised a home-catering service
that delivered freshly cooked Pakistani-Sindhi food.

Food was my safety.
My husband was gone. My brother was stirring trouble.
I'd begged him to help me with the business,
if only to make him let go of his rising poetry career.

If only I stopped him sooner.
Brother Abdul-Hafeedh went to prison.
I'd never seen him so broken.

But this is how you create a broken genius, you see:
you rip away their happiness and you
hand them tragedy.

Twenty-six

The sun had set. By the end of the pages, I was reeling from the knowledge—confused and sad, and trying to understand my family. I had the puzzle pieces but fitting them together was impossible.

I rushed from Aunty Farooqi's house back to our driveway. I wasn't sure if I should ask Amma about the letters. But an excitement jittered through me, of finally knowing *something*. I couldn't wait to tell Mamou, to ask him my questions. Would he answer any of them?

The aroma of reheated nihari lingered in the air. Uncle Jihad waved from the garage. "Oho, Nida!" Then his nose twitched, pointing up in the air. "Mmm, your Amma cooks up the best dishes. Just the way to a brother's heart."

"I can bring you a bowl?" I offered.

"Don't tell my wife." He patted his belly, but then his tone shifted. "I saw your interview on WhatsApp."

My smile dipped. "I *was* upset about it until I saw your tweets. You really blew up."

He beamed, pleased with himself. "That's what they get."

With another half-hearted wave, I entered the house, hoping to drown my exhaustion into a piping hot bowl of leftovers.

Suddenly, the blue string rose from my chest—dozens of the lines tangled into an intricate web, as if angry, as if hurt. I cried out from the sheer force.

The string dragged me forward against my will, toward the living room. I gasped out from the staggering force. My eyes landed on Amma, who was gripping her phone to her ear, tears streaming down her cheeks.

She turned, exhaled a sob, and dropped the phone.

"Amma!" I cried out in alarm.

"Inna lillahi wa inna ilayhi raji'un. It's your Mamou," she whispered, trembling in disbelief. "The prison called. They said he passed away. They said from pneumonia."

Dear Dreams,

Ever wake up from a dream only to forget?
Recalling colors and wisps
of images . . . Poof!
They vanished too.
My eyes shut. I really
was a girl who once had dreams
before all the good dreams were ripped
away from me.
A knife to the gut,
twisting one hundred different ways,
nudging closer and edging in.

I waited; waited
    and
    waited,
        for the bad dreams to wisp into the abyss,
        for the horrors of my life to transform
        into things I would never remember again.
        But no matter how many times
        I prayed away the terror,
        this wasn't a dream
        but a nightmare
        forged in reality.
        A dream of terror where

I waited and waited.
Kept waiting,
Kept
   W
     A
        I
         T
            I
             N
               G.

Dear Death,

It was the death of justice
when Mamou passed
to the world of the Unseen
and the dark cavern
of the grave, leaving four other brothers
imprisoned behind him.

The signs were all there,
from his coughing and hacking,
from his frail body,
from his scratchy throat.
Death in Islam was a bittersweet comfort.

    Inna lillahi wa inna ilayhi raji'un
    Indeed to Allah we belong and to Allah we shall
        return.

The promise of one end, and the beginning of another,
for the next time I would see Mamou
was on the Day of Account,
when justice about his imprisonment was dealt,
and the truth would be revealed.
For now, I would pray

    Please Allah, Please Allah, let me see my Mamou
    to be reunited with him in Jannah
        Inshallah.

Dear Dead Mamou,

Regrets filled the air
as Amma sobbed,
remembering all the unspoken things
said to her only brother, while all the spoken things
said, only hurt.

"He died," she cried. "He died before he could forgive me. He
     died!"
Aunty Farooqi and Nadia held her up by the shoulders,
but Amma sagged like the life
was draining out of her too.

"Amma," I whispered. I felt four years old again.
My voice small. My body hurting.
Aunties and uncles scrambled in and out the door like ants,
food piled sky-high in their arms,
with grievances, and prayers,
to return the favor,
because Amma spent the past ten years
feeding this community.
Al-Rasheed filled the fridge
with pots of karahi and puluo and chaana, shelves
     overflowing.
This was what Muslims did

in times of tragedy. We cooked.
Al-Rasheed was not rich. We weren't free with our time.
We worked long hours, owning shops, driving Ubers,
delivering boxes, manning cashiers,
taking care of growing families.
But when one was hurting, we used food as the balm.

At night, Amma's sobs made the house tremble
like the walls were sobbing too.
I held her but I could not cry,
numb to a pain that
had yet to hit.
Amma smoothed my hair back, uttering words
of grief I'd never forget:

This is why, Nida; this is why we can't write or take
risks. Why we must be perfect. I don't want you to
be like Abdul-Hafeedh, he had a bright future with
his poetry, but for that he burned.

Dear Al-Rasheed,

The mosque was dense with praying Muslims,
the janazah packed
shoulder to shoulder in condolences.
Aunties gave me their grievances,
Jawad promised to always make du'a,
I returned the favor,
knowing his uncle
was still behind bars.

My tears were dry.
My body was numb.
I was floating,
unable to feel,
unable to speak,
until Imam Abdullah led the prayer
and we were down in sujood.

Sujood was the act of bowing in prostration while facing the qiblah,
the humblest position to Allah,
an opportunity of private conversation
presenting all your concealed emotions.

I'm sorry, I whimpered inwardly,
I'm sorry I couldn't see the signs.

Twenty-seven

After my Mamou's body was lowered into the Al-Rasheed graveyard, we returned to the mosque for the midday Jummah prayer and sermon.

Al-Rasheed's street was congested with families who, in all their holy intentions, still exchanged insults over the last parking spots until no fire escape was left unscathed. Inside the polished building, green and gold Arabic calligraphy lined the walls, curving up toward the large green-domed center. The din of murmured prayers echoed across the musallah.

While we waited for the Jummah prayer to begin, we read Quran and prayed and prayed. Aunties were preaching and praying so hard, Allah probably okayed Mamou into heaven on Judgment Day (I hoped).

Uncle Jihad paced in front of me with his hands folded across his gut, shaking his head as he stroked his tear-drenched beard. "What a shame, what a shame," he kept repeating. He pinched my cheeks and placed his hand on my head. "Be brave, puttar."

Aunty Farooqi came next, her nails digging into my dupatta-clad neck. "He was gone so soon, so soon that poor soul. But to Allah we all return."

"Jazakallah khair, Aunty," I murmured into her shoulder.

I was still numb.

"I'm so sorry for what happened to him. But Allah is mercy." Aunty Aamiina also embraced me, and I stiffened. It wasn't me anyone should be saying this to. It was Mamou. I felt like I was stealing the prayers meant for him.

"On the Day of Account justice will come," she promised. And it was those words that ebbed some of the grief.

I was in a daze. The truth of my Mamou's passing hadn't hit me yet.

Aunty Sobia and her Ammi pecked my cheeks and handed me grocery bags full of paratha and freshly brewed chutney from the community garden. "Come by, okay? Anytime you need anything, just come. I'm here and I know a little something about grief." Aunty Sobia swiped my tears with her thumbs.

Eventually, after the adhaan—the call to prayer—was announced, Aunty Aamiina's husband, Imam Abdullah Abdi, in his white thobe, stood up on the minbar. "Brothers and sisters, stand in your lines."

We hushed and bowed our heads, but he paused. "I mean this literally. Please squeeze together and make room for the latecomers."

We all stood, collectively murmuring, squeezing against each other before sitting back down.

"May God reward you, bismillah." The imam raised his voice as he directed everyone to fit into the appropriate lines. "Bismillah," he kept repeating into the mic. "*Bismillah.*" He was gritting it out, as if any more *bismillah* was going to make the lot of us miraculously create more room on the carpet.

"*Bismillah, Bismillah.*" He huffed. Now it was embarrassing, I was getting out of breath *for* him.

Finally, the imam began his sermon. After reciting a short

du'a and greeting, he spread his hands, gazing at the worshippers with a soft smile. "These are trying times filled with slander and polarization. But it's not a time unique to the twenty-first century. Hassan ibn Thabit was the leader of the believing poets of the Islamic world, and the poet of the Prophet, Peace Be Upon Him. So much so that even Angel Jibraeel was sent down to help him. During encounters with the Quraish tribe, the Quraish would send their poets to slander the Muslims. In turn, the Prophet, Peace Be Upon Him, called Hassan to respond to the poetry. But the Prophet, Peace Be Upon Him, warned to be careful in criticizing the Quraish. Hassan would have to be clever with his poetry.

"Hassan was ordered to team up with the companion Abubakr, for Abubakr was an expert in lineage and history. This was an example of the Sahaba working together based on their logical strengths; they used their expertise of poetry and history to respond peacefully to the slander brought against the Muslims. The Prophet said to Hassan, *Write your satire against them for it hurts more than arrows falling onto them.*"

I blinked at the imam's words. The sermon was like an ironic sort of speech, the kind that had me wondering if God was speaking directly to me.

"Now brothers and sisters, apply the story of Hassan to the strength of Brother Abdul-Hafeedh and be inspired by it. His death should not be weighed down as a tragedy, it's a story of what he sacrificed for our ummah. Our tongues should not be idle during injustice. Speech is its own power better than any, especially in a world where hate has become a defining trait amongst the people. Before, we had peace and love to unify us. Now? Leaders hand their people hatred when the masses have nothing more to grasp on to. They're told the ones who hurt them are an invisible threat waiting to happen—not the leaders who steal their money and can't guarantee them basic rights. Even healthcare, poverty, education."

Imam Abdullah stood, imposing, on the wooden minbar. Behind him, overarching glass windows displayed the mangled skeletons of Al-Rasheed's houses. But the imam kept his eyes fixated on the audience and his words smooth. A hope to hold back cruelty.

Sitting cross-legged on the janamaz of the mosque, I admired the imam's effortless influence. With the right words, he was soothing a restless community. He didn't need to raise his voice to command the room. It reminded me of spoken word, every verse an intentional thread weaving in and around topics that were aimed to provoke emotional reactions.

After the imam finished leading the prayer, the masses began dispersing. Imam Abdullah approached my family with a soft, solemn look.

"I wanted to say, personally, that I am so sorry," he began. "Mamou Abdul-Hafeedh was like a brother to my family too. All we can do is remember that this isn't the end. This is just one life that serves as the prerequisite to the next. There is not a particular way to prepare for when one passes, especially in circumstances like this where the state murdered an innocent soul. But in Islam, justice is intrinsic to the cosmos.

"The Quran says in Surah Rahman, verse seven, *God raised up the Heavens and established the Scales of Balance*. Because Allah established justice. Let yourself feel, and whatever regrets you hold about Abdul-Hafeedh, release them. The beauty in death is when a person passes—all the anger you held toward them disappears like a clean slate. May Allah give you all peace and relieve you of this grief."

I glanced at Amma as she nodded, tears rolling down her chin. I'll never understand the relationship Mamou and Amma had, but I knew it was forged from the complicated parts of love. Each time they fought, it was *for* the love they felt toward each other.

Amma was weak, unable to stay standing, so Aunty Aamiina, holding her up, led her away to the back of the mosque. Before I could follow too, Imam Abdullah addressed me directly. "Nida, I've seen what the media said about Abdul-Hafeedh, your family, and especially you. All I can say is remember the story of the leader of the believing poets. The persecution around us has occurred all throughout time; Muslims have been murdered simply for their beliefs. But even in times of turmoil and grief, poetry was a clever weapon to respond to the slander."

"I tried," I tell him. "But it was used against us. Look what happened with Mamou."

He gazed at me with pity. "It's a trying time with your uncle passing, but remember the Prophet. He said, *the most noble struggle is to speak a truthful word in the presence of a tyrannical ruler.* Islam is a religion of activism, our roles are to enjoin good. Unfortunately, we have people who are bystanders to injustices around the world, especially against Muslims, even in our own community. What gives me faith is to see a young generation being vocal wherever they can."

He waited, so I nodded, murmuring an *Ameen* to show I was listening.

"The Prophet also said, whoever witnesses something evil, let him change it with his hand, and if he is unable, then with his tongue."

I nodded again.

"The Prophet also said—" he began.

"I get the point," I quickly cut in.

He cleared his voice. "Right. So, Nida, don't let them silence you. I know that's what your Mamou would say too."

"He did." I willed the tide of grief washing over my heart to cease. "One of the last things he said to me was, *The sharpest sword is the tongue.*"

Imam Abdullah smiled. "Then you know what to do."

———

By evening, with an air of bereavement clouding the house, I decided to bring Mohamed on a walk. After changing from my jilbab into a Bucks jersey, we lingered at the park. Around us, people trekked back to their homes. On the pavement, a group of teenagers began a scrimmage, playing streetball on the shabby court.

We watched them.

"Niiiida." Mohamed dragged my name out.

"Yeah, buddy?"

"Where's Mamou now?"

I eyed him. "What do you mean?"

"You know." Mohamed toed his foot around the grass, until his sneakers were stained green. "I know Mamou's down *there* but where is he now that he's dead?"

I flinched at how he said *dead*, but he was just a twelve-year-old kid. A part of me wished he'd asked this when Imam Abdullah was around. The imam was equipped to handle these questions, not me.

But I took my religiosity for granted. For young kids like Mohamed, it was different. They were born Muslim but didn't *understand* Muslim, if that made sense.

I was barely coping. I hadn't even properly cried. So, what did little Mohamed think of death? How did he interpret heaven and hell?

I straightened Mohamed's thobe, which was so ridiculously large, it dragged beneath his feet. "Mamou isn't in heaven yet, he's in the grave being asked questions by the angels."

"What? Will he go to hell?"

My eyes bulged. "Okay, relax. We're supposed to have faith in mercy. Mamou is a good man; he's charitable and he always stands for justice. He is . . ." My voice choked. Not *is*. Was. It stung to make that correction. It stung to see the man who I'd visited every month to talk out my grievances suddenly cease to exist.

"We just have to pray for him." I turned so he wouldn't see my moist eyes.

He's dead, Nida. He is dead.

When I turned back around, I witnessed the relief in Mohamed's gaze; it matched my own. It felt good to talk about our anxieties—death was so taboo, we didn't speak enough of it. Children were blunt, but that bluntness voiced the fears adults were too scared to admit to themselves.

After tugging again at my jersey, Mohamed insisted on watching the basketball scrimmage up close.

"Nida!" Jawad hollered from the court. "Are you going to join us or what?"

Mohamed smirked. "I bet Jawad will win."

"Aren't you supposed to be loyal to your family or something? It's a sad day! You're supposed to have extra pity on me!"

"Not my fault you're no good. And you're short. Jawad is over six feet!"

"*Mo-hamed*. Take that back!"

"We can bet on it."

"If I win, you're cleaning my sneakers. With. A. Toothbrush." I grinned.

He made a face. "If you lose the scrimmage rounds, you're cleaning *mine!*"

"Deal."

Mohamed climbed onto the wobbly bench on the sidelines. "Fine. *Go lose.*"

On the pavement, the players checked me the ball, saying the du'a for tragedy with a "Sorry for your loss."

No matter how many times I heard the Arabic verse, I never grew tired of it.

> *Inna lillahi wa inna ilayhi raji'un.*
> *Indeed to Allah we belong*
> *and to Allah we shall return.*

It was the most comforting phrase at times of grief because it reminded me that there was hope.

"Thanks."

I caught the ball.

"Let's play."

For a long, hard hour, I balled with Jawad's friends. By the time we finished the first game, his teammates were nodding at me in acknowledgment. See, I wasn't half bad.

"You a Bucks fan?" One of them, Bilal, swiped the sweat from his brow.

Jawad answered for me. "She worships the ball after God, I'm telling you."

"He's joking, but I'm actually a *LeBronsexual* for life, don't care what team. So hashtag LakeShow it is for now. My precious Raptors come second, can't forget my Canadian cousins. Bucks are tied somewhere in there, depending on if the team will actually support Giannis."

"Don't disrespect my Bucks like that. Bandwagon," Bilal said, which resulted in me slamming the ball toward him.

Calling *me* a casual? That's the worst insult imaginable to a baller.

"I don't understand you or Jawad for being LeBron haters. He's the GOAT after MJ," I said.

"Durant is better," Jawad said, with his Nets jersey.

"Weren't they swept against the Celtics in the first round not that long ago? Then he ran to the Suns."

He grimaced. "I'll make you eat your words."

By the end of the third scrimmage, most of the hoopers had left, leaving it to just a one-on-one between Jawad and me, with Mohamed still cheering. My brother was disloyal but adorable.

It felt like we were back in elementary school, battling each other in ball every weekend. A long time had passed, too long, since we used to sneak and play, or catch a basketball game, or listen to our uncles preach at the Poet's Block.

Jawad took advantage of my distraction by feigning right before crossing left, winning with a slick jump shot.

"Damn." I bent over to catch my breath.

"You can join us again if you want. Better than that snake, what's her name? Lexie?"

"Hey," I warned. "And it's Alexis."

He shrugged before squirting water from his bottle into his mouth. "Lord forgive me if this was backbiting, but I'm speaking truth. You need better friends."

"Yeah, whatever, it was messed up."

He snapped his fingers. "Wait, is it more messed up than that Pakistani place we went to owned by that Italian, who had butter-chicken biryani on the menu?"

I pretended to gag. "That was messed up. But was it worse than Ahmer's rap battle against you in the first week of school?"

"That was messed up," he agreed. "But is it more messed up than Mitchell Wilson deciding to hold one of his last rallies near Al-Rasheed?"

I gasped. "No way, is he actually?"

"For the Muslim vote, I guess."

"That's messed up. But is it worse than the interview I did with *Fifteen Minutes?*"

"That *was* messed up. But was it worse than *our* rap battle at MIST?"

"That was messed up." I grinned. "More messed up than your father preaching us into standing together in the prayer lines?"

That broke it. We laughed.

"One last one," I said, and I blamed my next loaded words on grief. "Was it more messed up than our uncles in prison?"

His smile disappeared. "Messed up," he said carefully.

But I couldn't stop, my lips parting open like I was about to projectile vomit. "Or more messed up that Mamou's dead?"

"Nida, what you're saying is really messed up."

"I know."

"You sure you're good?"

"I don't know," I answered honestly. "I think I'll be okay."

"After therapy," he muttered.

I dribbled the ball low to avoid his gaze. "You take it easy too, okay? I'm worried about your family."

"No kidding."

"Any word on your uncle?"

"Good, for now, I think. But my hope isn't lasting."

I grimaced. "I'm praying for him. And keep me updated if anything changes."

"Thanks, Nida." His smile was small and sad.

"I'm going to go now. But I'll watch today's Bucks game so I can grief tag you in NBA memes."

He wasn't looking at me though, he was spinning the ball on his finger, lost in his own thoughts. "Deal," he answered distractedly. "But after Isha prayer, you better come down to the

Poet's Block tonight. We're hosting a session in honor of your uncle."

"Maybe."

See? Al-Rasheed Block had its own way of dealing with grief. I just thanked Allah I was gifted a community who understood.

Dear Regrets,

Back in my room,
my left hand moved,
and the pen glided beneath me,
all scribbles.
I tried and tried
to write
but to no avail.

In movies, death
was romanticized where the hero
passed with smiles and wise words.

Mamou died weathered down
to his skinny bones.
His last words weren't hopeful, they were scared and full of
doubt,
hazed by an organized system of sickness and neglect.
He was so tired of hating the world.
All he had was his faith,
clinging to it until his last breath.
His sadness left me with regrets.

I was supposed to have legal aid
to afford a better terrorism attorney.

I was supposed to have saved him.
I was supposed to be writing and showing him my verses.
He was supposed to be writing too.
We were supposed to bond on this.
Not be cursed together.
He was going to be released.
I'd be waiting outside the prison
with Grandmother and Amma,
with Zaynab and Mohamed,
and Jawad and Imam Abdullah and Aunty Aamiina;
we were going to feast on Sindhi mutton biryani
and fight over every potato piece baked in it.
We'd pray together in thanks and read Quran.

He would be happy. He would be free. He would be—

I tore the journal paper to shreds
before the tears of frustration came raining down
unable to process his passing.

My wrists throbbed in pain from
the weight of the blue string taut against my arms.
I wished I could snap it in half.
I couldn't take it. I couldn't take this curse
that I didn't understand.

I'm sorry I couldn't save you. I couldn't even write
to please you because I'd messed up.
I rejected the pen,
a blessing I'd always taken for granted.

My insides began burning;
my arms stung red,

as if the blood pumping through me
was searing the folds of my skin.
This urge to write was pent up inside me
and I wanted to let it loose.

    But. I. Couldn't. Write.

    "Allah, tell me what I should do," I begged
    to the empty room.

    "I want this. I want to write.

    Mamou is dead. Can't I at least write? For
        him?"

The curse
wouldn't break,
even thinking of Mamou, and his dead body.
I picked up the pen, praying for it to speak.
The anger and grief thumped at my chest,
pounding and pounding.
The grief wanted to escape
the treacherous mold of my body
but it was imprisoned by me.

I gazed at the worn parchment of Amma's old journal, the musty smell wafting beneath my nose. The Urdu was faded and jumbled in Nastaliq script, unreadable. Too faded to discern even if I could. I was not perfectly literate in Urdu, not the way my Mamou was. And even if I was, how would the curse let me read poetry letters? Would the curse permit it?

God, if only I could read it to understand her, him, them—my entire family. If I could understand, maybe . . .

A sharp prick ran up my finger. I glanced down. The blue string shot out of my palms and plunged into the paper like a knife to a clump of ghee. Startled, I yanked back, but the string wouldn't budge.

What was it trying to tell me? Gritting my teeth, I pulled and pulled, but the string wrapped viciously until I was stuck to the old worn papers.

"Why are you here?" I demanded of it. "What do you want with me? I can't read the journal! All of this, it's useless!"

A voice rang in my head. It sounded like my Mamou.

Listen closely, Nida, and I stilled.

It spoke again.

Listen to the stories of the letters.

The blue string shot upward, thickening into a shroud. It blotted my sight and I succumbed to it. Something large and unfathomable was happening around me. I was helpless to ignore that voice and its inevitability, like a lamb on Qurbani Eid, knowing misfortune was soon.

The last thing I saw before I fell unconscious was a slash of the blue string.

———

The dream swallowed me into its dark mouth and vomited me out into the unknown. I knew I was dreaming in the vague way that I knew other details of the dream, as if some higher power was cramming the grim facts into my brain.

Images flipped past my thoughts like the pages of the old journal: my Amma, my Mamou, my grandmother, my grandfather, and other people I did not recognize.

Here, I wasn't Nida. I was a soul embodying the tales of the past. So, I shut my eyes, opened my ears, and listened.

Dear Dreams,

Strange dreams found me,
A strange dream with the blue string.
The string multiplied into a dozen thin strands,
looping in wide circles
seizing my torso,
wrapping around my throat,
stitching into my lips,
folding around my eyes,
binding me in blue chains.
I could not move.
I could not fight.
Listen to me, *it spoke,*
forcing my attention.
Then I was falling,
  falling through time and space
  and a kaleidoscope of realms,
  landing in a foggy room.
I could see my room but not.
  Like pattering rain
  wetting the planes of a window,
  blurring the sight.
Until the blue string spoke again.

Dear Nida,

I am the pen.

> Dear Pen,
> You reject me when I am sad.
> You reject me when I am mourning.
> You reject me when I crave you.
> You reject me when I am praying,
> hoping to let your ink loose.
> But . . . why didn't you reject me when I was angry?
> When I spoke in that rap battle?
> When I roared my rage to my best friend and teacher?
> Why do you curse me, pen?

Dear Nida,

I do not reject you, girl.
I reject your lies.
I let you use me:
  —only when your anger was honest.
You think you are the only one who was punished by fate
in their short, short life?
The original pen was God's first creation,
but now there are many ordinary pens on earth,

a precious responsibility.
Intellect was a gift to humanity
granted to no other creation between the Heavens and
    Earth,
before humans cursed
and abused it.
I was your pen,
young and new, just as you
before you misused me.
I have cursed many.

The blue string stretched high, expanding.
I realized it wasn't string
. . . but the finest strand of ink.

And I fell apart.

Twenty-eight

The blue string streaked across the sky, opening a vision to the past. The scenes blurred and rippled, the reflection of a murky pond. Time seemed to slow like a long, drawn-out breath.

Years passed in a blink. I watched my family's tale unfold.

British India

During the crux of communal violence, and a continent's nationalist movements determined to break away from their colonial overseers, there was a young couple who had just married. They resided in an unremarkable village north of the Swat princely state.

The region bloomed a green valley at the foothills of the towering Hindukush range, under the noses of the Soviets ruling the Turks of Turkestan and the booming revolutionaries of the Republic of China.

With another ripple, time darted forward.

I watched the couple move south to Hyderabad before sweating themselves in labor. Around them, the people talked. They worried about another famine. Worried about crops and goods shipped afar to Britain, a land where the people fattened themselves on riches produced by another's meager hands.

As I tried to process my surroundings, I was powerless to time, yanking me forward and backward, as if to tell me: *no, I am not linear. I follow my own story.*

Time mangled and fumbled and a new scene reopened.

The couple saved their earnings, attempting to open a fabrics shop. When that failed, the disappointment of it prompted the husband's Pashtun entrepreneurial brother to invite them to a bustling village in northern Uttar Praddesh, where Sikhs and Muslims lived in vibrant harmony.

Light splintered around the land, the sun rising into a red glow. A sandy path cut from the main route, where oily sewage water chugged down narrow lanes beneath the packed earth.

A village sat squat in a doab above the murky Indus, cleaving the green land in two, the tall arches of the rocky Himalaya chain north of the unnamed settlement. There, the wife gave birth to her son Ali Ehsan Baloch. Shortly after, she passed away from infection.

I watched Ali squealing and squirming as a newborn. Over the years, he grew, maintaining the sturdy, sure build of a man who knew his way around the mountainous terrain. With a smooth light complexion, and equally earthy eyes and puffy pink cheeks, my ancestor was his father's identical. I even saw a little of my grandmother in those features.

Eventually, Ali's father passed tragically due to a wild attack from a stray beast. Left parentless, Ali was raised by his widower uncle.

Together, mamou and nephew measured their living selling heeng and grain in a small square room shoved between the straw awnings of a butcher and a Kashmiri shop selling rare handicrafts. Ali ran the shop with the help of a kind Sikh moneylender. Across the bazaar, women worked the charkha in a fabric shop using cotton from South Punjab.

The hardy village was a steady fixture in the large British empire, en route to the bigger, bolder, more colorful cities rife with political banter that Ali spent little time understanding. He told himself that those kinds of matters were for bigger, bolder men.

His uncle would howl, *Lands will change, empires will topple, but buffalos are to be milked, and wheat to be milled, and children to feed.*

Every day, travelers trotted in and out of the village like hordes of ants.

I listened to the yaps about Muslim lands and Hindu lands; the dreams of a new caliphate but also of a secular nation separate from the grip of the British Raj; the stories of Jinnah protecting Muslim minority rights; the idea of a nation-within-a-nation.

I watched Ali listen too in silence. He could not parse out its meaning. He was still in his squat village, kneading maize and barley for bread on some days, and selling grain on others. But he heard it all, his village between everything but never at the center of anything.

Around Ali, a greater game was at play and his land was a piece on the chessboard. History was in motion: lands were becoming states, and people were thrust onto sides drawn by arbitrary lines called borders. The Japanese had declared themselves leaders of the Asian peoples. As new ideas were flourishing in the era of the white man's modernity, old ideas were burned like the Ottoman flag.

Between it all, my great-great-grandfather was a young, confused man named Ali.

But that was how all stories began.

———

The dream brought me to another afternoon.

Ali was laboring away, until he spotted a new woman at the chakki inside a spice shop. Ali fell in love.

She was a small, thin Punjabi woman but her sun-browned features were large—big lips and beaming ebony eyes, and swinging black braids tucked into her embroidered shawl.

The ones who knew nothing of her would assume she was quiet, but in the evenings, she spun words into heart-wrenching ghazals. Ali grew fond of her quiet ghazals, especially in Persian. He would guess at the meanings—the language familiar but unfamiliar in its poetry.

Ali had never given marriage much thought. But he smiled then, eyes brightening at the stark image of possibility. He rushed home to his uncle.

The next day, Ali and his uncle intended to bring forth a proposal for the girl's family. She lived with her paternal aunt and uncle in a two-room residence. The home was jammed in a complex of clay bricks in warm, earthy tones. Outside, the crop fields stretched outward like green limbs. Skinny cows grazed sparse yellow patches, their ribs jutting out along their long, ruddy bellies.

Inside, I watched the men sit back on embroidered cushions and, at the uncle's discretion, the girl served steaming, milky chai perfumed with cardamom. Ali took a sip and glanced down at his cup, waving away a buzz of flies. It was the best chai he'd drank in years.

The girl's name was Mehrnaz, named after a character from the famous Persian poetry epic of the Shahnameh. Curious, Ali asked why she lived with her uncle, and not her parents.

Mehrnaz spoke with a crease at the corners of her mouth: "I

will be forthcoming about my family. My father is a good man but imprisoned in Delhi. My mother lives with my brother in that city. I moved to my father's brother's home in this village for my own safety."

"Who is your father? Why is he imprisoned?"

"His name is Yousaf Reza Bukhari, a Persian poet from Delhi and a supporter of the Khilafat Movement. He was charged with sedition by the British Raj because he penned poetry against the British during a mushaira."

The thoughts rang in my head in my dream-state: *The British did not wish for a repeat of the 1857 mutiny. They pitted the Hindus against the Muslims and the Sikhs, seeing the benefit in having them turn against each other instead of joining together.*

"The British are arresting men for their words now, not their fists?" Ali was bewildered.

The girl looked at him calmly. "Well, poetry can incite violence in a way that fists cannot. They fear our words more than they fear our swords."

Ali asked more questions, and she answered them pointedly until he was satisfied, as if sighting a feast after a long Monday of fast. Mehrnaz's maternal grandparents had resided in Kandahar before moving to Quetta and then the port city of Karachi in the south. Her paternal grandparents came from a smattering of villages along northern Punjab. Mehrnaz descended from a long line of Persian writers dating back to the court poets who performed during the early Persianate Timurid-Mughal rulers. She spoke with an ocean of sorrow but a twinge of pride, as if obligated to be proud through her mourning. It was her family legacy, after all.

With the growing frenzy attacks, raids, and unrest in the city, that was why Mehrnaz's mother feared for her daughter. She sent her away, leaving her brother and imprisoned father in Delhi.

Ali's uncle asked, "How could your mother separate you from your family? You are their respect! Their izzat!"

She answered, "How tragic it was, Uncle! But my mother justified it with a simple reason: sons are for their fathers, but daughters are for their mothers."

The scene bled away like drops of ink.

Years had passed and Mehrnaz had given birth to two sons and two younger daughters. The children were savvy poetry performers, taking after the ghazals of their mother, and uncle, and grandfather, and great-grandfather, and so forth. They liked the poetry of Iqbal and Ghalib.

Ali grew fond of his sons. In the evenings, after their daily prayers outside the village's blue mosque, the children ran through a game called *Pakistanis versus Indians*.

No one wanted to be on the Pakistani team. *Pakistanis were the enemy and they always lost*, many of the children assumed. Pakistan did not exist.

When Ali heard the children saying so, he brought them forward and explained sternly what he'd grasped from the other merchants. That Pakistan was an idea of a homeland for Muslims. A Persian name that represented its ethnicities: Punjab, Afghania, Kashmir, Indus-Sindh, and Balochistan. Pakistan was not their enemy, even though Ali hardly understood what the idea of a *Pakistan* meant.

After that, many of the children felt okay to be on the Pakistani team.

The turmoil of British India made Mehrnaz protective of her daughters. She was fondest of the youngest: Nisha.

Nisha reminded me of myself. She was a tender, shy child as dusky as the colors of the red sunset. She listened more than she spoke, especially to the ghazals of her brothers. Reserved in nature, she kept more company with her seven roosters than her slightly older sister.

Often, her mother would spot Nisha climbing up the palms bracketing their small plot, swinging from one branch to the next, sucking on thumb-sized lemons until her lips became puckered and pruned.

One morning, Nisha sat with her roosters around the crop of foliage surrounding their plot. Hearing a rustle, Nisha turned. She spotted her mother burying jewels below those same lemon trees.

"Ammi, why have you thrown dirt on your gold set?"

Her mother straightened and smiled. If Nisha were any wiser, she would have spotted the sadness lurking behind Mehrnaz's pink lips. "It is better that I put dirt on it than let it be snatched by the hands of mobs and thieves. If we leave this village, one day, I will return and recover the buried gold."

"Leave where?" Nisha sucked on a lemon.

Her mother did not answer.

The dream passed, time shifted, and my family changed.

The children were older when their poet uncle visited from Delhi. It was Ramadan, a month for spiritual reflections.

My senses were invaded by a waft of strong spice, the scent of saffron tea. The famous poet uncle gathered the village's men after a night of prayer and spoke in verse to them about the ambitions of the Muslim League, of a new land that would protect Muslims, and end the era of their British overseers. The crowds clapped and cheered at each performance.

Partition was mentioned here and there but through huffs of laughter. Partition was a foreign idea to these folks out in the village. They had never anticipated it.

At hearing his uncle, Mehrnaz's eldest son, Umar, became curious. After a day of selling buffalo milk products, Umar joined the men in the fields. There, he watched the poets in a mehfil-e-mushaira.

Umar admired his poet uncle's education, compared to his limited schooling. So, when his uncle returned to Delhi, Umar decided to follow him.

At first, Mehrnaz objected. She rememberd how her father had been imprisoned. Her son had taken to politics the way her brother and father had, and she worried for him. But she remembered that sons were different than daughters. If Umar would take after the men of her family, so be it. She was powerless to stop it.

Instead, she would ensure that her daughters would never harbor the same dangerous ideals of the men in her family.

The day Umar packed his bags, Mehrnaz reached out before letting her arms drop. I saw my Amma in the wrinkle of her brow, the downturn of her pink lips, and the anger in her eyes.

Her son walked ahead through the door. She was good at this though. She was good at letting go.

———

After the night of Umar's departure. Ali awoke on his charpai for his nightly prayers only to find Mehrnaz cross-legged on the prayer mat below him, glancing at her arms. She twisted her wrists, seeing something that Ali could not discern. *What was on her wrists that kept her up late at night?* I felt him wonder.

But suddenly I knew. I was Mehrnaz, puzzled by a blue string wrapped around me—caging me, choking me. We both wondered if seeing a blue string meant that, at one point, our ancestors had too? Had the string cursed Mehrnaz's father during his imprisonment? Her brother? How had they overcome it?

I watched as Ali reached out to graze Mehrnaz's shoulder. In the slice of moonlight bathing the room, her eyes shone like shards of black glass.

"My love, are you crying?" Ali asked.

She recoiled and glanced at her upturned palms. "It's only the emotion of prayer overtaking me. I miss Umar."

Ali realized it had been months since his wife had last smiled.

"I search for my son," Ali began quietly, "far in the depths of the desert / What a pain he has caused me / He has ripped my heart for his love of the pen." Ali paused. "Won't you finish the poem?"

Mehrnaz blinked fast. "I cannot."

Ali interpreted her words as her unwillingness to engage with the couplet. He hadn't realized that she was cursed and could no longer speak poetry.

Ali stood and walked to the clay pitcher in the corner of the room, lifting its lid to pour out water for his ablution. He spoke softly, "Then let me join you in prayers."

Mehrnaz smiled faintly, finally.

———

Time leaped and I tumbled with it. Mehrnaz rarely smiled. Grief over her son's departure drove her to forbid her daughters from attending any poetic symposium that would attract unwanted attention.

But her fears came to fruition. Mehrnaz received an alarming letter from her brother in Delhi. Her son Umar had been arrested.

Umar, deep in the waves of anti-colonial politics, had contributed to a series of controversial student writings. They called for the defense of revolutionaries who attacked landlords collaborating with the British. Umar's strong poetry led to a charge under sedition for the *incitement of violence*.

Like many anti-colonial activists, he had been inspired by Jinnah when he defended Tilak, a nationalist who'd been charged with defending violent militants.

But in the nationalist tide overtaking the subcontinent, jails were wombs for political theater, full of imprisoned poets, activists, and politicians. Before Mehrnaz's father had died, he'd told his family that jails never worked as disciplinary institutions of subjugation. In the fight for freedom, revolutionaries sought deliberate arrest so that prison became a space reserved only for anticolonials. It created political celebrities, martyrs, and new heroes.

But I knew like my own Amma, Mehrnaz did not wish to see the day her eldest son would become a martyr. What mother could stomach witnessing the sacrifice of their child's young life full of so much promise for the burden of words readily taken on by others?

With the pain of motherhood, Mehrnaz had all but quit reciting poetry. With her eldest son's arrest, she partitioned herself from poetry altogether.

———

The dream rippled across the subcontinent into a flash of scenes: Ali departing to arrange bail for the release of his son Umar. Mobs and violence in Delhi. Muslim massacres in Kashmir. Looting and raping and a siege in Hyderabad. The killings of Hindus, Sikhs, and Muslims.

Finally, a return to my ancestor Mehrnaz's village.

Her elderly uncle ordered the family to pack whatever belongings they could carry. Mehrnaz looked unsurprised as if she'd resigned herself to this possibility some time ago.

Her youngest daughter, Nisha, was confused. Then she recalled the game of Indians versus Pakistanis and she understood. The subcontinent had been partitioned.

Tension strung the air as if at any moment, a match would be lit and ignite a roaring fire that would consume them all. Neighbors that had long coexisted with each other turned on one another.

Partition: the mutual genocide of Hindus, Muslims, and Sikhs. And many, to save themselves from this fate, dying by suicide.

At last, the match was lit in the small village whose name did not matter, and that stood at the center of nothing but between everything. A mob that traveled from the ring of neighboring settlements invaded Mehrnaz's village. It began during an animated poetic symposium, which alerted the mob. Engulfed in a tide of ethno-religious enmity, mobs shouted to slaughter every Muslim man on sight, to capture any mothers and daughters.

In the following weeks, as hordes of Muslims escaped to moth-eaten Pakistan, and hordes of Sikhs and Hindus escaped to India, communal riots drowned cities in torrents of blood.

The British withdrew without a hand of aid, leaving a torn continent and its bloodied peoples to sort themselves by the hastily drawn borders of the Radcliffe Line—decided by a British judge who'd never stepped foot in the region prior—which cleaved two new nation-states into pieces.

And as Nisha escaped her village by foot, a home overrun by riots, she glanced one last time at the dark packed earth beneath the lemon trees and she wondered when she would return for her mother's jewels.

Ordinary men had become murderers. What had they done to deserve such an evil fate?

———

The dream pushed me through time and generations. I saw my ancestors escape to Pakistan, with a pocket of survivors, trekking to the Sindh state, crossing through the border of two newborn nations.

I saw my ancestors attempt to board a train, a ghost of a vehicle. The insides were drenched in red, the passengers all massacred. Bodies were strewn across the seats. The urge to vomit overcame me but in this horrifying dream, I could only watch.

The refugees simply entered the train flowing with corpses. They closed all the windows, so they could not see outside, and no one could peek in. A tactic to avoid attack. Mehrnaz's relatives lived in Karachi, so they traveled there.

I saw the city, bloated by the influx of refugees, swelling and swelling, like an infected limb. Underneath the railway tracks in the waterlogged slums of Karachi, I saw my grandmother, Nisha, as a little girl witnessing children relieving themselves in the open. Pumps of smoke filled the air, tasting of metal.

I couldn't imagine this city as a home. And my grandmother wondered at it too, half-dazed. She wondered if she would ever see her father and eldest brother, trapped in Delhi, again.

But her great-uncle found it easy to leave behind their village. He instructed his family to never speak of their infamous grandfather, uncle, and brother—all imprisoned poets who had perished during the riots.

Do not mention it. None of it.

Mehrnaz had lost her father, uncle, son, and husband to a revolution. She had borne the silence of a daughter. And later, she bore the silence of a mother. She learned: silence was a legacy too. So she passed that new legacy right down to her daughters.

I watched as Mehrnaz, my great-grandmother, took her family's journals and burned them, as my Amma would do decades later. To Mehrnaz, it was foolish to possess the manuscripts in Pakistan and remind them of a lost past. To my Amma, it was foolish to possess her family's writings in America.

In the years passing, the governments of India and Pakistan told their people to keep quiet. To almost . . . pretend the failures of partition had never happened. To forget the British and their role in the violence. *This is important*, they said, *for peace. No matter who was made a victim, no matter how many were abducted, murdered, sold, or scarred, your silence is important.*

"To admit that you were violated is to concede defeat," the people around me boomed in their ethnic chauvinism. What had happened to them was unacceptable—but to pave their way forward was to bury the scars of the past, because to speak of their own suffering was to bring shame to their honor.

In the cities and university campuses and unions, silence was met with the heavy hand of the military. Sedition never disappeared. It was only replaced by a new government.

But Nisha was wiser than her siblings and uncles. She heeded her mother. She learned to forget her family art. She never attended a political poetry symposium nor the poetry mobs to protest General Zia-ul-Haq. She discarded her old identity as one would shed their dirtied clothes. The rest of her siblings—older and poisoned with remembrance of their former home—could not forgo their memories of family and poetry as easily as Nisha.

Adapt, this is your new land, the world demanded, like a soul squeezed into a new mottled body, forced through the sinews, beneath the skin, stretching along the arms and fingers, rubbing a mouth that wasn't its own, testing a tongue and language that didn't belong.

Asia was a dark open wound, but eventually it marbled into scars that would never heal right, into thick purple scabs that would bleed from time to time.

The day they arrived in Pakistan, my great-great-uncle told Nisha, *homelands are like the tides of the sea, they change and leave you stranded but eventually you find your shore.*

And Nisha did. Eventually she married a man, also a poet, in a traditional red and gold shaadi. She birthed four children, three daughters and one son. Her second daughter, Zuha, resembled her mother. Her son, Abdul-Hafeedh, resembled her late brother, an intellectual and poet, fluent in Farsi, Sindhi, Urdu, and Punjabi.

Nisha survived. Her children were living proof. But still, her mind would wander sometimes to her mother's jewels still buried under those lemon trees that she hardly remembered swinging from.

Long ago her Amma recited: mitti bulati hai.

The motherland beckons.

Dear Cursed Nida,

The pen murmured
in this strange dream.
Now do you see,
the story of . . .
your mother, uncle, your grandmothers, your grandfa-
    ther, your great-great-grandfather, so many great-
    uncles . . .
And more. All sorts of people, outside your family,
once had a blue string attached to their wrists.
You must know this.

Dear Myself,

I heard the truth,
I saw the deaths,
I witnessed the violence.
Oh . . .
the long history of my family,
Mamou warmed me,
of colonial legacies.
Many poets were arrested by white men with looming batons,
called the British Raj,
who persecuted people through crackdowns,
as poets rebuked their fellow brown men,

for seeking appeasement from white men.
These native writers were opposed to Europe's modernity,
concepts of materialist regularities,
they were cracked down
on charges of sedition,
and incitements of violence.
In fear, artists abandoned their writings,
abandoned the pen,
they were cursed—
once upon a time
—just like me,
sharing in cursed legacies.

Some broke the curse, *the pen mused.*
*Some died before they could. Like your Mamou. Like your
    great-great-uncles.*
I have heard your cries:
you've wished all your life,
to step out of your Mamou's shadow
yet you beg to Allah to be able to write,
for your Mamou's sake?
You are a dishonest poet.
You promised to never abuse your words,
only to write for someone else's use?
Why do you write, Nida?
You are one in a long list of poets.
But they returned and found their voice again,
*they broke their own curses by believing in faith through
    their pen.*
*Everyone has a pen. We are thousands. I was your
    responsibility*
but you broke me.

Dear Foolish Me,

The pen's pleas flowed like leaves in a river,
bending through old dirt-paved paths,
creating new streams for me to wade through.
If only I would take the first step.

Dear Black Hole,

The anger writhes inside
the black hole of my soul,
crawling and clawing
with no release.

I am a pent-up ball of energy;
I will find my escape like a cosmic explosion,
all starry rays before darkness claims me,
hope ablaze.

Dear British,

Sedition, *you proclaimed,*
in an empire reeling from famine,
tens of millions dead by your greedy hands.
Thousands more sent to jails,
to divide resistance movements,
but they mistakenly assumed
that art was
a terrain easy to conquer.

White men speared divides,
shooting us down with metaphorical guns
until the metaphorical became physical
pointed right down our noses.
They claimed to be our knights,
riding the dawn as our saviors,
but all I read of colonial India
was famine.

Sunken cheeks, poking ribs.
Skeleton bodies.
Eyes cast black as crow feathers.
The British weren't knights but hawks,
circling above,
ready to pounce.

These colonial regimes
live on through history,
through their bloody legacies,
rising all around us
in new countries and unfair laws,
controlling our bodies and arts,
calling themselves civilized states and liberal democracies.

I fell from above, in this dream state,
passing Mamou and his blue string,
My fingers
   S
     T
       R
         E
           T
            C
             H
               out, ripping away the blue string.
I fell,
  to the world
past cursed uncles, and fathers, and brothers, and sons, and
  mothers forced to endure it all.
So many lineages, so much violence;
for a second we are each other
through this string connecting us in a curse.
"Peace," we greeted, hand to chest.
  "This curse, we are not alone
  in bearing its legacy."
But that snipped too.
And I am again, Nida.
A girl alone with her pen.

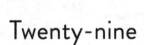

Twenty-nine

awoke from the dream, my face pressed against the desk. I peeled off the crumpled papers stuck to my cheek and checked the time. Seven o'clock. I'd only fallen asleep for half an hour.

Was that dream real?

The dream didn't vanish from my grasp like on a normal night. Instead, it was stark and vivid, etched into my memories, a fleeting sensation that was like the orange of sundown plummeting into night, when the shadows grew long, a suspended moment that was sudden but out of reach.

The dream had to be true, right? Its vision contained real names that I'd heard from my grandparents. Some of those stories Mamou had mentioned in passing, of an old village his great-great-uncle had lived in. But these bits of my history had been spoken of only ever in pieces, never fully realized until this dream. What did it all mean?

I put my arms out.

The blue string was still bound to my wrists, heavy and persistent.

Why do you write, Nida? the dream string echoed in my head.

For the first time since the contest, I wondered.

Why do I write? For Mamou? To always live in his dead shadow? For my legacy? For my ancestors who endured so much yet persisted?

Or did I write for me?

But I wouldn't find the answers here.

Opening my phone, I texted Rayan from MIST. Since the pen was trying to tell me something, maybe I could gift someone else its blessing and opportunity.

NIDA

Salaam, if you're still interested, every week a group of poets get together at Al-Rasheed. You mentioned your interest in the Poet's Block. We drink chai, share some poetry, and rap battle. Want in? I'll send you the address. If you have a prepared piece, bring it tonight, and perform. I'll make sure they let you.

She texted back almost immediately.

RAYAN
Hell Yeah.

Dear Poet's Block,

At the Poet's Block
Rayan clutched her journal against her chest.
Cleared her throat, looked me in the eyes, and said,
"Wow, this is a lot of people. I'm kinda nervous."
"Don't be," I reassured her. "It's just Muslims around here.
    Say your piece, wallah, I'll be snapping."
The reassurance made her sit straighter,
like a rod to her back,
made her smile real big, an infectious grin
that had my lips widening too.

We watched the poets perform,
their verses like relics paused in time.
Finally, Rayan stood behind the podium,
she glanced once at me, but I gave a thumbs-up.

Now I was nervous for her, a rock-sized weight on my chest
that wouldn't unclench.
I tried to breathe to shove the weight off,
but it was for nothing because when Rayan opened her lips
I didn't even need to snap,
Because the hands around me
were shooting up to clap and snap.

Heads nodded, people murmured their Ameens and
   mm-hmms.
Rayan's gestures moved in rhythm,
emphasizing the verses put out.

"I lived through that," I told Rayan later.
Her eyes widened. "Really?"
"Really," I repeated.
It was a simple compliment, but it made her world.
This was poetry,
this was the family I was missing.

After the performance, as poets began trickling out of the tent, Jawad sat beside me on the carpet around the low table.

"You made it," he said, a little shocked.

"We had a deal."

"Still."

I glanced away and admitted, "To be honest, I was kind of scared no one would want me around anymore, after what I did."

He shook his head and passed me a chai cup. "Of course we would. Welcome back, Nida."

I sipped the cardamom-scented warmth. It was good to be home. "Can I ask you a question?" I said after a short silence.

Jawad looked up. "Sure."

"Why do you write poetry?"

"That's a strange question."

"Well, I had a strange dream. And I'm starting to reevaluate a lot of assumptions I had. So please, tell me. Why did you pick up the pen?"

Jawad thought about it. "Let me ask you a question instead because I'm tired of telling you what to think, Nida." When I didn't protest, he went on. "If you could get rid of an emotion, would you? Your happiness, sadness, pain?"

I didn't have to think. "No," I realized. "Even when those emotions hurt me."

He shrugged. "There's your answer. Asking me why I write is like asking me why I have a certain emotion. It's a part of me. I just do it."

Ahmer called Jawad over. He left before I could ask him more.

I found Rayan and asked her the same question before she could leave.

"It's not why I write," she answered. "It's like asking, why am I me?"

On my walk home, the longer I thought about their answers, the more memories tugged free.

My first memory with poetry was when Mamou taught me calligraphy. I was eight and tracing peacock designs. Instead of trying to write in English, I wrote a verse in Urdu. Just thinking about it made me smile bittersweetly.

I missed that simplicity. When I could write with no judgment, make all the mistakes in the world, and be carefree. It didn't matter if anyone read my work. Because it was meant for my eyes.

Oh.

Oh.

It hit me. Poetry wasn't Mamou. It wasn't mine or anyone's.

People expressed their emotions in different ways, and maybe for poets, this was our way.

Maybe the pen's curse really was a blessing. Maybe I needed time away from writing to realize what I was missing. I'd missed writing for more than just the sake of Mamou.

At times when I was happy from eating Amma's delicious food, at times when I'd return home from praying inspired to write praises. At times when my frustrations spilled over after losing a ball game against Jawad because the Bucks beat the Lakers.

That was my poetry. It was *my* truth. Not anyone's objective version but mine alone.

I straightened, determined to get this right.

Running to my room, my hands trembled, skin still burning. I grabbed a fresh piece of paper. My stomach clenched, but my instincts told me to keep writing.

I took a careful breath and made my intentions clear because in Islam, no action is without intentions.

The sharpest sword is the tongue.

I gripped the pen, closed my eyes, ignored the blue string and its curse, and

    pushed

       the

          words

            out.

My eyes shot open. The blue string trembled, lifting from my limbs before rising and rising against the ceiling.

It began shedding until dozens of strings unraveled around me. They shimmered in their indigo strands before snapping into broken seams and disappearing.

The pen in my hand was heavy, shy against my fingers, uncertain in its trust in me.

Nevertheless, it glided across the white surface of paper, scrawling intangible letters. Strangely, the burning inside my skin found relief, subsiding the more I scribbled in blotchy ink.

An hour passed. I didn't dare stop.

My art was my only honest communicator. All this time, people, even well intentioned, were trying to shove me into molds, ones created by systems set up for me to fail. But when I spoke in the way that truly speaks to me . . . the words came forth.

When I was done writing, the paper was a series of close-knit scrawls. I crouched lower, recognizing the faint lines.

The pen had written an Urdu verse. It was messy, rusty from years of disuse. I couldn't remember the last time I'd written in Urdu, the Arabic-like script a clunky series of lines and curves. It was barely words, but my brain, recognizing the language, re-arranged the ink.

Stop thinking, I could imagine the pen's voice berating me.

When I was young, I'd said to my journal,

I write to you, and you write to me. I had murmured the hushed oath to myself, a promise careening past time until it became ageless.

So, I held out the pen and I spoke that promise again: "As I write to you, you write to me."

With the curse gone, I was acknowledging the pen for what it was. Something to be taken care of, something to be treated right, not manipulated by the Mr. Wilsons out there who used their words to lie, and spew hate and abuse to the masses. If I made the same mistakes from before, lying with my art, I'd be no different than him.

The pen was right. I'd been a dishonest poet.

That night, I continued to write with no filter in messy script, pressing away at the paper in a language only made for my eyes. The blue ate at the white, until nothing remained.

I wrote and wrote,

I wrote and wrote,

I wrote and wrote—

Dear Me,

My hand stitched around the pen,
hieroglyphs spinning into stroked
    shapes,
worked into private words.
To the world?
To the room
    —to myself.
Strangers' eyes trying to peek in,
greedy for a taste of paper,
pressing against me to rip those pages
in two, then more pieces.

But I command my own order,
letting the verses stream out
                    down
                        down
                            down
a crashing river of ink, wearing
on paper, then on me.
Piecing together into words
that cut sharply into the white,
punching their strings of ink
into blue edicts.

Let them look, let them judge,
gavel thudding their podium
as I scribe names,
    names of poets who'd been cursed like me,
joined together from sweat and blood,
pieced in my historic shelf.
Art, you see, can never be chained
—forever a reminder to myself.
Letters for my poet self.

Dear Ancestors, Mamou, and Amma,

I broke the curse.
I could write again.
What would you think?

Dear Baba,

Remember how we rode through the bazaars,
coiled in pockets of Lahore and Karachi,
past the shrills
of Urdu, Pashto, Pahari, Sindhi, and Punjabi?

Zipping across corridors,
curses falling from the mouths
of alleyway entrepreneurs
in more languages than my tongue knew.
I wondered, what is Urdu?

Urdu encompassed the vast mosaics of lost cultures,
lost cultures wrought into bent shapes
by the hammers of colonial men.
Smashing. Smashing. Smashing . . .
molding Asia into "civilization."
Urdu in its complexity
is the bazaar of linguistic resistance.

Dear Book,

Naked is the book
bereft of ink,
without life or desire
to paint its barren white lands,
and empty too is a man without art;
his heart has hardened without words to soften it.
What makes us human if not the free will to speak our love?

Thirty

My eyes were red and bleary from scribbling into my blank new journal for half the night to make up for lost time. I had a plan now and no one would stop me (Inshallah). If Mitchell Wilson would be having a final stretch of political rallies in our state to secure the Muslim vote, then we couldn't miss this last opportunity, especially with Election Day on Tuesday.

First, I texted Jawad my plan. We had four days to spread the word. Then I went to Zaynab.

"You sure about this?" Zaynab turned from watching Hum TV. "You'll be putting yourself out there, and it could be a repeat of exactly what happened the first time."

"I don't care anymore," I admitted. "I'm tired of doing nothing. I have a chance here to fix my mistakes, to bring attention not just to Al-Rasheed, but to all the Muslims suffering because politicians refuse to understand our community."

Muslims weren't just in America. There was the New Zealand Christchurch shooting; the Muslim Canadian family mowed over like rodents by a car steered by a white supremacist, orphaning a nine-year-old; the mother and daughter frisked and arrested by cops; the hijabis criminally charged on the beach for wearing burkinis; the ban of hijabs on university campuses; there were the New York Muslims mass profiled by the FBI; the MSAs visited by cops and spies; and countless mosques vandalized on the daily.

The list went on. There were too many cases to name.

"You seem too confident about this after everything that's happened. This can blow up in our faces again," she warned me.

That was true. Maybe I was being too optimistic.

Zaynab leaned back against the mattress. "But if I had a chance to speak about how I was spied on, I would. So, no matter what Amma says about this, I got you." She stood up and rummaged through her closet.

"What are you doing?"

"We have to make sure you look good. We'll make you a modest hipster hijabi." She held up two jersey hijabs, one orange-brown, the other nude pink. "Now which one?"

I pointed at the orange-brown.

"Good choice."

My phone pinged. Based on my notifications, Jawad had made a WhatsApp group with poets from all over the city, informing them of our idea.

After a moment of hesitation, I sent Alexis a text, asking to meet at five o'clock outside the Al-Rasheed Block where the rally would take place.

Now, I had to tell Amma.

Dear Amma,

Tacked on your bedroom wall
was an old family photo, a timeless snapshot.
My aspirations were there but tainted by the world.
My hijab was clipped embarrassingly
in two crooked layers,
showing a glimpse of my widow's peak.
I bared my teeth in a version of a smile
    —all innocence and dreams, staring up at my parents
        eagerly.

From that confident tilt to her chin,
you'd believe that girl was ready
to take the world by storm:
study hard, befriend all the Pakistanis,
visit the sick aunties,
drop food at their door and attend the mosque without fail.
She'd probably be an exceptional student with A+'s,
excelling at mathematics and the sciences,
be accepted into top colleges
with some kind of engineering degree.
She'd venture out and run for executive positions
at the local Muslim Student Association
in high school and college.

She'd embrace discomfort. She'd be exceptional.
She'd be smart and the perfect picture
of an immigrant kid who'd made it big.

I hated the idea of buying into all of our system's meritocracy,
thinking we can succeed,
but that was what our
immigrant parents dreamed up for us
and we all went along with it.
To hell with it. All those plans, all those hopes could go down
    the drain.

There was a lot that was murky
    —a lot that I never realized was all up to me.
Yes, I had dreams, but Amma had to open her eyes
and realize I couldn't just do what she wanted for me
because of some concept of honor and izzat.
The same way I could never be what my Mamou expected.
My future was up to me.

Thirty-one

I found Amma in the kitchen.

"Hey, jaanu," she said, her tasbih dangling from her right fingertips. In her left hand she gripped a marker to label the plastic jars. She'd spent the entire day emptying, washing, drying, then labeling her bulk orders of imported spices to begin recipe testing.

I watched her scribble *Chili* on the label sticker, admiring her work ethic. Amma was always a hustler. It was what Amma needed, work to throw herself into to ground her grief. What else could she do except shoulder it alone? But sooner or later she'd break from the weight.

That was why I came up beside her, wordlessly joining in the rhythmic emptying, washing, drying, then labeling.

By the time I'd finished a row of jars, Amma began cooking her first recipe. She shoved a spoonful of mixed vegetable curry into my mouth, to appeal to the new vegetarian clients.

I rolled the grease around my tongue before swallowing. "More ground coriander."

She nodded and rubbed at her cheeks, swollen from another night of weeping.

As she dug around for the coriander jar, I attempted to imagine everything from her shoes. I thought about how this was my last year of high school before I'd be gone. I thought about all the relationships I'd been failing to keep intact, beginning with my mother.

My throat closed. Amma froze and sensed my gaze, her own silent but searching.

I was in pain. And I had no way of telling her.

Instead: "You will always hate everything I do."

"Not hate," she said weakly, but it was a small attempt at consolation.

"If I performed poetry publicly, how much would you hate it?"

She immediately looked alarmed. "What are you doing?"

"Something I should've done before."

Her mouth opened and closed like the argument was exhausted out of her.

"Amma?"

Still no answer.

"You hate poetry, don't you, Amma?"

She didn't answer.

"Why do you hate it when your father and brother wrote it all the time in Pakistan? You even performed in your wedding. You stopped because of your Amma too, right? She was scared after Mamou's arrest."

Her eyes widened. "Who is telling you all this?"

I wished I could speak my heart, about everything—the dream, the old journal letters—but some things would forever stay unspoken between us. I'd accepted that.

She took my hands, sandwiching them between her own. "I don't hate it. I fear it. There's a difference. If your poetry was about the moon and flowers, then yes, Nida, write all you want. If the poetry is about politicians, then no. Don't do it."

"Did you write about the moon and flowers?" I knew the answer, but I wanted to hear it from her.

She pressed her lips together. There was more gray weaved into her hair than ever before. "No. Even if I wanted to . . . I wrote to be closer to my brother, and father. There's no point now that he's dead. I can't do it." She sighed. "For once, I wish you'd listen and stop."

"No," I decided. "I won't stop."

I expected protest, but Amma only rubbed my hands between her own, teeth biting into her bottom lip. She was scared to lose me like Mamou.

It took me a long time to realize what Amma was really fighting—she was never fighting me; she was fighting herself. But that's the thing with parents, they live through their children's aspirations. Maybe in another life, Amma would've stuck by spoken word. Maybe she would've enjoyed going to the Poet's Block as much as I did. I took a chance on that *maybe*, praying for the best.

So, I told Amma what I would be doing with the poets at the rally. I explained that we were going to stage a poetry mob, like what the Pakistani women did decades ago under General Zia, a Pakistani military dictator friendly with America, who'd enacted terrible laws. Elders and youngsters staged poetry mobs, spinning words into clever nazm, appealing to masses through Islamic motifs.

Like then, we'd create a poetry mob at the same time as Mitchell Wilson's rally, to send a loud and clear message, using Islamic motifs.

I told Amma that I already had the support of Muslims from across the country, I just had to be brave enough to accept it.

Amma's hands balled into clenched fists.

"You remind me so much of my Baba," she said.

I blinked.

She rarely talked about my dead grandfather, so when she spoke next, her Urdu came out in a rush, as if speaking about him pained her. "My Baba became famous for his poetry along with my Amma's brother. There was a lot of violence and uncertainty in both Pakistan and India—a whole country had just been created. I was told they organized a poetry mob, a symposium on campus. My Baba told us, *Our words aren't about peace. Our words aren't about fighting. They're about healing.*"

"I don't understand. . . ."

"If you're going to this protest, understand that it's a sensitive time for Muslims and non-Muslims—when people are scared, they look for groups to blame. That's exactly what happened during partition; different religious groups were attacked and blamed. Here in America, people are scared." Amma shook her head. "They're scared because there are fewer jobs, their health is being jeopardized, and they don't feel safe. So, politicians blame immigrants or other groups and put all that fear on to them. Then the story becomes that *we're* stealing their jobs, *we're* a threat to their safety. That's why we're called terrorists—it's by people whose wounds have never healed right."

I'd never thought about it this way.

I couldn't save my Mamou with my poetry. But maybe I could save my Amma. Amma couldn't string together words, not like she once did as a child. But she could learn to appreciate them like she did many other things. She wasn't the composer, but the listener.

It would take time, but I was ready.

Amma gripped my hands harder. "Please, rethink this, Nida. The election is almost over. Everything will quiet down. You have school. Your future to think about."

"I can't."

Amma would never like poetry. Not now, not in a few years,

not ever. Not as she did before the world tainted her love black-and-blue. And she was not regretful of this, but I could see that she was regretful of how she couldn't force herself to accept the things I pursued.

"Amma, at least tell me more about my grandfather. Mamou is not here to tell me anymore."

Her eyes creased with hesitation.

"Don't let this be too late, either. You're here, Amma. He isn't. And I learned the motherland beckons."

Her eyes shone in confusion—about how I knew things about our family that I wasn't supposed to know.

My offer was a way of compromise. I didn't need the letters, letters that I couldn't read anyway. Not when I still had my living and breathing mother and her tongue that could weave the history of many stories.

Amma's shoulders dropped in resignation. She opened her mouth. My hopes crouching low finally stood up. And I listened.

Thirty-two

It was the day before the election and word of our mob had spread across our group chats on social media. One street over from Al-Rasheed Block, a crowd was gathered for the rally, police securing the perimeters. We stood on the outskirts, watching Mitchell Wilson's volunteers positioning the voting signs for his evening speech. I was already breaking into a cold sweat, but I was dressed smart in a Raptors jersey, practically sweatproof.

Around me, poets were raising megaphones and banners, non-Muslims and Muslims alike. My nerves were singing, making me nearly drop the journal clutched in my arms.

The plan was to stage the mob outside the perimeters of the rally, on public property, which was the park. Then, the poets of Al-Rasheed, beginning with Jawad, would say a speech to galvanize the protestors and disrupt the rally.

Originally, Jawad and I brainstormed the potential setbacks that could hinder this protest—such as the police shutting us down. And it seemed from the tight security . . . this might be a huge possibility.

Before I could dwell on this more, my phone pinged.

ALEXIS
Where are you? You brought me to a rally?

NIDA
I'll meet you at the bus stop.

When I saw Alexis, she was bundled in a fall coat, tucking half her face inside the collar. "Hey Nida," she said impassively, without meeting my eyes.

"Hey," I said.

It was silent as I tried to dig around for the right words, but she beat me to it.

"I've been doing some thinking," she spoke up.

I waited.

"I know what I did was screwed up. I took pictures of your journal. And I know I shouldn't have brushed it off like it was nothing. I told my mom about it, and she freaked out, telling me I should've apologized to you from the beginning. So, I want you to know that I'm sorry. I'm really sorry."

"You told your mom what you did?"

She tucked her face back into her coat. "I would've told her sooner, for advice, but with the divorce, she hasn't talked to me much. Until I told her what I did."

"Your mother had to tell you to apologize to me?"

"That came out wrong. But . . . I heard about your uncle's passing. I'm sorry about what happened. When I heard the news from school, it put a lot into perspective. I was so caught up with the result, I didn't realize the damage it caused. . . ." Her voice trailed off before she looked me in the eye. "It doesn't matter. I'm sorry, Nida. I know sorry doesn't make up for anything, I know we'll probably never be friends again, but you have to believe me when I say I had good intentions. I never wanted to hurt you, I just wanted to do *something* because I felt helpless."

"You took out your helplessness on me. I'm not a charity case," I finally managed. "I never was. I appreciate the apology, I really do. I appreciate you owning up to it, but don't look at friendships like something you need to fix. You think hearing about your parents' divorce made me feel helpless for you? Absolutely. But that doesn't mean I'll try to fix it. I *will* listen because that's what friends are supposed to do."

"I know," she said bitterly. "But divorce isn't something that can be solved. When I heard about the NSPL competition from Mrs. Sophia's email to you, it seemed like an obvious solution to help with your insecurities and the financial issues. And to bring you out of your shell."

"You assumed," I corrected her. "You assumed a lot about me, my religion, and the consequences. If you had misconceptions about Islam, you could've just asked me instead of saying what you did at school in anger. I was your friend. I don't care if you hold biases about my religion as long as you're honest and open-minded. A lot of people accidentally have prejudice. The difference is if you try to learn more about me."

She was crying now. "I know." She wiped furiously at her cheeks. "I know and I hate myself for it. The worst part is I wish I'd owned up to it before. I wish I'd understood where the boundaries were, but I didn't. And that's not your fault, I just . . ." She shook her head. "I'm sorry about what I said about your poetry and the jihad thing. I won't pretend that I understood most of it because the truth is, I didn't. And I still don't."

I nodded but I couldn't speak more, my anger had lodged in my throat.

She squirmed on the spot. Then said, "I think I should go."

There are times in your life when the awkwardness of a situation hits you square in the face. It was how I felt with that conversation.

When the Christchurch shooting occurred, one of the Muslim victim's family members forgave the shooter. I never understood it. His wife was shot in cold blood and even after the shooter did something that awful, he openly declared his forgiveness. I hadn't agreed with it, but that didn't matter.

Right then, I understood the choice of it. The shooter would plague his thoughts for the rest of his life, so he decided to do something about it. He chose mercy because no one else could but him.

Staring at Alexis, my choices were clear. I didn't call after Alexis and ask her to stay and explain more; I didn't go to her and reassure her that everything would be okay or that she was forgiven when I would see her in school. She had her problems, and I had my own. But I prayed that I had the strength someday to forgive and forget her because it meant that the incident no longer mattered. That I no longer cared, and I could tuck it behind me, living a life free of what she'd done.

But that was for another time, I hoped.

Thirty-three

The mob participants lined up along the block, surrounding the perimeters of the political rally, holding up their banners, waiting for Mitchell Wilson to walk onstage to his podium. The posters were scribbled with different poetry verses. One of them said, *No to War, No to State Terrorism,*

Before the protest could begin, it was Maghrib prayer.

In my earlier high school years, I went to a handful of protests and my favorite moments were the masses praying together while the non-Muslims guarded our worship lines against the authorities. It was a type of rare solidarity.

We lined up in rows. A group of non-Muslims formed a human shield to barricade the worshippers. Jawad, who'd completed his Hifz, led us in prayer, and by the end of it, during the du'a, he raised his hands to the sky and recited, "O Allah, to you belongs all praise, Lord of the heavens and earth and all that is between. O Allah, we submit to you, we repent to you, so grant us forgiveness and strength. We ask you for Paradise. We ask that you forgive us, the ones alive and the ones who've passed and bless our martyrs. Please grant Abdul-Hafeedh afiyah in the hereafter and light in the grave. Give us the strength to protest and speak before our oppressors. Save us from ill friends and snakes. Ameen."

"Ameen," we echoed.

When he rose, I came up beside him and muttered, "Did you really have to add the *friends and snakes* part? I just know that was a jab at me."

"Don't know what you're talking about, Nida," he said, as he swallowed a smile. The nerve.

Before he followed the protestors, I pulled at his arm. "This is hard to say and I am very late," I began. He waited. "But I'm grateful that you kept reminding me of what I could've done, even if it took a very public rap battle to make me understand."

But Jawad, bless his LeBron-hating soul, gave me a crooked grin that made my stomach flip, even at my sad attempt at an apology. "It's cool. I was hard on you though. I felt bad."

I gave him a crooked grin in return.

As we walked back to the bench to begin the mob, he said, "I don't know if you heard but the MSA decided they'll be protesting the school board's Muslim policies at the next board meeting. I'll be performing there. It might be a lot to ask after everything that's going down, but it also wouldn't be the same without my partner in crime." He nudged me.

If he had asked me a week ago, I would've declined. But I knew what I wanted.

"Yeah, I'll be there. Suspended or not, they'll have to drag me out of that protest."

He grinned, straightened his Nets jersey, and climbed onto the bench. Bushra handed him the wireless microphone that the MSA had let us borrow.

Right on time, across the street, Mitchell Wilson took the rally stage. We waited with bated breath as he greeted the audience with waves and a charming smile.

"Good evening," he spoke into the microphone.

But those were the only words I was able to hear because the protestors along the intersection began a preliminary chant. It grew louder and louder, shouting "Hypocrite" as Mitchell Wilson spoke into his mic about promises and progressive change and equality.

Cars that were swerving on the street honked at us in support. The cameras that were positioned to televise Mitchell Wilson's rally pointed toward us as the chants echoed across the rally. The street began filling up with more news vans, reporters flocking to the scene.

The crowd circled the block.

By the five-minute mark, Jawad nodded at the first round of poets to be on standby. But then he did a double take.

"Nida, do you see that?"

I glanced up at the fringes of the crowd.

Was that . . .

Uncle Jihad, Aunty Sobia, Aunty Farooqi, Uncle Khalid, Aunt Aamiina—I lost count. Almost every Al-Rasheed elder was present, phones out as they accidentally filmed the crowd upside-down for their WhatsApp statuses. What stunned me more was seeing . . .

"Amma?"

Amma stood right beside my favorite tobacco-chewing aunty.

"Nida baby!" Aunty Farooqi shouted, waving before swiveling the camera at me. Amma looked embarrassed on her behalf.

Jawad shook his head beside me.

I envisioned Amma's WhatsApp status influenced by Aunty Farooqi, though I doubted she'd actually post it:

Bye Bloody Mitchell, We Paki Proud #Resist #Protest #Racism #Islamophobia #ThatsMyDaughter

Seeing Al-Rasheed standing strong reminded me of why we were here in the first place. There were uncles in the audience who were fresh immigrants, and others who'd been residing in America for over a decade.

Al-Rasheed's residents looked tired and angry. It was the same routine. You arrived in this country with eyes bright, full of promise, applying for job after job, only to come home disappointed. You'd bear it all with a grin, as you accepted a customer service or a factory job, or any employment that didn't come with benefits, insurance, or a contract.

You would wonder if the immigration was worth the sacrifices but remember being an immigrant was a point of honor for your izzat.

You'd gaze down at your young kids and think, maybe the schooling they received would make up for it. And every time you saw your next-door neighbor struggling with the same hustles as you, making ends meet with five side jobs or a small business down the avenue, you'd silently acknowledge that you were in this fight together. The world was grating at your resolve, but your neighbors' small talks, mosque, and *salaams* kept your head strong.

It was the life of an immigrant. Past the glamor and American dream, there were communities struggling to make ends meet. That was Al-Rasheed.

They showed up at this protest with the same resolve echoed across other ethnic enclaves in America—they would continue fighting to be acknowledged as equals.

Gazing at the chanting crowd, I began to believe it. We were loud. We were doing it. We were *really* doing it.

Until cops swarmed the streets with flashing lights, after the first poet's speech.

"This early? We've barely begun the mob!"

This couldn't be happening.

We watched as they streamed down the road in our direction. But the protestors only began chanting louder.

Jawad gripped his mic tighter. "We have to move."

"But we just started!"

"If the police are here, they're coming regardless of what we say," Jawad said, helplessly.

He was right. But if they shut us down now, our protest would only be a tiny blip during the political rally.

We watched in horror as the cops, reaching the outskirts of the protest, zeroed in on protestors. They began to usher residents of Al-Rasheed from the scene. When anyone resisted, the authorities began forcing them.

"We have to do something!"

"We *can't*. They're justifying it for Wilson's safety. This is how it always is until we're dragged away," Jawad said.

This wouldn't work.

This wasn't fair.

My eyes pricked. Across from us, I could make out the bleary figure of Mitchell Wilson onstage. Beaming.

Mitchell Wilson wasn't a hero. He was a hypocrite, a desperate, pathetic man standing on a podium, dressed up in pretend, appealing to the same people he'd hurt to gain votes.

I wouldn't shut my mouth. I would say this and more, and more, and more, until my tongue went dry and my lips cracked and my throat ached.

I wasn't a headline. I wasn't entertainment. I was a girl. I was a poet. I was Nida Siddiqui, the niece of the notorious Abdul-Hafeedh, making her own legacy.

And I was done taking orders from people who never cared about me.

"Give me the mic," I demanded.

Jawad whipped his head. "What?"

"Forget moving, we have one shot at this," I said before my nerves could get the best of me. "We have to take advantage of the media presence."

"What are you going to do?"

"Perform."

My hands wrapped around the hilt of the microphone without waiting for his reply. But he was my partner in crime; he understood.

Like always, the rush returned before any spoken word performance. Maybe this would be my last . . . or one of many to come. But I acted like this was my first performance—understanding the loss of a gift when it was stolen from you—asking for permission from the pen I hurt, hoping to be accepted.

But I wouldn't recite my *Dear Mitchell Wilson* letter, I was more than just one letter. My letters were pieces of my existence but never the whole picture. When I penned it, I was upset, but since then, my world had grown more. It wouldn't be defined by the Wilsons of the world. I knew what letters I would say—I would tell my story.

From below the bench, Zaynab squeezed my ankle, nodding her support. Behind her, other Muslim Student Associations from across the city shouted into the night with their creative banners. There was even a prison abolitionist group and other organizations that shielded us from the police lining up on the road.

After Jawad passed me the mic, he splayed his hands, offering to prop my journal up like a makeshift podium.

I shook my head. "It's okay, I have my words memorized."

His brows shot up, but he put his hands down.

I didn't have any practiced speech. Just a girl, her notebook, and her tongue.

I cleared my throat into the mic, suddenly aware of the camera crews pointed toward us, recognizing who I was. My lips trembled and my legs shook like a toddler attempting her first walk, unbalanced and unsure. You'd think my insides were doing turns from how hard it was to catch a single breath. Was that how far away I was from my words?

But I closed my eyes, imagined I was in my bedroom, and envisioned the verses scrawled in my journal. My hands brushed my hijab, the fabric my safety against the stares.

And I spoke.

"Assalaamualaykum, I'm Nida Siddiqui."

The crowd paused.

A chorus of *Waalaikumsalams* greeted me in return and my confidence expanded from my stomach to my throat.

"Many of you recognize me as the Muslim girl who was frisked by Mitchell Wilson and his security personnel. Soon after it happened, I penned a public poetry letter about Wilson and what he said and did to me. But America couldn't take the heat."

Another chorus, this time of whistles, boosting my determination.

"I was called a liar. I was called a radical. I was called an attention-seeker. But it wasn't just me. They defamed all of Islam; they justified their Islamophobic beliefs. Until I became afraid of my own letter. But nothing in that letter was a lie. I stand behind it. Because they're *my* words. My story."

I whispered a bismillah.

Begin it slowly, I reminded myself. I had to trust the poetry would accept me as much as I was accepting it.

"*Dear America.*"

Then I was speaking and speaking and speaking.

I let the words past my tongue, imagined they were needles

bobbing into anyone who stared at me wrong. And I kept going, bringing more and more force into my gestures. Shouting at some moments before easing my voice into a gentle swell.

It wouldn't bring my Mamou back. It wouldn't fix the fact that four innocent men from Al-Rasheed were incarcerated too. It wouldn't solve anything. But they were words, and if they were just heard . . . maybe that would be the beginning of something more.

I continued to speak. I spoke about immigration; I spoke about expectations. I spoke about the way I was frisked, about Wilson's racist messages, about his manipulation, about his tricks, about my friend's betrayal, about my love for Al-Rasheed, about the pains of my Mamou, about his wrongful incarceration, about his murder in that federal prison, and finally . . . about my fears and dreams.

I owned those words, refusing to take them back.

The eyes of the audience never left my body.

Wilson's speech at the rally was drowned out by the torrent of my words.

I felt heard. I felt seen.

For the first time, I felt free.

Thirty-four

After my performance, the police shut down the protest with threats of arrest. But the damage was done. That same night, video clips of my spoken word went viral. News stations played the performance, declaring how rowdy students bombed a political rally.

To my surprise, Amma immediately forwarded the video of my spoken word to her WhatsApp groups, bragging in English, *Look my daughter, look her performance!*

That same night, I received an email from the organization Muslim Legal Aid, who proposed an attorney to represent my family pro bono after seeing my performance. They said we had an opportunity to sue for the wrongful death of Mamou.

Muslims and non-Muslims flooded my inboxes, sending me waves of support. Some accused me of being unpatriotic. People sent threats. Amma was scared, all the time. It was clear, there would be people who always villainized Muslims. But there were also people who accepted us. Other communities, just as brown as my skin, had our backs. And others who were white.

I didn't have to assimilate, no matter how much Amma or

anyone justified it for our own safety. No matter how much Amma stuck to her philosophy that no consequence was better than some. Amma was also a mother, and mothers would bear a world's pain to protect their children from the hurt of others, even if it made them a villain.

But I had Muslims behind me—other spoken word artists from across the country, reaching out to collaborate. They believed in me. Eventually, Amma would too.

Epilogue

On Election Day, I awoke to the strangest sound.

Bleat, bleat, it rang around the bedroom.

"Nida, baby, touch the goat," a familiar voice said.

"What?"

I looked down the mattress to see Amma and Aunty Farooqi leading a baby goat toward me.

"What is this?" I shouted before scrambling up my bed. "You guys are crazy! Get that thing out of my room!"

Bleat, bleat, the baby goat cried. It nudged against my foot.

"It's charity," Amma answered simply like this was supposed to make sense.

"Gotta get that evil eye out of this house!" Aunty Farooqi declared. "I told you that Sister Ayesha, she cast the evil eye on you."

Bleat! cried the goat in agreement.

"Ugh!" I groaned and covered my eyes with my blanket.

"Nuh-uh, Nida baby, touch the damn goat and we'll go," Aunty Farooqi sang through her chewing tobacco.

Is this even legal? I wondered. *Where will the goat go?*

Zaynab woke up across the room, took one look at the goat,

and groaned too. "I hate when you do this, Amma. This isn't Pakistan! This is America!"

But Zaynab and I obliged, sticking our right hands out to touch the goat.

"Don't any of you have plastic bottles? Where do I spit my tobacco?" Aunty Farooqi shouted as she ventured into the shared hall bathroom.

"Zaynab, I'm not going to clean whatever tobacco mess is about to end up in our sink."

She groaned again.

Amma called Mohamed into our room. His eyes widened. "A goat!" He practically launched himself at it, petting the white-and-brown fur too enthusiastically.

"Wait, Mohamed, stay right there," Amma ordered as she positioned her phone.

"Amma, are you seriously taking a picture?"

"Respect your elder, *stooopad*."

I didn't know how Amma had the energy this early in the morning to insult me so gracefully.

After fiddling around with the camera app and managing to capture a picture, she handed me the device. "Write my caption in English, and don't forget the emojis, jaanu."

Oh, so I was jaanu now instead of stupid girl?

"The caption should be, *Looks like tonight we're eating goat karahi*," Zaynab offered.

I gasped and covered Mohamed's ears. "Don't say that in front of him!"

At Amma's expectant expression and loose chappal on her right foot, I typed a caption.

Can't have sadaqa without the best goat in the house on

election day? #Sadaqa #Spiritual #MuslimsInAl-Rasheed #GetRidOfThatEvilEye

During lunch, Amma sat Zaynab and me down before we drove to the polling station.

"So, we're voting for Mitchell Wilson after everything?" Zaynab said.

"We all saw this coming," I admitted. "I mean just look at his policies, especially on immigration, minimum wage, and Medicare."

Amma sighed and spoke in Urdu. "That's the truth. We even had this problem during elections in Pakistan. Politicians can make so many promises, but their actions act against it. The truth is, we have to choose between the two options—a party that has policies against healthcare and immigrants and prioritizes guns over people or a party with Islamophobes, but sometimes, a spectrum of policies. It doesn't make it right, but that's the choice we have in this country."

"It doesn't seem fair," I muttered. "This doesn't feel like a choice at all."

Amma looked us both in the eyes. "It's not necessarily about who's in power now—it's about the promise of who could be in power tomorrow."

I thought about some of the politicians I'd seen online, even some Muslim women braving American politics. There were more like them who existed. No, there were more like them who *could* exist.

For now, I wouldn't get to choose a miraculous option in this election. Perhaps I could never even hope for politicians that treated us as human beings because neither political party ever had the best interests of people like us at heart.

Amma was correct: we couldn't vote for the people we liked, we voted for who we thought was the less evil option.

That evening, I voted for the first time in my entire life. But it was bereft of the sense of empowerment that the citizens around me felt. Voters snapped pictures, proud at exercising their rights. But some of us, tucked into those long winding lines—we cast our votes bitterly. Reluctantly. Some from Al-Rasheed voted against Wilson. Others voted for him.

I did what I always did. At home, I scribbled those frustrations into another letter. Then I dialed the number of the attorney from the legal aid organization that had contacted me to set up our first meeting. I worked on my spoken word for the protest at the next school board meeting. And I texted Rayan to meet at the Poet's Block for another performance.

I still had to finish my college applications. I would succumb, eventually, to the expectations that came with being a Pakistani girl who wanted to go to college. Which meant pursuing good physics programs that universities had to offer. But throughout this, one thing was certain: I'd stick by my pen.

I'd reconsider Jawad's idea of publishing an anthology, using all this newfound support people had for me; I'd start venturing to more slams outside the Poet's Block, taking on the offers of the poets who'd reached out after my viral protest speech.

You see, after everything that had transpired, I was living, I was breathing, and I was hoping. Because that was all I could do.

Sincerely,
Nida Siddiqui

Acknowledgments

Alhamdulillah. I cannot begin this without thanking Ar-Rahman, Al-Kareem. All success is due to Him.

I want to begin by acknowledging the many, many wrongfully detained Muslims around the world. Dr. Aafia Siddiqui has been wrongfully imprisoned for more than a decade. Other detained Muslims at the time testified that they heard her under torture in the same CIA black site they were held in. Her child, who was abducted alongside her, is still missing. Khurram Parvez is an exceptional Kashmiri activist detained under false terrorism charges. Due to intimidation tactics, many outspoken people (who I know personally) are viciously threatened into silence and can no longer speak for his freedom. Dr. Aafia and Khurram Parvez are two examples of individuals imprisoned under the false notion of supporting terrorism. I hope you can remember their names and look into their cases, because the rest of the world has forgotten. Terrorism is a label used unjustly against many Muslims in order to discredit their causes and silence their voices.

Writing a book is a solitary experience. It's surreal to have a lonely activity turn into a project supported by countless extraordinary individuals. Putting out a book about Muslims was very scary—because of the fear of pushback, but also because of the possibility of being censored and told to rewrite Nida's scenes in a certain way. However, that did not happen. Many people supported the importance of an unapologetically Muslim story. First, I am so grateful to my agent Paige Terlip at Andrea Brown Literary Agency for understanding my vision and intent from the first draft, and for always supporting me through all the painful hurdles that this industry puts us through. When I was paranoid about where to take the story, you pushed me (kindly) to look past my fear. The submission process felt so brutal, but you never stopped encouraging me.

A big thank-you to Vicki Lame, my amazing editor, for acquiring this story. From day one, you encouraged all the Islamic and speculative aspects. You always believed in the story and made editing such a fun, chill experience. Your editorial insights are genius, and they propelled my writing in ways I didn't think I could accomplish. And alongside Vicki, Vanessa Aguirre, thank you for your wonderful insights and help in every editorial and production stage of this process. You both are brilliant.

A big thank-you to the entire Wednesday Books team: editorial director Sara Goodman; publisher Eileen Rothschild; jacket designer Olga Grlic; mechanical designer Soleil Paz; designer Michelle McMillian; the marketing team, Alexis Neuville and Brant Janeway; publicist Meghan Harrington; production manager Adriana Coada; production editor Cassie Gutman; copy editor NaNá Stoelzle; audio producer Elishia Merricks; audio marketer Maria Snelling; and audio publicist Amber Cortes.

A big thank-you to my writing community. Chinelo Chidebe, where do I begin? You had faith in me from the start. You are the kindest soul. I owe so much of this to you. Umairah, you were my first reader, thank you. And I love our absurd manga and JJK theories. Emily Varga, you are the best CP and friend a writer could ask for. All the way from the mentorship to now, we did it! I am so proud of us! Gigi Griffis, you are like a sister, I could not have survived publishing without you. Thank you for reading too many drafts of this story. On that note, Angel di Zhang, Piper Vossy, Sami Ellis, Chandra Fisher, and Elora Ditton: thank you for helping me plot this story from the very start. Sami, you are a rock to me in publishing and always support my wild campaigns. Vaishnavi Patel, I cherish our friendship so much. L.C. Millburn, thank you for being such a sweet human being. Kate Dylan, your knowledge helped me survive this industry, and you always stop me from panicking! The entire Slack crew, you are my ride or die. Deborah Fayale and Ciannon Smart, you plucked me from the trenches and mentored me to become a better writer. Thank you. Deborah, our phone calls about life and plots never fail to inspire me to be a more ambitious writer! June Hur, our book talks always make my day. Liselle Sambury, Kristin Dwyer, and George Jreige, your constant advice and generosity is so appreciated. Hanna and Tigest, go us! S.A. Simon, A. M. Kvita, Noreen Mughees, and Rosalie Lin, thank you! The Writers Forge, I'm grateful that you supported me when I was a freshman and just starting out. Aqsa and Namra, thank you for the art insights. The APIpit team, thank you for your warm support.

I want to express special gratitude to my professors Dr. Dylan Clark, Dr. Bharat Punjabi, Dr. Joseph McQuade, and Dr. Arafat A. Razzaque at the University of Toronto in the CAS and NMC departments. Most of this book was edited between attending college classes. My professors have zero clue this book exists, but their courses changed my life and inspired me to incorporate so much research into my writing.

This book was in some ways a love letter to my local Muslim community. I never had a community like this growing up until recently, and I never want to take it for granted. The Muslim community's never-ending advocacy and efforts leave me in awe, and I would be lying if I didn't say that parts of this book were inspired by the heartfelt community I have today.

With that being said, a giant thank-you to every member of MIST, past and present. It doesn't matter if you are Muslim or not, look for a local MIST competition in your region—they were some of the best experiences of my high school career. And the spoken word goes *hard* there. I loved it.

To my Kashmir crew, our work encourages me to never give up the good fight. You know exactly who you are, and no matter how much they try to silence us, we'll keep trying. To Brother Mehmet and Kayum, thank you for your work. The hospitality and warmth from the Uyghur community moves me so much, and so many characters here are inspired by my love for the Uyghur community.

Thank you to my entire family. First, my twin sister Sidrah. We both grew up reading books rather than socializing. It was that love of books that helped me become an author today. And thank you to my older sister for being a role model for me. I promise both of you, none of the characters in here are about you. And lastly, my wonderful parents who sacrificed everything to give me an education and home. My mother really did off-screen my goats for curry. All my family back home, you are amazing cheerleaders, and I love coming to see you in Pakistan. This book is an homage to our beautiful religion, land, and family—flaws and all.

If you are South Asian and reading this, and if you have the opportunity to ask a family member who survived partition (only if they're comfortable), please do ask about it. It's a dark chapter and its ramifications are felt to this day. Many of our grandparents in the diaspora felt they had to remain silent about this part of history. Or they assumed we didn't care, so they could never explain what they endured. Our generation should not be ignorant about this part of history nor the bloody legacy of British colonialism.

Lastly, no matter who tries to silence you, continue speaking up for good causes. There is so much darkness in the world, but there are also many inspiring people who will remind you to always have hope.